FINDING WOODSTOCK

ESSEX PRESS

Books by David Tillman

IN THE FAILING LIGHT
DINNER FOR EIGHT
FINDING WOODSTOCK

To order, write to:

Essex Press
P. O. Box 914
North Andover, MA. 01845

FINDING WOODSTOCK

DAVID TILLMAN

ESSEX PRESS

For information contact:
Essex Press
P.O. Box 914
North Andover, MA 01845

ISBN 0-9668972-1-8

Printed in the United States of America

TO MY DAUGHTER, KAYLY, WHO
I JUST LOVE TO PIECES.

September 7

I belong to the suburbs. This is not my doing, really. The suburbs are where I was born.

My father was born on a farm. He left the farm to fight the commies in Korea. He was a sharpshooter, so they stationed him in Hawaii to put a bit of ocean between the enemy and his eagle eye. Americans believe in fair play.

After the war, my father didn't go back to the farm. He moved to the suburbs. Perhaps he was shell-shocked.

He married someone like himself in so many ways – age, race, religion, politics – which was only proper. He married someone entirely opposite in sex – which was also only proper. I was born soon after in a clean white hospital among a crowd of well-scrubbed nurses, then whisked off and circumcised without my approval. My mother was unconscious throughout the whole affair. My father was unconscious in his own way; he was at work. He looked up quickly from his desk when his secretary entered and announced my arrival, but he paused only briefly, greeting the news of a son with a smile and a fistful of cigars before returning to work.

In my youth, we moved quite often. When they searched for a new neighborhood, my parents always had their ears tuned to the drone of lawnmowers and their nostrils flaring as they sniffed out the aroma of a Sunday afternoon barbecue. To go beyond the familiar sounds and smells of the suburbs was unfathomable to them, like Christopher Columbus setting off for the giant snapping turtles that inhabited the ends of the Earth.

My mother's shouted fanfare, *"Here's our new home,"* was usually my first clue that we had moved again and were not just out for a Sunday drive. Once installed among the Sheetrock walls of my new bedroom, I barely noticed a difference. Some places it snowed, other places it didn't. I learned new words: Cul-de-sac, Gunite, Har-Tru, liposuction.

Each time we arrived in a new neighborhood, my parents would smile at all the welcoming faces that lined the street; pale white faces that watched us curiously as we followed the exhaust of a nationally-franchised moving van to our new home.

My parents smiled again as they settled comfortably into the familiar floor plan of the freshly minted house. My father smiled each morning as he stepped into the sunshine in his gray suit and saw the other husbands step into the sunshine in their gray suits.

Then a quiet Saturday; and the rattle-pop-boom of four pickup trucks brought my mother and father to the living room picture window where their smiles faded. Hillbillies were moving in across the street.

Nobody ever knew where they came from, or from where their money came. A modest lottery winning or an insurance payoff, maybe. Perhaps their half acre of marijuana finally slipped past the watchful eye of the DEA, and the husband came running home one day to their tarpaper shack on a Vermont hillside, tossing hundred dollar bills into the air, shouting, "Look, Edna, we's rich! We's headin' for the suburbs!"

Lucky us.

"They must have followed us," my mother sighed, thinking back on the hillbilly family we had just left behind in another suburb in another state. But these were different hillbillies. I could tell because this time only the daughter was pregnant.

My father cringed as the lead pickup, overflowing with mattresses, missed the driveway and drove across the soft grass. The other three pickups didn't even try for the driveway; they drove directly onto the yard. All morning the pickup trucks came and went, churning up the lawn until they had created an environment they were more comfortable with – mud season in the Green Mountains.

My mother counted the many mattresses with their rusty-brown urine stains. Small children were moving in. "How many kids do you think they got?" she groaned.

A red-and-blue pickup truck delivered a large wooden spool, the kind electric companies use to keep their spare cable in order. Three men flipped the spool on its side. A big pink woman hoisted up a mildewed umbrella and threaded its shaft through the spool's center hole. She forced it open with sweaty palms until its tattered fringe flapped in the light breeze. She released her grip and the umbrella tipped, jutting from the oversized hole at an odd angle, spinning, spinning while the woman fetched four chairs – all of different sizes and designs, all made of new-and-improved recycled plastic – and set them around the improvised picnic table.

"They're not going to leave that in the front yard, are they?" my mother wondered. But of course they would. She knew they would, because they always did.

Another pickup truck churned through the gelatinous mud.

Two teenage boys, forever trapped in cutoffs they had long outgrown, hopped out of the cab and into the back of the truck. They started tossing spare fenders, mufflers, and a transmission into a bed of pachysandra beside the front stoop. They had the entire makings of another pickup truck with them. When they had emptied the pickup, they threw a black plastic tarp over the pile of debris and held it down against the wind with four leaky car batteries.

"Eight children I count so far," my mother moaned. "Perhaps some are cousins or something." Nobody had eight children in the suburbs anymore, not since the arrival of the pill, anyway.

As it turned out, three were cousins. But they were to live there, too. Their parents were in prison for beating each other up in a drunken rage.

One of the pickups backed too close to the front stoop and knocked a supporting column loose with its rear bumper. The family patriarch looked up at the small roof that hung out over the front stoop. He kicked out the damaged column and tossed it on top of the auto parts. The dangling corner of the roof dropped slightly, and the old man smiled smugly. Much better now. Just like home.

Come winter, the snow brought the whole stoop roof down and blocked the front door. For two years more, the hillbilly family used the back door, until one day the youngest boy – an unscrubbed toddler whose first spoken words were "aw sheeeeet" – carted off the debris to make a fort.

I looked down the length of the street. There were no smiling faces greeting this family. Everyone was hiding behind their curtains, staring out their living room picture windows. Horror shuddered through the neighborhood.

"Why don't they put that junk in the back yard?" my mother cried.

Why did she say that? She knew the answer. The back was where the chickens would go, and the rabbit hutch. And they would try raising goats there until the animal control officer wandered over to remind them about one of the rules in the suburbs: no livestock.

They would grow corn along the back fence and tie three dogs out back to guard it from wildlife. They didn't know that squirrels were the only wildlife in suburbia. Birds, too. But the dogs would never bother about the birds or the squirrels; they'd spend most of their days lying in the dirt, licking their balls.

The family never had a name. Everyone called them "those people." Mr. Harris once let slip that he knew the husband's name. Jimmy Bob, he called him; and everyone grew rather suspicious that Mr. Harris was being a bit too friendly with "those people," on the sly perhaps. The suburbs were never quite as affectionate toward Mr. Harris after that; no longer the cheerful, smiling place it had been the day he and his charming wife moved in, driving up in their matching white Mercedes with their "HIZ" and "HERZ" vanity plates.

I left for college the day Jimmy Bob grew impatient for a hotdog and blew himself up pouring gasoline on the barbecue grill. It was his blood-curdling screams and the wail of the ambulance that came flooding back to me on Graduation Day when my father intoned to me the immortal words, "Son, given any thought to where you'll live, what you'll do?"

I did not return to the suburbs; not that day. I married a city girl instead. Together we bred two city children and pretended nothing existed beyond the range of the subway. I think we were happy.

But today that has changed. The suburbs have a way of sucking what they want from the city. They decided they wanted me back, so here I am. Suburbs are what I've known best. I have returned home.

My wife's name is Beth, but I never call her that to her face. I call her *Love*. My name used to be Harry, but now it's *Honey*. Children sometimes call me Mr. Lascome, but when they do, I look behind me thinking my father must be hovering somewhere in the background.

Beth and I are spending a busy Saturday morning in our new home. We have just bought our first house. Before that, we lived in a large apartment complex in the city. The TV is plugged in and the cable has been installed – it was the first thing we attended to. We are gathering tips from Martha Stewart as we unwrap the dinnerware. We hear a rattle-boom-pop and go to the living room picture window. There are three pickup trucks pulling onto the lawn across the street.

"What is that?" my wife asks. She is new to the suburbs and doesn't understand.

"Those are our hillbillies," I explain, and hurry back to Martha Stewart just in time to hear her say, "It's a good thing."

"Oh, cool," I hear our son shout. "That kid's got a rifle."

"It's just a toy," my wife suggests. But then she sees the boy point his toy up toward the telephone line and fire a shot at a fat crow. Pow! The bird flies off as the telephone line flutters to the street. "Honey! Call the cops. They're shooting real bullets."

But of course, the phone line is dead.

September 8

Beth spots them first and calls me to the picture window. "Honey, I think we have company."

I look out the window to where Beth is pointing; our homestead is being invaded by a neatly dressed couple and their two offspring – an 8-year-old girl in white patent leather shoes and a 12-year-old boy with his hair laid to one side with the aid of salad oil and a broad-tooth comb. Like a little army on parade, they march in single file, tallest to shortest, up our driveway and along the dirt path where slates will soon go. As if on cue, they rise on tippy-toes when they see they have wandered upon my newly seeded lawn.

"They're either Baptists or Jehovah's Witnesses," I observe.

"How can you tell, Honey?" Beth asks. My wife still has much to learn about the suburbs.

"They're always first to move in on the new family, Love. They get extra heaven points if they steer you to their church."

I spot a Bible tucked under the man's arm. Baptists. Jehovah's Witnesses would have a wad of loose literature they could leave behind.

I see the woman is carrying a fruitcake. It's the neighborhood fruitcake. If I brought it down to the police station and had it dusted for prints, I could learn the whole history of the neighborhood; who arrived first, who moved in next and received the fruitcake when it was still fresh, which neighbor got the fruitcake after that, and so on. The whole chain of command, right up to this important moment and the cake's pious march up our dirt path in the outstretched hands of the Baptists.

I gather my clan together. We look scruffy. My son Justin is fourteen. Being fourteen and looking scruffy go hand-in-hand. I've given up on changing that, but Beth hasn't. She wets a fingertip and tries to rearrange his hair while he throws karate chops at her wrist.

My daughter Kathleen is seven and is normally pretty, but she's been playing dress-up and has on my big shoes and my pajama top.

"Take those off," my wife whispers to her.

"I can't," Kathleen shouts back.

I open the front door at the exact moment my wife pulls the pajama top over Kathleen's head. She sees that our little girl is naked underneath, but doesn't react quick enough to prevent the neighbors from noticing the same thing.

The Baptists are embarrassed. Their son's stiff hair has shot straight up at the sight of the bottom half of a 7-year-old girl. He no longer looks like the other three. The serenity, that pious stare is gone, and he is now a boy with a strange new sense of hormones.

The husband frowns. He does not approve of nudity. He showers in a bathing suit and changes his clothes in a dark closet. He and his wife always make love under heavy blankets, and he only touches her breasts by accident. She sighs when he does and wishes they could do more. Sometimes she wishes she wasn't a Baptist.

She is the first one to speak. "Oops, caught you." She giggles, then thrusts the fruitcake forward, breaking the invisible seal created by our vinyl door frame; the precious seal that separates us from the outside world.

Beth accepts the cake with a cautious smile.

"We'd like to welcome you to the neighborhood," the woman chirps. "We live next door. We're the Greenleys. I'm Evonne, but everyone just calls me Eve, and this is my husband Adam." She pulls the two children forward by their reluctant hands. "And this is Cain, and our daughter, Sarah."

My son eyes the other boy suspiciously. He takes notice of his thin arms and trembling chin, and knows he'll be beating this boy up fairly regularly.

Kathleen has run off. It's hard to face people who have just seen your nakedness, especially when they're Baptists. She peeks down the staircase from upstairs, thinking perhaps if she makes a new entrance – properly dressed, this time – they'll think she's a different little girl. She walks slowly toward the doorway, then hides behind my legs. Our visitors are clucking "for shame, for shame" without actually making any noise. They do it with their accusing eyes and their pouting mouths. Except for the boy; he's too busy wondering what just happened within his own body.

There's an awkward silence. My family does not know the suburbs. They know the anonymity of large places; cities and tall apartment buildings. No one has brought us a fruitcake before. They are stricken in awe by this strange ritual. I am the first to react because I once knew the suburbs. I recall words like *neighborliness*, *family-oriented*, and *proselytizing* as I step forward.

"Hi. I'm Harry." I stick my hand out and let the Baptists

fight over who will shake it first. "This is my wife Beth, and my son Justin, and my daughter Kathleen." I forget to tell them that as a group we are the Lascomes, but I know they'll discover that next Wednesday when they scan the local newspaper, checking the real estate transfers to see how much we paid for our house.

No one else shakes hands. They just nod their heads at one another and smile as if the suburbs give them gas.

"We'd invite you in," I say. "But the house is a mess. We still haven't unpacked."

The Greenleys seem relieved that they don't have to enter our home. The front stoop is neutral territory and there is comfort and safety in that.

Adam clears his throat. "Well, we just wanted to welcome you to the neighborhood." He wants to say more. He wants to tell us about his wonderful church and the fellowship we would find there, but...the naked girl, that worries him. We could be a den of heathens. His church is happiest when all its members are thinking the same. He doesn't want to destroy that harmony by bringing us there.

Beth looks into the hallway, her eyes darting among all the unopened boxes. She scoots over to one and tears off the packing tape. The Greenleys have turned to leave. She digs inside the box and yanks out a ceramic flower pot, then scurries to the front door. "Yoo hoo," she calls.

Eve turns back to face us. She smiles, thinking perhaps my wife is going to do something to cement together an everlasting friendship. Perhaps we will have a group hug.

"This is for you." Beth holds out the flower pot. A sprinkling of potting soil leaks from the bottom through the drainage hole.

Eve hesitates, then reaches out and takes the pot. "Thank you." She rejoins her family, who are already marching single file down the driveway.

We wave slowly, our smiles frozen painfully in place.

"Why did you give her a pot," I say, trying not to move my lips, not wishing to destroy the friendly effect of my false smile.

"I don't know. I guess I panicked," Beth whispers. "This is all so new to me. I thought maybe we were supposed to exchange gifts."

"This is the suburbs, Love," I reply. "Not an Indian reservation."

September 9

We had planned to move in June; that's a rule in the suburbs. Right after school ends, the yellow school buses disappear from the streets and are replaced by orange moving vans. Perhaps somewhere someone is converting buses into vans in a concealed body shop.

Despite our well-laid plans, we were not able to move in June. Our house was not finished then. There were delays. The roofers walked off the job, hightailing it to Florida to repair hurricane damage at exorbitant rates, and our builder had to import crews from Canada to finish the work. They were paid in American dollars and were very happy, but they were paid by the hour and did not work fast. Then it rained in August.

It is now September. School started last week, but we had not yet moved. We were sitting in our apartment waiting for the paint to dry. The paint crew sprayed the interior of our new house all in one day. Everything is yellow.

No, the building contractor tells us, it's eggshell white.

It looks yellow to me. Yellow is not a good color for a ceiling.

Justin is strutting down the street toward the bus stop. He is going to high school this year. He's a freshman. He has pubic hair. He has a child's brain. Pubic hair and a child's brain – that is a dangerous combination. Mother nature, in all her wondrous glory, sometimes makes mistakes. Justin doesn't know it yet, but he is an outcast. Three days of school have passed without him – now he will be the new kid. He will be the new kid for the entire school year because he is three days late.

Another boy will start school in two weeks. His father will be a CPA. They will have Midwestern accents. My son will become friends with the other new boy, and together they will be "the two new kids." The other boy will be shy of twelve – he is smart and skipped some grades. He doesn't want to be a CPA; he wants to be a spaceman. He doesn't have pubic hair yet. Justin will go to the other boy's house to hang out, and the other boy will show him his G. I. Joe doll. Justin will think he's in hell.

"Kathleen! Get down here!" Beth yells up the staircase. She has made us a wonderful breakfast. It is lightly poached eggs on a whole-grain muffin, topped with a sprig of parsley. It is a city breakfast, not a suburban breakfast. Beth has been to the local supermarket, but she has not yet discovered the corn flakes. She still brews jasmine tea. She will switch to Maxwell House coffee soon. Instant. You've got to move fast in the suburbs.

"Kathleen, you'll be late for school," she calls again.

Kathleen is crying. "I can't go to school."

My wife wipes the tears from the girl's eyes and squeezes her chin. "Why can't you go to school?"

"I don't have a uniform."

"Kitten, you don't need a uniform," Beth coos.

My daughter looks at me, and I nod my head in agreement. "No uniforms."

Kathleen cries louder. No uniforms. It's all so strange here.

"You can join a dance school and wear a ballet uniform," my wife tells her.

"Or you can join a soccer team and wear a gym uniform," I suggest. It will never be clean when she needs it. We'll rush around, hand washing it in the kitchen sink, pulling it from the dryer halfway through the permanent-press cycle. She'll wear it damp to her first game. She'll be the new girl on the team, so she'll spend the entire game sitting on the bench next to the crippled girl that serves as the team mascot. Beth and I will stand behind a fence, our fingers curled through the wire mesh, waiting futilely to see her enter the game. We'll see the Baptist girl, Sarah, kick one of the boys in the nuts when she thinks no one is looking.

Kathleen is no longer crying. She is smiling bravely.

"I'll take you to school, Kitten," I say. I take her hand, and we walk out the front door. Her school is only three blocks away, but I drive her there in our car.

See? Already the suburban ways are coming back to me.

When I return, my eggs are cold. The yellow yolk dripping artistically over the edge of the muffin has turned hard. I drink my tea in one swallow then hurry out the front door. It is getting late, and I have a train to catch.

***

I sit alone in the dimly-lit train. It was years ago when last I lived in the suburbs. There was an oil embargo then. People took trains. Now I am sitting alone, staring out the window at the miles of highway clogged with a colorful array of stationary vehicles. There is an accident somewhere. There will be an accident everyday, and everyday I will ride past the idling cars and stare at them from the window of my train. Some days I will see my neighbors waving to each other from their separate vehicles. They exchanged fruitcakes once, but they will not ride to work together.

At the next stop, a blind woman gets on the train. She has a Labrador retriever with her. She calls out, asking if there is an empty seat anywhere. I say nothing. There are eighty seats, and seventy-nine of them are empty. What are the odds she'll sit on my lap?

A woman in a wheelchair also enters the train. I recognize her. She panhandles in the city. Apparently, she commutes from the suburbs. She tells me she forgot her wallet. "Do you have two dollars for train fare?" she asks. She gets a handicap discount.

I give her two dollars. It is hard to ignore a panhandler when you are together on a train with no one else but a blind woman.

We get closer to the city. Many people get on the train. An elderly gentleman sits next to me. He is retired, he tells me, but he goes to the city three times a week. He goes to teach welfare mothers about computers. He teaches them to become data entry clerks. Most of them will fail, he says. Most of them go to school merely to keep their welfare checks coming. But two of them are going to make it – two out of twenty-two – and that's what keeps him going to the city three times a week.

I tell him I work for an investment company. I tell him I don't do anything useful. I tell him I go to the city because they pay me a lot of money to do nothing useful.

The old gentleman is paid nothing, and he has to pay his own train fare.

The train is full now. People are standing in the aisle. They sway back and forth as the train enters a rough section of track. The Labrador retriever is lying in the aisle. His soft paws are very near the shuffling shoes of the strap hangers, but he does not seem concerned.

I see my old apartment building. We are very close to the city now. It has taken me an hour to get this far. I used to walk to my office. It would take me fifteen minutes. When it rained, I took the subway. That took seven minutes, if I didn't have to wait too long on the platform.

The train drags itself slowly through the train yard. The track is rough, but we are moving at least. Cars are stopped on the overpass; sporty cars capable of going one hundred and twenty miles per hour sit idling as butterflies flutter past. Again, I see my neighbors.

My neighbors have new jobs. They have come to my suburb because it was pointed out to them when they first visited the city, arriving in new suits to be interviewed for their promotions. They were flown in from distant lands and assigned a trusted real estate agent who showed them around. He showed them my neighborhood. "This is where most of our junior executives choose to live," the agent told each one, not thinking it at all inappropriate to use the word *choose*.

The interviews were mere formalities. Each neighbor's fate was scratched in stone long ago, well before they ever went to work for their company, perhaps as far back as that distant Saturday when they sat in quiet terror in a crowded cafeteria and took their SATs. The promotions have come more-or-less on schedule, the timing varying only slightly depending on heart attacks and other deviations from the mortality tables, but the courses themselves have all been prearranged, and little can be done to change them.

My name was etched deeply upon the surface of my desk the day I started work. That was fifteen years ago. Most people around me have no idea what I do. I do it very well.

My boss is cruel. Sometimes I see the shadows of Auschwitz in her cool, blue eyes. I see her standing guard in a dark tower, eager for the chance to kill. But she is too young for that, isn't she? Too young to have been there? Perhaps she is a vampire and doesn't age.

People say she has never been laid; that's what makes her cruel. I believe it. She is taut, rigid. She would pinch the dick off any man who tried to enter her. Her vicious thighs would squeeze tighter and tighter until...pop.

She is standing beside my desk when I arrive at work. She is smiling at me and tapping her watch. "The work day starts at eight thirty," she says. "You're late."

I look at my watch. It is eight thirty-three. She might fight me for twenty minutes over a three minute sin, and I'm not sure I have the strength. "No, I'm early."

"You're late!"

"Today is Wednesday," I explain. "And I'm here for Thursday, so I'm early."

"What are you talking about?" She glowers at me, making no attempt to hide her hatred of everything I am.

"You aren't a time traveler," I reply, "so I could never explain it to you."

She storms away from my desk. That is the last I will see her today. I will hear her attacking others, screaming like an Indian scalping settlers, but she will ignore me.

She doesn't know what I do here; she just knows I'm supposed to start it at eight thirty. She will call down to personnel and ask for my file. She will get to the bottom of this. *Who is this man? What does he do? What strange powers does he hold?* The file will arrive empty, and this will worry her even more; she will leave me alone. *He must be important – they have expunged his records.* I am not a secret agent. My file is empty because I have not done anything for the last ten years.

I sharpen pencils, mostly. I have eight pencils, and I start off each morning by sharpening them. My mornings are busiest when the pencils have gotten too short and I have to go to the supply room for more. When I was younger, when I first started working here, I had to sharpen my pencils several times a day. Once I even had a mechanical pencil. Lately, only one pencil ever needs sharpening. But I do them all anyway to keep in practice. Some day I might be busy and dull the tips of all my pencils again.

A middle-aged man stops by my desk. He is lost. He knows me from somewhere but can't quite place my face.

"Hey, how's it going?" he asks.

"Great, great," I say. I show him my pencils. He and I went to orientation together when we came here straight out of college. He is now Vice President For Public Affairs. That means he's a pretty good liar. He was a business major in college, but he does not use any of that now. Now he uses unscrupulous skills the college wouldn't teach him.

A spark of ancient recollection strikes him. "So how's the Lipnitz account going?"

"Fine, fine," I say. Mr. Lipnitz died seven years ago. Poor Mr. Lipnitz worked fifty-five years as a weaver to accumulate a tidy little nest egg. After his death, his son-in-law cracked the egg open and spent it all in one year.

"Say, could you tell me where Mark West's office is?"

I shake my head. "No." Mr. Lipnitz's whereabouts is the only one I know for sure.

People here gossip about me. They say I'm the brother-in-law of the President. The President of the company, not of the United States. If I were the brother-in-law of the President of the United States, I wouldn't be sharpening my own pencils.

Some people toss around ugly rumors. They say I'm sleeping with the boss. There's a horrible thought. She would pinch my dick off, no sweat, then laugh about it afterward – maybe keep it in a pickle jar as a souvenir. I don't listen much to rumors.

When I started here, I was in the Department of Inactive Accounts. There were seven of us. That was until one of my co-workers had a brilliant idea: let's see if we can't get our inactive accounts active again. We sent out Christmas cards with little jingles. "Tis the season to be jolly. Better start saving now, by golly." We signed them "From the crew of your jolly investment vehicle at..." It was very successful. Accounts became active and fell out of our jurisdiction. They laid off my co-worker – the one possessed of brilliant ideas. As more and more accounts became active, the department of seven became a department of two. Then Sally retired and the department sign came down altogether. They left me behind to tidy up. Then they forgot about me.

I stay out of trouble. I make no mistakes: I'm good at sharpening pencils. Each January I get a decent raise, and once or twice a month I get a phone call from my only client, Mrs. Finch of Harmony Mills, in the Catskills of New York. I send her a Christmas card every year; address it myself and sign it with my real name. She never liked our jingles, so I get her one that says "Happy Holidays." When she dies, a computer somewhere will click into action and terminate my job.

The phone rings.

"I didn't get a statement," a voice crackles.

"Mrs. Finch? Is that you?" I ask.

"Who's that?" Mrs. Finch replies.

"Harry Lascome."

"Harry? Oh, Harold!" She tells me about the weather in New York. She tells me how her husband used to be an air raid warden during the war, and how her daughter is in a bad marriage. "He beats her, I know, but they say, 'Mind your own business, old lady, or we'll have you put away.' A fine way to talk to one's mother."

"And how are the grandchildren?" I yell into the phone. I take the lone file from my credenza, open it to a page of notes, and read off their names. "Little Vicky and Scott." I think Vicky must be in her thirties by now, but I still call her Little Vicky.

"They want to lock me in a closet!" she hollers. "They say if I give them the farm, they'll take good care of me, but I know them! They'll lock me in a closet!"

She is angry now. I worry about her blood pressure. There will be repercussions if I kill my only client. "How can I help you today, Mrs. Finch?"

She asks me what the balance is on her account. She's thinking of retiring and is taking inventory of her assets. She says this every time she calls. She's eighty-seven. Her last day of work was in 1968. She wore a mini-skirt that day.

"Seventeen dollars," I say.

She thanks me. It was sixteen dollars last year. Her investments are paying off.

Sometimes the phone rings and it's a wrong number. I'll ask them where they're calling from. *Utah! Wow! Get any rain there lately?*

I look at the clock. It is nine twenty-two. I wish Mrs. Finch had waited until later to call. Now I have nothing to look forward to until lunch. Maybe she'll have a memory lapse and call me again.

I eat lunch with Roger. I have eaten lunch with Roger for fourteen years and still don't know his last name. He has never worn a clean tie. I sometimes wonder if being around Roger is the reason my career has never really materialized. His shirt tail is always hanging out, and his socks rarely match. He is odd baggage to drag with you through the halls of destiny.

He talks as he eats. I watch the chunks of tuna fish grow smaller and smaller in his mouth. He has an overbite and the process is slow. "So my wife says, 'You go tell your boss you need a raise.' I say, 'A raise? What happened to the two percent they gave me January?'" He laughs, and tuna fish falls onto the table. He scoops it up with a finger and plops it in his mouth when he thinks no one is looking. "Fuckin' two percent."

I don't tell him I got three percent for sharpening pencils.

I only vaguely remember how I met Roger. It was in the cafeteria. My department was seven then, and every day we went to lunch together and sat at a table for eight. One day Roger sat in the empty chair. Year by year, the seven of us became six, then five. Four. And so on, until Sally retired, and it was just Roger and me. He is an accident in my life.

Roger works in the mail room. He knows more about the company than the President. He can tell a lot by just looking at the outside of an envelope. For seven years, one particular Senior Vice President received mail from a particular woman associate addressed "From Ms. Raines, To Mr. VanBuren." Then one day it changed. "From Becky, To Danny VanBuren."

"He finally bagged her," Roger said.

Sure enough. A week later, Mrs. VanBuren walked out on Mr. VanBuren. A week after that, Mrs. VanBuren returned home with a new diamond necklace and a fur coat, and Becky became Assistant Vice President. Becky mailed Danny a thank you note: "From Assistant Vice President Raines, To Mr. VanBuren." Roger says there were photographs included; he didn't see them, but he could smell the developing fluid.

Roger asks me if I'm going to eat my potato salad.

"No," I say.

He sticks a plastic fork under the scoop of potatoes. It wobbles as he lifts it, threatening to jump to its death rather than enter his gaping mouth, but Roger keeps it from falling with his fingertips. Safely on his plate, he noisily sucks each fingertip clean.

"I got to get back to work," I say. "See you later, Roger."

"Don't do anything I wouldn't," he cackles. There are few things Roger wouldn't do, I imagine, as I look upon his grinning mouth, showing me the current state of the suicidal potato salad. It is a sad end to such a noble vegetable.

I try to smile back, but I have never been able to smile in Roger's presence. There are two ways I imagine Roger's life going once I am gone from here; he will eat lunch alone for twenty more years, his hungry eyes darting from one table to the next, hunting for abandoned food; or one day a beautiful woman will sit down next to him – "I was hoping to see you alone," she will say – and they will have children together. The world is funny that way.

At my desk, I take down a three ring binder. It has a label on it: Inactive Accounts. Inside is a National Geographic neatly punched with a set of three holes. I visit Africa and watch elephants die until it's time to go home.

***

Beth greets me at the door, brushing hair from her face with exaggerated aplomb. "How was your day?"

"Fine," I say, not touching my hair as I set my briefcase on the floor. I have not needed to do much with my hair in years, ever since short hair came back in style.

"How was your walk from the train station?" she asks, tossing her hair further from her face with a casual flip of her head.

"Fine," I reply after a cautious pause. Beth is trying to tell me something. She wants to seem blasé, but I can tell; she is searching her mind for the right words. I smell onions burning.

"Why don't you take the car?" she asks. She smells onions, too. She trots into the kitchen to the stove and turns the gas down a little.

I trail after her, watching the periphery for signs of a trap as I explain, "If I took the car, you wouldn't have one." We own one car. Some days it was one too many when we lived in the city.

"Well, I was thinking." Beth pauses to stir the onions. She is being fair – she's had all day to think. She is now pausing to give me time to think. "Perhaps I should get a new car. A minivan, maybe."

In the suburbs, one car seems to be one too few.

"It's a short walk to the train station," I respond, feeling the tension ebb from my feet now that Beth's plan is revealed.

"Yes, but when it rains."

"I can take an umbrella." I weigh the cost of an umbrella in one hand, and the cost of a minivan in the other. It is only in my mind, but my shoulders still tip a bit.

"How about when it snows?" Beth asks calmly.

"I'll wear a ski cap," I reply, snatching an onion from the pan with a fork.

She swats playfully with her wooden spoon at my retreating hand. "It'll be dark when you come home in winter."

"I can carry a flashlight."

She stirs the onions again, slowly; this time for her benefit as she struggles to recall this conversation as she'd practiced it earlier in a mirror. She sets her wooden spoon aside and takes up a salad fork. "What if a dog attacks you?"

"I'll carry mace."

"It would be so much easier if you took the car." Beth pokes one of the onions with the fork to see if it's tender.

"What if someone steals it?" I say as I watch her set her fork aside and turn the stove off.

With her task now finished, our voices quicken.

"You could install an alarm," she suggests.

"I might get a flat tire."

"Make sure you have a good spare."

I am fighting a power too strong to resist. We are suburbanites now. It is required that we have a minivan.

***

I have never heard Justin swear. I don't swear, at least not at home. Sometimes I swear at work, but I do it softly so no one will hear; just a little curse sent out to hang in the air and haunt the halls, if only for a moment.

I walk into the garage. It is filled with boxes. There are many boxes still waiting to be unpacked. Beth needs a cheese grater.

"It's in the box marked 'kitchen,'" Beth yells.

There are a dozen boxes marked "kitchen." The garage door is open, and I can hear two boys talking in the driveway. I walk to the open doorway planning to say "hi" to Justin and to meet his new friend.

"That is fuckin' awesome!" I hear Justin say.

I am too embarrassed to step into the light now. I retreat. Then I stall, rattling among the kitchen boxes until I'm sure Justin knows I'm near. Finally I walk out onto the driveway.

"Hi, son. Who's your new friend?"

Justin winces. He hates it when I meet his friends. He hides them when he can. Many times I hear their voices, but they don't seem to have a physical form. I sometimes wonder if he has invented them, if he's invited back his invisible friends of early childhood and is doing make-believe voices so we won't know how lonely he is. I wonder if we should be seeking professional help.

This friend is real. I knew him many years ago. He has never aged. He is a farm boy. The suburbs have moved in on him and made him an outcast on his own land. His father sold most of the farm, and now they raise Christmas trees on the remaining six acres. They will sell that, too, when taxes have run their bank account dry. Then they will be gone.

"This is Frankie." Justin doesn't tell his friend who I am. He assumes his friend doesn't need to know another father – he already has one of his own back home. They are hunched over a motorcycle. Frankie is sixteen. His father bought him the motorcycle because the barn was torn down to make way for a four-bedroom colonial. Frankie can't raise pigs anymore. He can't go to 4-H shows anymore. His father bought him a motorcycle to cheer him up.

Frankie will not grow up to be a farmer. He will be first an outcast, then a hoodlum, and finally a prison guard. He will be injured in a riot and get a good disability settlement, but he will drink himself to death before he can spend it.

Both boys look down at the bike. They each stroke a handlebar.

"Hey, Justin!" Frankie says. "You want me to take you for a spin?"

I see Justin's chin jerk up slightly. Excitement glitters in the corners of his eyes. He tries to suppress a childish grin, but he can't. Then he sees me, and the smile fades. He will have to ask my permission. In front of his friend, he will have to whine, the pitch of his voice wavering, fighting a discordant battle between two octaves. *Daddy, can I go for a ride with my friend? Please? Pretty please?* He can't do that now. He is fourteen. Hair is gathering like moss in dark regions; it has colonized his armpits. He is a man.

"Justin's helmet is still packed away," I say. "So don't get too crazy. Okay, Frankie?"

Justin looks up at me. He gives me a special smile. *Thanks, Dad. I love you, Dad. I didn't realize you were so cool, Dad.* It's a rare smile, and I treasure it. I forget about the cheese grater.

Beth is in the kitchen still. She has given up on me and is grating the cheese in a pepper mill.

"I thought you were kidnapped," she says.

"I was checking out Justin's new friend."

She sighs. "Frankie?" She says a lot in those two syllables. She doesn't like him. "He doesn't go to school."

"Where'd Justin meet him?"

"After school. We saw a sign for fresh eggs," Beth explains as she cranks the pepper mill with a hint of aggression. "Frankie was selling them through the kitchen window."

It will be the last time Beth buys eggs from a farm. She will buy them at the supermarket in the future. She will buy white eggs until she hears that brown eggs are better. Brown eggs are local eggs and are therefore fresher.

The pepper mill idea is not working. The holes are gummed up with cheese. Beth takes out a knife and chops the cheese into course chunks. "I can't wait until we get everything organized." She says nothing more about Frankie. She doesn't like him; that's all she has to say. Even that, she didn't actually say.

Not to worry, Love. Frankie will be gone soon. Somewhere out there is a senior accountant or an insurance executive waiting anxiously for another promotion. They will have a son and perhaps a daughter, and will move in down the street. Frankie will fade away, and Justin will play with the son – a future spaceman. Beth will like him because he is young and sweet and always says, "Thank you, Mrs. Lascome." I will hate him because he'll talk too much about his father and their Corvette.

September 10

It is the children's second day of school. I have taken the day off to finish with the move. Beth and I have been unpacking linens and bedspreads. There are linens and bedspreads scattered all about our bedroom, but none have made it onto the bed. Beth and I are on the bed, on the naked mattress. We are naked. There are no sheets covering us – we are not Baptists.

It is late summer, but it is still very hot.

We have already kissed. Passion is gone – it is now raw sex. A mirror leans against a wall, ready for hanging. It is set at an odd angle and I can see my hairy ass pop into view as I hover anxiously over my wife's perspiring body. It is not a pretty sight.

Two beads of sweat form on my chest and roll to my nipples. They are going to fall – together, simultaneously – if I can just time it right. I line my nipples up, align them with Beth's breasts. This is something new; I have not tried this before.

Beth's eyes are closed. She will not see the creativity of my lovemaking. Her eyes are shut, and she will dream that the falling droplets are the tears of Mel Gibson as he confesses his love to her.

My eyes are open, but they do not want to see the hairy ass bouncing about in the mirror. I look toward the window instead. There are no shades yet. No curtains. If it weren't for a small tree, we would be exposed to the world. I imagine the tree gone. I imagine the Baptists standing on the sidewalk, watching, each one slowly licking an oversized lollipop with their serpent-shaped tongues. I get harder.

Beth does not notice. She doesn't moan. She says nothing. She wishes Mel Gibson were a better lover.

A door slams shut. A boy's voice calls, "Mom, I'm home!" The words echo along the barren yellow walls, and I wilt.

I roll off Beth and onto the floor. There is underwear somewhere among the bed sheets. There is a tee shirt and a pair of cutoffs, too, but I can't find them. Beth digs frantically among the pillows. She has found a bra, but nothing more. You can not greet your son wearing only a bra in the suburbs. Probably not in the city, either. I find my sneakers and put them on. There are footsteps on the staircase.

"Mom?"

My sneakers flap against the bare floor as I scurry to our bedroom door and grab the knob. The door will not shut. There are boxes stacked against it. The top box is full of sun screen. We have never been tan, and that is why. I rush back to the bed, many things flapping as I run – sneakers against floor, flesh against flesh. I grab Beth's hand and together we run to the master bathroom.

Justin hears the bathroom door close. "Mom?"

I nudge Beth, and she calls out. "I'll be right there."

He doesn't respond. I hear footsteps on the stairs again. I look down and see that I'm hard again. I reach out with my lips and kiss Beth.

"Not now," she whispers, and pushes me away.

We sneak into the bedroom and dress in silence, then stroll downstairs to greet our first born.

"Dad?" Justin did not expect to find me home.

"So, Jussie, why are you home so early?"

Beth calls Justin "Jussie" when she forgets he is fourteen. She calls him that when she thinks he is angry at her. Apparently, she calls him that after she's been making love.

"Teacher's workshop today," he replies. He looks at both of us with a queer stare. There is something wrong – he can feel it in the air. A strangeness has infiltrated the house. Pods have replaced his parents – we are not his real parents. He looks away, and spreads peanut butter across a slice of bread.

"But school just started a week ago," I complain.

Justin shrugs. There is no point in questioning good fortune. He looks at us again and his eyes narrow; we are not moving. People normally move, but Beth and I are standing still, watching peanut butter accumulate on bread as though it were an Olympic sport.

"Any mail?" I ask and walk to the hall table, breaking the spell, restarting the normal motion of a healthy household.

I forgot – we are in the suburbs. The mail does not make it inside any longer. I have to go out to the street, to the mailbox.

Kathleen is returning from school. We meet on the front stoop. "Hi," I say.

She says nothing, but she's not crying, and I take solace in that. In the city, she went to a Catholic school. We aren't Catholic, but the parochial schools were more orderly. They paid very little in wages, but somehow attracted better teachers than the public schools. Kathleen cried every day, though. It was always something different. The other children got to eat a cracker, but she didn't.

"They're holy crackers," I explained. "Here, have an Oreo."

One nun made the Catholic children say "Hail Marys" when they made mistakes, but she bopped Kathleen on the head with her pointer when Kathleen couldn't spell *Mississippi.*

"Kitten, when you're older, you'll understand freedom of religion is more important than a bop on the head."

She stopped crying long enough to look at me like I was from Mars.

Now she enters the house in silence. She is silent from terror; terror of the unknown world into which she has fallen. I could like terror – her silence, anyway – but I don't think it's a good emotion for a 7-year-old to build a life around.

I follow Kathleen into the house. "Justin, could you get the mail for me?"

Justin stares at me, a stare he learned from his mother when he was a toddler. He needs the magic word.

"Please," I add, and say a *Jesus* under my breath.

Kathleen is in the family room watching TV. She has no interest in good posture. She doesn't care from what angle she views her show. She is lying on her back upon the carpet, with her feet up on the sofa and her head tipped straight back so she can see an upside-down television behind her. She isn't watching her show though. She is staring up at the ceiling.

"Is there something wrong?" I ask.

She moves her mouth slowly, saying each word distinctly so I don't miss any of it. "I don't like my new school."

I think back on my school days, searching for some clue of what she might be going through. I remember one particular grammar school in a town where the weather was always hot and steamy, and all the children spoke with languid accents. They laughed at me because, moving so often, I had no accent at all.

"Are the children mean?" I ask.

"No," Kathleen replies impatiently.

I recall another school where at lunch the boys told jokes about hot rods and mouths that I didn't understand. I laughed at the punch lines anyway to hide my ignorance.

"Are they too smart?" I ask.

Kathleen laughs at that. "No." She rolls over on her stomach and stares at me with a look of shear amazement. "They're all white. It's creepy."

I am confused. We are white. Or car is white. If we had a dog, it would be white. But then I think of what it must be like for a little girl encountering such uniformity for the first time. How would I feel if I moved to a town where everyone was named Harold and no one ate anything except boiled eggs? What would it be like if everyone was a clone of Albert Einstein or Mr. Rogers? I pat her foot. "You'll get used to it."

"I miss my friends." She starts to cry. We are making headway.

She misses Rahana. Rahana was – is – black. She taught Kathleen Swahili words when they were six. Kathleen said something in Swahili to a black man in a convenience store.

He glared at her. "You mocking me, girlie?"

After that, Rahana and Kathleen spoke Swahili only to each other. They invented their own secret world and let no one else in.

"You'll make new friends," I say. I walk into the kitchen, but behind me I can hear Kathleen sobbing. Then I hear her whispering little bits of Swahili.

The city is calling her home.

September 15

Kathleen is in the den. I hear the tippy-type of quiet keys as she sits facing the wall, the eerie glow of the computer framing her flowing hair with a technological radiance. She stops typing, then laughs. She does not hear me as I walk up behind her. I stare down at the computer monitor, expecting to see a knock-knock joke.

"8 or 9 inches," the screen says, "depends on how hot it gets."

"Kathleen!" I shout, unsure of the quickest way to end this seductive exchange. I reach down and pull out the power cord. The screen goes black.

"Daddy! Why'd you do that?"

"Who were you talking to?" I shout, holding up the cord to show her the power that I wield.

"Some girl in Michigan," Kathleen says, the irritation in her voice showing that she does not understand a parent's fear of technology.

Some girl? There is nothing on a girl that is eight or nine

inches long. I hope she will never know a boy that has something that is eight or nine inches long.

"She was telling me about her snapdragons." She grabs the cord from my hand and jabs it into the socket, clucking with disgust.

"Snapdragons?" I say.

"Yes, Daddy. Snapdragons. She has a garden." With a few expert strokes to the keyboard, the screen comes alive once more; a blue flash, and then a cacophony of colorful pictures. The mouse slides, buttons click. Both hands work feverishly. If she had a garden of her own, she would have weeded it by now. Nine-inch snapdragons. Bah! Baby, go for twelve. Mice across America hear wires crackle as Kathleen reconnects to a Michigan gardener, one of limited skill.

"Phooey," Kathleen says, and lays her weary hands at her sides. "She must of logged off."

"How do you know that, Kitten?"

"Because the chat room is full and won't let me in. If she was still there, everyone would be gone, and I could get in." She looks up at me as if she were lecturing a naughty puppy. "No one wants to talk to her. All she ever talks about is her snapdragons, all day long."

"Why do you talk to her then?" I ask.

"'Cause it's cool," Kathleen says. She flicks the computer off by its switch and grabs a piece of gum out from under the lamp shade. "I'll try again later."

"No. Show me," I say.

"Show you?" She laughs. "Daddy, this is a computer." She blows a bubble and pops it with her teeth.

"Yeah, I know it's a computer." I reach over and flick the power back on. "You don't think I know about computers? My generation invented them."

"Yeah, right." Kathleen nudges my hand away from the keyboard.

"You still program in Cobol?"

Kathleen snickers, but does not reply.

Beth wanders in holding a sheet of paper. "It's the strangest thing," she remarks. She slides up beside me, then jumps back as the computer screen bursts forth with bright lights. "Someone taped this to the front door." She chuckles again. "An anonymous letter saying we're tacky."

"Let me see it," I reply.

She hands it out toward me, and I shudder. A sprig of crabgrass has been taped to the bottom. That's like pirates handing out black spots. Whoever did this means business.

Beth sees my worried look and stops chuckling. "It's just some old crank."

"No," I reply as I rub my fingers across my sweating forehead and through my hair. "We've done something. Think."

"Done something? What could we have possibly done." Beth backs out of the room, retreating from Kathleen and the spooky glow of an unfathomable future.

I follow her as she glides into the kitchen. She moves about, happy to be among the familiar appliances, unaware of the danger we are in. She pours tomato sauce into a pot, then goes to throw the bottle away.

I see the trash compactor is empty. "Where's our garbage?"

"Our garbage?" Beth shakes her head in amusement. "The bag was full, so I put it out."

"Put it out?" An image of a forlorn trash bag sitting between the driveway and the sidewalk flashes through my mind. "But today's only Tuesday."

"So?" Beth seems unconcerned as she places the pot on the stove and flicks on the gas.

"Trash pickup isn't until Thursday. You never, ever put the trash out more than twenty-four hours ahead."

Beth laughs. "Don't be silly. You put the trash out when the bag is full."

I pick up the phone and punch numbers. "I'll get Adam over here and see how bad the damage is."

"It's not like we stuck pink flamingoes along the walk," Beth sighs. "It'll be gone in a few days."

I don't have time to explain about pink flamingoes, that they're okay now, especially if you're the neighborhood's token gay couple or very very rich so everyone knows its a put-on. I explain hurriedly to Adam what has happened. He does not wait for me to finish; I can hear his phone swishing against a wall as I spot him exit his back door and rush across our lawn.

He bursts through our back door without knocking. "Let me see it," he shouts. There is an unnatural quality about him, as if none of this surprises him. He is a bad actor playing an uninspiring role.

Beth brings him a root beer as he scans the letter. The only sound he makes is a crinkling noise as he shakes the paper, hoping to knock the note's meaning out and onto the floor where we can see it.

"Well, I don't think the damage is too severe," he announces, his voice much deeper than normal. "It's not like you let a visiting relative park their RV in your driveway."

"No, no. Nothing like that," I reply, eyeing Adam suspiciously.

"What's wrong with RVs?" Beth asks absently. She unwraps a package of fresh linguine and drops it into a large pot of boiling water.

Neither Adam nor I respond. In time she will learn about RVs. She will learn about boats under blue tarps and playhouses on front lawns. She will learn about grass that is too long, Christmas lights that are too bright, and house paint that is too pink. But right now we are discussing garbage that is too old.

"I think we can fix this," Adam's deep voice continues.

"Adam," I say. "You knew about this letter."

Adam freezes, then his voice returns to his normal drone. "The whole block knew. Something had to be done. I mean, two Tuesdays in a row, man. Are you trying to destroy the neighborhood?"

"Beth didn't know," I explain.

Beth rushes up and grabs Adam's hand. "Really, I didn't know."

Adam smiles kindly at Beth as he pats her hand. "Well, like I said, the damage isn't too severe."

"So what do the neighbors want for penance?" I inquire fearfully.

Adam retreats toward the back door. "Some landscaping. Two azaleas and a yew under the living room window should do it. Mr. Firestick was demanding a boxwood, too, but three shrubs should be enough. And some cedar mulch." He opens the door and steps out, then turns back. "And no more garbage on the front lawn until Wednesday nights."

The glass rattles as the door slams shut. I look at Beth and try to smile. "That's not too bad."

"No? What else could they have done?" Beth asks as she chops angrily at a block of sourdough bread.

I slide over to the stove and dip a ladle into the bubbling tomato sauce. "They made Mrs. Raddcliff spend six Saturdays in a row handing out literature for the Republican party, and all she did was hang her laundry out in daylight."

October 5

Beth holds up a black evening dress. She wore it to a Christmas party several years back, but tonight it's a different crowd; no one will have seen it.

"Too formal," I say. We're going to a neighbor's for cocktails. We have lived here a month now; this is our first invitation to a neighborhood function.

Beth is visibly excited. The dress shimmies seductively as she holds it up, its sequins glitter in the bedroom light – it is her hands shaking with anticipation.

"Too formal?" she replies disappointedly.

It is her favorite style for cocktail parties. It accentuates all the right features. It reminds me of old movies – of clumsy men dropping olives down women's cleavage.

"It's too formal for the suburbs," I say.

She is saddened. What is the point of going out if you can't dress up? She holds up an old sweat suit – she stenciled the bathroom in it, and there are splashes of salmon and cranberry on the sleeves. No, not food – paint.

I laugh. "Getting warmer," I say.

She finds a pair of gray slacks and a red silk blouse and puts them on. She doesn't ask my opinion – she has run out of options. I was going to wear my gray slacks and a red polo shirt; but matching outfits – we would be too cute then – so I choose a green shirt with crossed golf clubs on the pocket. There is the name of a country club underneath, but I don't read well upside-down.

Beth checks her lipstick one last time in the foyer mirror. "Justin, take care of your sister," she calls.

"Kathleen, keep your brother out of trouble," I call.

They do not respond – they are in the family room fighting over the television remote control. We leave anyway; we have to be at the Greenleys at seven and it is now six fifty-eight.

The party is at the Andersen's, but they don't know us. They weren't the ones to invite us, either. Eve invited Beth.

We walk down our driveway, through the early evening air.

"How did this come about?" I ask again, still not sure that the Andersens will welcome us.

Beth retells the story:

She had called me this morning at work; she was bored.

Take a walk, I had said.

She couldn't, she replied. All the houses looked the same. She was afraid she'd get lost. Besides, there was nothing to walk to.

"Well, go visit Eve next door," I suggested.

"Can I do that?" she asked.

"Yes. Just go ring their bell."

So she did.

The two women talked. They talked about their children and

other things. Eve revealed that she sold cosmetics in her spare time, but they didn't know that at her church. She baked sometimes, too, she said. She had just made some macaroons – they were an experiment. They came out of the oven flat, the edges crisp and black. The two women laughed. "Oh well," Eve said. "I've got some Ring Dings."

Beth doesn't bake. We had three bakeries near us in the city. One was Portuguese, the other was Italian, and the third I guess you'd call American. We ate perfect macaroons.

"There's a party tomorrow at the Andersens." Eve cut her Ring Ding in half because of her diet. She ate the other half after Beth left. "Are you and Harry going?"

"No, Beth replied. "We aren't invited."

"Of course you are," Eve giggled. "You'll be our guests."

As we approach the Greenley's driveway, their garage door opens with a clack and a whirl. We watch from the street as the tail lights of their car go on and their vehicle backs down the driveway.

The car reaches the end of the driveway and stops. The window rolls down and Adam's face pops into view. "Hop in," he commands.

Adam is not smiling, but Eve is giddy. She is in the back seat waiting for Beth. I share the front passenger seat with Adam's Bible.

"I thought this was a neighborhood party?" I say, not sure why we are getting in a car.

"It is," he replies, swinging the car onto the street.

We drive past three houses before the crush of parked cars indicates this is as close as we will get to the Andersen's. We will have to go the rest of the way on foot.

The two women are laughing as we climb from the car. Adam

silences his wife with a frown, then leads us past two mailboxes before turning up a driveway.

Mr. Andersen is standing at the front door, quietly counting guests as they enter, measuring the success of his party. He greets us under the glow of an orange bug light. He is a smiling young man, boyish in appearance, a blond wave on top of his head. He is holding a martini. I suppress the urge to ask him whether his father lets him drink.

"This is Harry and Beth Lascome," Adam explains. The martini boy does not react, so Adam adds, "The colonial-blue Wilmington."

"Oh, the Wilmington." He puts out his hand. "Troy Andersen," he says, then indicates his own home with something of a flourish with the martini glass. "Ours is the Remington model, as you can see." He steps aside and lets us through. We are friendly, he knows – the Wilmington and the Remington are the same house, except the Remington has a mud room where the Wilmington has a laundry room. It seems quite a contrast when one thinks too long about it. "Donna!" he calls. "The colonial-blue Wilmington is here."

A pregnant girl shuffles into the foyer. "Come in! Come in!" she shouts. "Make yourself at home."

I look about at the familiar surroundings and feel that that will be quite easy.

The party is in the living room and the kitchen. There are two children in the family room. They are wrestling on the floor, each one struggling for control of the television remote. They are too old to be from the pregnant girl's womb.

"Due Christmas Day!" Donna pats her stomach and smiles at Beth.

Beth has not asked about the pregnancy, but Donna assumes all women are interested in pending births. I never ask about pregnancies – not since the incident with the secretary at work, the barren one with the thyroid condition.

Beth tries to follow me into the living room. “Faux pas,” I whisper, and point toward the kitchen.

“What is this? Stepford wives or something?” she whispers back.

The women have wine in the kitchen. Hard liquor is set out for the men on a card table beside the living room fireplace.

“It was a four thousand dollar option,” Troy announces proudly as he steps up beside me and points toward it – the fireplace, not the card table. “But what the hey.”

He asks me what my pleasure is, but I don’t tell him the entire truth. “A beer,” I say.

“One beer. One beer for the colonial-blue Wilmington.”

There are a dozen men in the living room. Half are wearing red polo shirts. I'm glad Beth forced my hand on that one. Adam knows most of them and abandons me. He dives into the group and is laughing before he’s had a chance to absorb the conversation.

I poke my head into the kitchen and see Beth surrounded by women. That’s one of the major differences between men and women. Women take the new person in right away – add them to the pride right off. Strength in numbers. Men, they have to sniff around a bit before they’ll accept a new member. They send a scout out occasionally to give me a whiff.

“So Harry, you see the fight the other night?”

Couldn’t. Had to spar a few rounds down at the gym that night. That’s what I should say, but instead I say, “You mean boxing?”

“No. Hockey. Jeez.”

The scout returns to the group, his nose slightly curled from the stench of my ignorance. The men huddle, and there’s a bit of laughter that I imagine is at my expense.

Troy comes up and gives me a beer anyway.

In the kitchen, Beth is talking. She is still nervous. Her voice is loud. "I was thinking of going back to work," she is telling someone. "Do you know if there's a feminist bookshop in town?"

In the city, once the children got older, Beth worked in a little book nook that sold mostly women's literature and some poetry. She does not consider herself a feminist, though; she is "modern."

There are no feminist bookshops in the suburbs. There are no feminists. No socialists, no atheists, no anarchists. Not out in the open anyway. They are all in hiding – the closets are very deep in the suburbs. They will come out, though, and mingle with the rest of the neighborhood at the Fourth of July picnic. They will even "ew" and "ah" as fireworks explode overhead. But when talk turns to politics, they will excuse themselves; they will volunteer to flip burgers or play bartender to their friends; anything to avoid the droll banter of bickering Democrats and Republicans.

"You don't want a job," I hear Eve say. "If you're bored, you can join me at the fitness center."

Another woman squeals in delight. They are a minority – the housewives. They see an opportunity to win another convert to the noble cause of homemaking.

There is a small table between the living room and the family room. I set my beer on it and fill my hands with salted peanuts.

The two children turn off the television and go upstairs. They are brothers – nephews of my host, perhaps. They are too old – teenagers – to be his children. The party is lame, and they are disappointed. They have porno hidden among their mattresses. One has a bulge under his shirt – he has swiped my beer. They will pass the bottle between their bunks and whistle low at the size of women's breasts.

"Damn, Harry!" Troy sees I'm without a drink. "You can sure suck them down!" He grabs my hand and pulls me to the group. "You should see this guy drink," he announces to the others.

I'm in.

***

The women have been discreetly counting the men's drinks. They know their husbands well – know their limits – and the time is ripe. The music starts, and the women flood the living room, grabbing anyone but their own husband for a dance partner. Beth grabs Troy's hand – his freckles have turned bright red from the effect of his fourth martini.

A scarecrow with buck teeth takes my hand. It is obvious she is anorexic, and I shrink visibly from the sight of her. She thinks it's the beauty of her slim figure that has startled me. She smiles back. "Don't be shy." She clacks the words out on skeleton lips.

I am dancing with death.

The tempo changes; a slow song plays. First one man, then another, spins off from his original dance partner and joins his wife. It was a thrilling moment – a bit risqué – this mixing of spouses, but we must nestle our heads once more between the familiar breasts of our betrothed before someone gets carried away. There is no more gentle flirting – Beth does not squeeze my biceps and coo, "such muscles," as the scarecrow did to me.

There is one man among the group who has come stag. He claims his date got sick, but he is probably gay. He drinks Dewars, though. "Come on, let's liven this party up!" He pushes a few buttons on the stereo, and "Louie Louie" blasts across the room.

The dancing stops.

He sidles up to several women and shakes his shoulders at them – pretends he's got titties – but they ignore his advances. He realizes the moment is gone and he is being a fool. Dejectedly, he pours himself an extra large glass of Dewars and flops across a yellow armchair.

"Everyone! Everyone!" Troy is swaying on the hearth of his four thousand dollar fireplace. He clinks a spoon against his martini glass. "Now that everyone's good and drunk, it's time for the entertainment." He points toward the dining room as Donna marches into the room with a large placard balanced on her pregnant belly.

My vision is blurred, but I can still see the bold green dollar signs scattered about the margins of the sign; and along the upper border, the bright red letters A M W A Y.

October 6

The shades are drawn, but the light in our bedroom is still too bright.

"What time is it?" I ask.

"Ten," Beth says. She is sitting cross-legged on our bed, picking through a pile of home cleaning products.

"What day is it?"

She smiles. "Sunday."

Good. I didn't miss the rest of the weekend. I look at her booty, stretching from her knees to the foot of the bed. "Where'd the Tupperware come from?"

"Julie came on after Troy and Donna finished with their Amway pitch. You were asleep."

"Julie?"

She stares at me. "Julie. You know. The one you danced with."

"Not..." But I don't have to finish; Beth nods her head knowingly.

"Where'd the cosmetics come from?"

Beth picks up a lipstick and twists it open so we can see the color. She was a bit drunk, too, apparently. "Eve sold them to me while we were waiting for you to fetch Adam home."

After the party, Eve wouldn't let Adam drive, so he insisted on walking. We took the car; Eve drove. She tried to follow him, urging him along with the glare of the high beams, but he stopped beside the road and wouldn't move until we had left. When he didn't arrive home, Beth sent me out to find him.

"What happened to him, anyway?" Beth asks as she examines the lipstick under the table lamp.

"He stopped to piss on the Simpson's azalea bush," I explain. "He was returning the favor their dog does for him."

Adam drank ten beers and didn't piss once at the Andersen's. He is a camel. Moses should have ridden him to safety when he fled Egypt.

"Took awfully long," Beth replies.

"Then he passed out in their rock garden."

There is yelling outside our window, but it is good-natured yelling. Adam is calling us to church. He has never called us to church before. What have we done? I open the blinds and look out toward the Greenley's driveway. He is dressed up more than usual. The children are lined up beside the driveway. Eve is lined up. They each have a bright red Bible. They are a perfect family.

No, he doesn't really want us to come with them. He is embarrassed about last night's antics. He is putting on a show for the neighbors, to let them know that it was all a big mistake. He is not a drunk.

I open the window. "You go on, Adam," I yell. "Beth's busy with inventory."

He salutes me, and the four Greenley's march into the garage. They drive off honking and waving. The car does not smell like vomit, but the Simpson's rock garden does.

"I hope he looked better than you do," Beth says.

My mouth is dry. I don't have a headache, but if I shut my eyes tight enough, the world turns blood red. If I open them again, little stars dance around my forehead. I swat them away, but they ignore me and keep dancing. "I think I'll take a shower."

The water falls noisily upon my neck and shoulders. I feel fat and puffy all over. Except for my dick, which feels tiny – he has gone into hiding, a little acorn desperately trying to preserve his health while the poison works its way out of my system.

Come out and play. I flick him with the tip of my finger, but he is dead. I have killed him. My brain is dead, too. I have killed all that I love of me. My toes are tingling – they are still alive – but I don't love them. Perhaps if I were a ballerina, I would.

The bathroom door opens. I do not hear it – the water pounding against the back of my head prevents that – but I feel the cold air roll into the shower stall. Perhaps Beth will join me in the shower. I listen carefully, and hear the faint tinkling of urine, then the flush of the toilet. There is another cold blast. Beth has left – she will not join me in the shower. I look down at my shriveled penis – it is just as well.

I feel refreshed as I rub my hair dry. The little stars come back anyway. There is nothing to be done about that. I toss the towel into the hamper and step from the warm moisture of the bathroom into the chilly air of our bedroom. My entire family is on my bed. Beth has given Kathleen one of the lipsticks – bright orange – and the little girl is busy coloring her face. Justin is asking Beth if she can sew a biker's patch on his sweatshirt. I am standing before them naked. They do not understand that at first – it is not something they normally see. They cock their heads as they try to figure out what it is that's different about me. The reality sinks in, and Kathleen hides her head among our pillows, spreading orange across the pillowcase with her lips as she burrows deeper and deeper.

"Jeez, Dad." Justin grimaces as he averts his eyes. He hopes that his will not become so puny as he grows older. He has just gotten used to the idea of it getting bigger.

I step backward into the bathroom. I will not expose the rest of me. I will not show them my hairy ass. Another shower is needed. Perhaps when I return fully dressed, they will think that I am a different daddy.

***

Outside, the sun is bright and summer won't give way to autumn although it is October already. The grass seed has not germinated. Chemical companies have noticed this and call me on a regular basis, but I am determined to do it on my own.

I am spreading more fertilizer when Adam returns from church. Redemption is his, and he is smiling broadly. His necktie is in his hand, for inside the church was hot. Someone once suggested air conditioning but was shot down.

"We do not challenge the wisdom of God when he created summer!"

"But we heat the building in winter."

"Only to remind us of the eternal fires of hell!"

They've got a very large furnace at Adam's church.

Adam steps to the edge of his property, where the lush green of his spring labors contrasts with the dry dust of my summer-long delay.

"Have you tried lime?" he asks.

I shake my head no.

He kicks my dust with the end of his polished shoe. He is now an official trespasser. "They took your topsoil, you know."

"They took my topsoil?"

"Yeah. They came here with dump trucks and a bulldozer and scraped it all off. You have to buy it back if you want anything to grow." He points off toward a vacant area of the development, to where two huge mounds overgrown with Queen Anne's lace lay like women's breasts under a summer nightgown. "That's where they dumped it."

Now I'll need a wheelbarrow. I have to reclaim what is mine, a shovel full at a time. Scrape away the weeds, fill the wheelbarrow, and roll my dirt home. A thousand trips perhaps – but I will not pay again for what I have already bought. Let the builder spot the telltale trail, the sprinkling of dirt that escapes the wheelbarrow on each bumpy trip, gradually paving a brown path across the black hardtop, pointing the way to the home of Harold Lascome, soil thief!

Adam kneels down and examines my dirt. Nothing is going to grow this year; there is no harm in him marching across the lawn to where I stand. He stands up and strides to my side. "Beth told you about the two boys?"

"The two boys?" Beth has told me nothing about two boys. We talk about bills and laundry. Sometimes she asks about hillbillies, but we rarely mention boys. We have one of our own, and any reminder of that can be painful.

"Last night, at the Andersens."

"The brothers?" I ask.

Adam nods his head. Ah, those two boys. "They're Donna's nephews. They're orphans."

Orphans. It's such a strange word. Something from Dickens' era. Is there really such a thing as an orphan in this modern age?

"Their parents die in a plane crash or something?" I ask.

Adam smiles. "Car crash, Donna says. But there was no car crash. There was never even a father." He moves up closer to me, and whispers in my ear. "Their mother was a hooker. She died of AIDS."

I say nothing.

Adam nods his head again, dispelling any doubts I may harbor, daring me to disagree. There is wickedness in this town, his thin, smug smile says. He will battle that wickedness from the shadows; the two boys will never know who their enemy was. They will not know why they were sent from this comfortable neighborhood to the boys' school in Kansas. They will watch the dusty wheat fields from their dorm room window, never knowing that it was Adam, waving cheerfully to them from his well-kept lawn, who smeared disgrace across their family name and forced them into exile.

I do not mention the beer swiping incident. Underage drinking will add unnecessarily to Adam's arsenal. AIDS and illegitimacy are enough already to invoke the maximum sentence: lifetime banishment from suburbia.

A basketball bounces inside the garage. The sound of it echoes through the neighborhood. Justin strolls into the driveway, dribbling the ball in front of him as he goes. He stops and shoots. The ball goes straight up, and he leaps into the air to catch it. He is prodding me in his gentle teenage way. *Dad! Where's the basketball hoop you promised me!* The words ring out with each bounce of the ball. *Dad! Dad! Hoop! Hoop!*

Promise! Two syllables. That's a double dribble, son.

Justin is wearing his sweatshirt. I see that Beth has already sewn the biker patch on the back. Adam's eyes lock on the patch each time my son spins away from an imaginary opponent; Adam does not see a youngster engaged in healthy athletics; he sees a future gangster.

Frankie drives up on his motorcycle; he guns the engine to draw attention to his arrival. Justin rolls the basketball into the open garage as he tosses me a, "Dad?"

It's a courtesy "dad" – he is not really asking permission, and he is not waiting for an answer. He bounds to the end of the driveway and leaps on behind Frankie.

"Be back in time for dinner," I yell, but Frankie revs the bike and drowns me out.

The two boys sit there a moment, Justin bouncing up and down on the back of the long seat, grinning; and Frankie practicing "cool," sitting rigid, slow deliberate hand movements, looking straight ahead, his eyes and face hidden behind the darkness of his new visor. Justin taps the top of Frankies' helmet, Frankie gives a thumbs up, and they're off.

"Don't forget dinner!" I yell once more.

Adam's eyes widen – it all makes sense now. The naked girl, the feminist bookstore, and now the son with his motorcycle gang. We are the neighborhood's closet liberals. Perhaps he was too hasty befriending us. "Ah, I've got to get back to the family, Harry." He steps backward, carefully retracing his footsteps across my failed lawn.

October 11

Justin is looking out the picture window. He has the curtain drawn across his face so that only his eyes and hair would be visible from outside the house.

"Who you spying on, Son?"

He puts a finger to his lips. He is on a top-secret mission. His hand releases the curtain as he slides back against the wall.

"Is someone after you?"

He nods, then gulps. "Bernie Ickman."

Bernie Ickman is a little Jewish boy. Justin can whip him with his shadow. Fatherhood confuses me. Perhaps Bernie knows karate or something. "The skinny redhead everyone calls Icky?" I ask.

Justin nods. "They got something called a Sadie Hawkins Dance, and his sister wants to ask me to it."

Now I understand. Bernie is such a skinny little guy because throughout his life, his sister has been hogging all the food. Hormones have exploded within her, and pimples decorate her face with their own unique tint of purple creating a distorted display of color that only Picasso could match. At school, she hovers on the fringes of Justin's group, eyeing him quietly until he feels something must be wrong and reaches down to check his zipper.

She is too horny for her age. The weigh of her body rubs against her, putting pressure on her insides that causes juices to flow. She knows she is not attractive, but she has learned from older girls of ways to get a boyfriend, things she can do to keep him coming back for more. She only needs to get Justin to that Sadie Hawkins Dance, drag him out the back door, bring him behind the dumpster, and...

Oh, God. I must help Justin on this one. If she gets him, he will be trapped. He is too young – he will think he has found a girl who can do things no other can. She will hang out on our front stoop, talking trash and chewing huge wads of gum. The scent of her needs will attract panting dogs to our yard. She and Justin will slip into the basement, the garage. He will follow her with a stupid grin on his face. One Saturday, I will go to steal back a wheelbarrow load of my topsoil and find them together behind the dirt piles, among the Queen Anne's lace. The image will repulse me; it will be months before I can work on the yard again.

I look out the picture window.

"They'll see you," Justin hisses.

There is no one out there. Then I see her. She is big. Icky is lost in her shadow. "I'll tell her you've been grounded."

"Thanks, Dad."

I hear a familiar motorcycle. Frankie pulls up beside the two Ickmans. He says something funny, and the girl throws back her head and laughs. Her huge breasts jiggle, and Frankie's eyes bug out at the sight. He shifts uncomfortably in his seat; he hasn't seen such tits since the milking cows were sold off. He pats the back of the seat, Justin's spot. The girl acts coy at first. She darts her eyes toward our house and almost spots me in the window. Justin is cute, she thinks, but this boy is sixteen and he's got a motorcycle. He can rev his engine and send vibrations clear through to her toes. *All right*, I see her say. She hops on the back, and the two bags of hormones rage down the street and out of sight.

Bernie Ickman looks around. He is Justin's friend at school, but he has never been to the house. There is a big difference there. He puts his hands in his pockets and turns back toward his own street, one nearer to the synagogue.

"What's going on out there?" Justin asks.

"Your friend Frankie got rid of her for you."

"That Frankie," Justin says. "He's such a good friend."

***

Kathleen is in the dining room doing homework. She has crayons scattered across the shiny wooden surface of the table. She hears my footsteps and slides a piece of paper over the one she's been working on.

"They have you coloring for homework?" I ask.

"Uh huh," she says. She doesn't look up, but keeps scribbling. She has drawn a dozen circles. They are children's faces – black, brown, purple, green, and pink. They appear to be singing. I imagine they are singing "We Are The World." Above the picture, she has written "I Love My School" in bold black crayon.

"But that's your old school," I say as I slide the sheet to one side and reveal another picture. There are six circles. They are all colored pink. None of them are singing; they are frowning. Kathleen has written "My School" above the pink circles.

"But you didn't like your old school," I say. "You always

came home crying."

"I liked my school. I just didn't like Sister Roberta," she says.

I can't argue with her there. I didn't like Sister Roberta, either. I suspected she was born a "Robert." One of the older boys at the school told me he had seen her Adam's Apple, but every time I saw her, she had a scarf tied around her neck.

"Isn't there anything good about your school, Kitten?"

She taps a crayon as she thinks. "Well, we have a swimming pool."

"There. See."

"But we can't use it."

"Why can't you use it?"

"Because Maple Avenue School doesn't have a pool, and the teachers said it would be unfair if we went swimming and the kids at the old school didn't."

"Well, just write 'My school has a pool,'" I say. "That'll at least sound like you're saying something nice."

"It rhymes, too," Kathleen says. She smiles. It is the first time since moving that I have helped her with her homework.

November 7

Frankie is gone. He never told Justin he was leaving. Justin bought a helmet with his savings – a real motorcycle helmet to replace the bicycle helmet he had been using. He walked to the farmhouse, swinging the helmet at his side, ready for a spin on Frankie's motorcycle, but the farmhouse was no longer there. A big hole had swallowed it up.

Eventually, a huge pillared house with a granite facade will rise above the hole – with a six-car garage, a swimming pool, and tennis courts. An athletic man and a mousy wife surrounded by little amber-colored bottles will live there. He will sleep with underage girls and she will swallow handfuls of pills. They will both be searching for something, but whatever it is will not fit on the six acres of the former Christmas tree farm.

Justin is sprawled on the family room floor watching reruns of "Gilligan's Island." Kathleen is lying beside him crying because she wants to watch "The Flintstones."

"Justin," I say. "You didn't rake the leaves like I asked you."

He doesn't respond.

We have one tree. Our neighborhood was once a forest, but the contractor knocked all the trees down, built the houses, then planted a single maple on each lot. The price of the maple was worked into the landscaping charges, so I don't know how much it cost me.

The tree has been dying since the day we moved in, and ended the season with seven leaves. One remains stubbornly attached to an upper branch; it will still be there come spring. The other six leaves are scattered around the base of the tree. I bought Justin a rake and asked him to clean up the leaves. "And throw them in the trash," I had said. No point in making a bonfire.

He isn't responding, so I walk to the television and flick it off. He has the remote and zaps it back on. I reach behind the console and pull out the plug. "Rake the leaves," I say.

Kathleen runs crying to her room. She really wanted to watch "The Flintstones," but "Gilligan's Island" was better than nothing. Justin slams the door as he goes outside. I plug the TV back in and watch "Gilligan's Island" to the end. Once again they are not rescued. They remain castaways on an uncharted island.

November 8

The garbage man refuses to take our trash. There are six maple leaves near the top of the trash can. He has spotted them: he won't take lawn debris. I am already late for work, but I am arguing with him anyway.

"You take lettuce leaves," I reason.

"That's food," the man replies.

"We're from the west coast," I lie. "We eat maple leaves there."

He shrugs his shoulders and dumps the trash into the back of his truck. He is in a hurry and doesn't have time to argue; the sooner he's done with the route, the sooner he gets home. He gets paid for a full day even if he does his route in three hours. He works quickly and is sloppy, spreading newspapers and gum wrappers through the neighborhood, but he is rewarded for his fast work with an afternoon off.

The hillbilly across the street has been watching the proceedings. He waits for the garbage truck to move on to the next house, then walks over to me. "If you leave out a six-pack of beer, they'll usually take anything."

That's one beer per leaf.

"Thanks," I say. "I'll try it next time."

He sticks out his hand. "I'm Bill Abernathy, but my friends call me Nat."

I shake his hand. "I'm Harry Lascome. I have no friends."

He laughs. "Well, come on over for a beer, and we'll fix that." He puts his hand on my shoulder and coaxes me toward his driveway. There is a mailbox lying across it; his son knocked it down with his all-terrain vehicle and they have been driving around it for three days.

I smile. It is seven fifteen in the morning. "I have to go to work."

He releases my shoulder. "Want one for the road?"

"I'll take a rain check," I say. I walk down the road toward the train station. I look back and see he's leaned the mailbox up against his maple tree. I doubt that the mailman will spot it there.

It is autumn, and I smell leaves burning. It is an old smell from my youth. We did not burn maple leaves in the city. Tobacco and the occasional scent of marijuana; that was what we had in the city. The sun is bright and there is a clarity to the air. My wife has her new minivan, but I still walk to the train station.

"Take the car," she implores me each morning.

"When it rains," I say, but I never do. There is freedom in walking – there is no dependence on technology or Arabs. There is no need for mental concentration. There are no laws telling me what to do. I know a short cut through the woods. I am Thoreau, and somewhere beyond the tree-line is Walden Pond. The pathway is paved with pine needles; it is soft and quiet. Even in the rain, it is soft and quiet. There is a small trail branching off; I will explore it on the way home, but now I have a train to catch.

A truck has spilled diesel fuel on the highway. There are red lights flashing on top of fire engines. There are white lights flashing on an ambulance. Blue strobe lights flash from the top of police cars. It is a light show – red, white, and blue. It is America calling.

A crowd has gathered at the train station. They can not get through the fuel spill, and have decided to take the train. They will get to the city quickly and conveniently, but tomorrow they will return to their cars.

I am not late this morning. My boss frowns and stomps off to her office. She is unhappy because she has nothing to bitch about.

The phone rings.

It is too early for clients, but it is Mrs. Finch anyway. She has been up since dawn. She is so upset she has barely slept. Her cat won't eat.

"I'd take her to the vet, but it's so expensive," she sighs.

I am seized with panic. She will cash in her mutual fund to pay the vet. She will close the last account in my credenza. "Maybe she's eaten a hair ball," I suggest. "I wouldn't worry."

"Are you a cat lover, Harold?"

"Yes," I tell her. I have never had a cat. I don't like it when cartoon cats outsmart cartoon dogs.

"I've had Mittens for eighteen years," she explains. Her voice crackles with emotion. "I don't know what I'd do if anything happened to her."

I think for a moment. "Tell you what, Mrs. Finch. Take Mittens to the vet, and send me the bill." I am not a generous man – it is a business decision. My entire career is dependent on the health of one Catskills farm cat.

Mrs. Finch lets out an ancient gasp. "Oh, you are an animal

lover, aren't you?"

I am embarrassed now and brush aside her remark; a flippant comment, something like, "Aren't we all, Mrs. Finch. Aren't we all."

"You have children?"

"Two," I reply.

"Children. They're a blessing, but then they grow up," she groans. "And they turn on you. A cat, though, will always be there for you."

Unless they're an 18-year-old cat who's choking on a hair ball. I ask her if she'd like to know her account balance.

"No, no," she replies. She asks me if I'm interested in her weather, then tells me, not waiting for a reply, that they had a heavy frost last night and she thinks the tomato crop has been ruined. "There really isn't enough sun for tomatoes to ripen properly this time of year, anyway, but I find comfort in keeping things going as long as possible."

You should have thrown quilts over them, I tell her, but she just laughs that off. "At my age, I need all the quilts for myself."

She is silent for a moment, thinking back on a day when her husband was an air raid warden. They had many quilts then, she says, one covering each window of their farmhouse. "Black outs, you know. Wouldn't do for the warden's house to be the one to guide the enemy planes in." They were made from scraps of cloth that could not be donated to the war effort. Her children took the quilts as mementos after her husband's death. They took a lot of the furnishings, too; her grief had made her powerless to stop them. She has a rocking chair and a small TV now. She sits nights with her cat curled in her lap, rocking, watching news of a world she no longer knows. There are no rugs left, and the floors are cold in winter. Her bed is in the dining room because the stairs scare her at her age. She doesn't know what, if anything, is left upstairs.

"Perhaps there's a Monet hanging up there?" I laugh gently, and I can feel her smiling briefly at the other end of the phone line.

"No," she says. "I think my daughter has smuggled most everything out by now. She took the drapes to be dry cleaned, but she never brought them back. She thinks I forget, but it's only the little things I forget."

My boss walks near my desk and frowns.

"Let me read you your balance," I say too loudly into the phone, pulling the Finch file from my credenza.

My boss goose steps away, still frowning; she's found me properly engaged in business. She mumbles something that sounds vaguely German as she scans the nearby cubicles, searching for another outlet for her anger.

Mrs. Finch ignores my offer. She doesn't want to know about her balance; she asks if my children are a blessing.

"Well, they're too young to steal drapes," I say. I don't tell her, but I am beginning to worry about the security of my condoms, though.

"No, they wouldn't steal drapes," she replies. "But I bet you're a better father than my husband was." She sighs. I think I ought to reply – demean myself slightly – but she continues sadly. "We didn't marry for love back then. He had a farm and I had sturdy hips, and that was enough for a marriage."

She has an intelligent side to her that never showed in our prior conversations. She is a woman whose mind has gone to sleep in front of daytime television, but I feel it slowly waking up now. She has a story to her life that isn't the suburbs, and it isn't the city. It's a slower, more relaxed place. Rugged, course, though. Lives with rough edges and unpredictable turns – a place where my father once lived until he went searching for something better, and found tract housing with central vacuums and automatic garage door openers.

"But I'm wasting your time," she says.

"No, no. Not at all." There is an eagerness in my voice that surprises me and inspires her.

"I really only have one plant, you know."

"One plant?" I ask.

"Tomatoes. I talked of my tomatoes like there was a whole field, but that's because that's how I like to remember it. I only have one plant now, next to the porch."

I try to imagine what this woman looks like. An old farm woman. She would be skinny, no doubt, having toiled long hours in the fields beside her husband. Or perhaps plump – not working the fields, but cooking for a dozen field hands and sampling all the dishes beforehand; eating all the leftovers afterward because she hated seeing waste, knowing the effort that went into producing such meals. White hair, wrinkles; and had dentures because dental care was a luxury on the farm.

I leaf through her folder. Her age, birthplace, address, date of husband's death, children's names – they're all there, but there is no picture of the woman I am talking to, not even an old one.

"What do you look like?"

She laughs. "I'm an old woman. You wouldn't be interested."

"But I am," I reply.

There is silence, then she cries softly.

"I'm sorry," I say, not knowing what I might have done to upset her.

"Don't be," she says softly. I have only reminded her, she tells me, of the last time someone thought about her looks. A hairdresser. The woman had given Mrs. Finch a perm, and said Mr. Finch would fall right over when he saw her new look. Mrs.

Finch had snuck into the hairdresser's while in town on chores, using money she had saved taking shortcuts with the meals, little shortcuts that her husband wouldn't notice.

He didn't notice her hairdo, either.

"Perhaps that was my punishment for being so sneaky," she suggests. "But I just wanted it to be a surprise, nothing more."

That was so long ago now. Recently, only she has cared about her looks – occasionally. She looks in the mirror and sees an old woman. Sometimes she first catches a glimpse of the young lady she once was. Briefly. Then the wrinkles come into focus, and she knows that true love has passed her by.

"It's all my own doing, though," she says. "I let my husband set the tone. He didn't know how to show love. Your children aren't going to learn it later in life." She laughs, but it is a sad laugh. "If only I had died first. Then he could be the lonely old sourpuss rocking his days away with a dying cat in his lap."

It's the wrong note to end on, but she says good-bye and hangs up before I can think of a cheerful remark.

My day is disturbed after that. I see that Mrs. Finch and I are not so very different. She sits day after day with a dying cat in her lap, and I sit each day with my job dying on my desk. We collect our checks – and we wait. And my family; do I show them love? Or do I hand them rakes and cheese graters and think that passes for love?

Before I sink to far into a morass of self-pity, I am alerted by a surge of excited people passing through the hall. They are remarkably eager and possessed of determination. It is obviously lunch time.

As usual, I eat with Roger, but he can not disturb me today. I even laugh when he blows milk out his nose.

I have to learn to show more love. As I stand up to leave, I look at Roger, his red cheeks bulging as he tries to eat too much sandwich at once. No, I don't have to show love right this minute – just friendship. I pat his shoulder. "See you tomorrow, old buddy."

My boss is hanging around my desk, checking her watch against my allotted lunch hour. She sees me smiling at her and checks her blouse and skirt, thinking a bit of something is showing that normally shouldn't.

"It's a beautiful day out there," I say.

My cheerfulness sends her into a panic. She scurries into the women's room where she knows I can't follow.

***

I walk the pine needle pathway homeward, but stop where the smaller trail branches off. Curiosity is urging me to take a detour. Perhaps Walden Pond is out there somewhere, pulling me toward its cool waters. A cedar bough partially obscures the trail's entrance, adding to the mystery. I push it aside and slide my feet sideways down the narrow way. It opens up onto a clearing; a forest glen, dramatic rock formations guarding one end that could have been placed there by Vikings or ancient Druids, but were most likely sculpted by glaciers. It is a place of serene beauty.

But then the signs of human contamination come into focus. Beer bottles smashed against the rocks. Cigarette packs: soggy, fading in the dirt to the point where the brand name is no longer obvious. I look between my feet at a condom – used, the fluid of a recent encounter still visible. I step back in disgust; but then I think of the pleasure represented there. Perhaps the sperm are still alive, swimming futilely against a wall of latex, determined to extend their existence and – remarkably – become a child. Perhaps the encounter was so recent that the screams of the orgasm still echo through the trees. I wonder if Beth might not join me here some time under a clear night sky, and we too can send shrieks into the forest.

No. We are parents now – and suburbanites. We will take our pleasures quietly, civilly, with the eleven o'clock news playing in the background, our bedroom television turned up just enough to make sure the children can't hear us.

This forest clearing, though. It is not a place for adults. Teenagers come here. Bored, suburban teenagers. They drink beer and abandon their virginity: the boys eagerly; the girls with hesitation, then regret. I look down at my feet and see how it all happened.

The boy with his practiced lines: "But baby, if you loved me, you'd do this for me."

She moves her fingers toward his crotch and offers to take him in her hand.

"No, not that," he whispers. "I want to show my love to you, baby."

She pushes him away. Gently. She just needs time to think.

He pouts, his lower lip quivering irresistibly. "Well, if you don't want to go out with me..."

She panics – it is lonely in a house full of brothers, with two parents who barely speak. She nods her head slowly, and they lay down in the pine needles together. She closes her eyes and grits her teeth, praying for it to be over. There is a brief feeling of intrusion, then he rolls to one side. After all this, he doesn't know what he's supposed to do, she thinks. But then she sees him pull off the condom. She sees the thick liquid I am now staring at, and she realizes it is all over.

"That was great, baby, wasn't it?" he says.

She wipes the pine needles from her hair, but says nothing. Later in life, she will meet her true love. She will already be married to someone else, so they will rendezvous in stuffy motel rooms. The musty odor of their love will quickly permeate the darkness. Hours later, they will fall back into the pillows – exhausted, spent – and she will smile. She will laugh gently as she thinks back on all the boys who poured their tension, their anger, and their frustration into her and called it love.

I think of Justin. Will he use these corny lines? *Baby, prove your love to me.* I try to imagine him saying such things. His lips take on the look of Mick Jagger as he reaches out with them to kiss the girl, and I can't help laughing.

And what about Kathleen? Will she fall for such drivel? I remember her crying about uniforms. She is so sensitive and fragile. I imagine a skinny boy with pink hair and a nose ring saying, "Baby, I'm the only one who understands you." She'll cry gently, then nod her head as she says a sad, "Yes." Afterward, she'll cry for days in her bedroom, refuse all phone calls, and eat nothing but dry toast brought up to her by her compassionate mother....

I must leave this clearing in the woods – quickly. Madness takes hold when adults dwell too long in the world of their children.

***

The house is quiet when I enter. I set my briefcase down and scan the interior for signs of abandonment; but the furniture is still there.

There is a quick burst of canned laughter from the family room. Bare feet are sticking out into view. I can tell they are Justin's: he doesn't cut his toenails. He lets them crack from shear weight as they hang out over the ends of his toes. When he sleeps, mites journey down from his eyelids – a family outing –

and use his toenails as springboards, doing back flips into the puddles of his wet dreams.

I step quietly up beside him as he slouches in a recliner, hovering near an abyss of unconsciousness. "Hi, son." I wrap my arm over his shoulder and give him a big kiss.

"Daaaaaad!" His voice starts low, but then shoots up high. I have created a whoopee cushion. He glares at me, then grins sheepishly. He's not sure; it's been so long since I touched him.

I'm not sure, either. He's gotten so old. I think of a summer day, in a park. We rolled together in the grass, down a long hill. And at the bottom, we tried to stand but couldn't. We were dizzy and grabbed each other for support. We laughed and fell backward into the grass where it was cool, and it was sunny, and I felt full. But he was a little boy back then – that is much too far to have to reach for a pleasant memory of a father and a son.

"How was football practice," I ask.

"Soccer, Dad," he groans. "I play soccer."

"Soccer," I say. "But don't they call that football in Europe?"

He shrugs his shoulders, then aims a remote at the television, switching from old reruns to a music channel. It seems a strange concept – needing videos to enhance the music. When I was young, the music itself inspired its own special images. I would lay on the sofa – headphones on – and close my eyes so that nothing from the outside world could interfere with how the music played within me. Hollywood can't create what I saw.

"Where's your mother?" I ask.

He shrugs again.

I tussle his hair and kiss his cheek. *He's my son!*

"Dad!" He flicks the TV off with the remote and storms barefoot to his room.

I can see I'll have to take it slower.

The garage door opener engages; rumbling, clanking like the

coupling of box cars. It promises reliable service, but can that be true when there is so much disturbance in its mechanisms each time it performs the simple task of opening a door? I hear the minivan pull into the garage and bump a trash can. The metal fire door in the kitchen swings open and the smell of pizza rushes through the house.

"Sorry I'm late," Beth calls. "Kathleen's soccer game ran late on account of a fight."

I glide into the kitchen and spin my wife in a circle as the pizza totters on her fingertips. She gives me an odd stare as I kiss her on her lips.

"Little girls and boys were fighting?" I ask as I threaten to sweep Beth off her feet.

"No," she stammers. "The parents were fighting." I am beginning to frighten her.

I push her hair away from her face. "No shiner." I kiss her eyebrow.

"Kathleen never gets to play," Beth explains. "So I was left out of it." She sets the pizza box on the counter and pushes me away. "Cut it out," she says gently. "Pizza's getting cold."

Justin smells the pizza from the far corner of his bedroom and, taking the stairs two at a time, shoots toward the kitchen. "All right!" He throws his body into his accustomed chair and waits to be served.

The fire door opens again, and Kathleen struggles into the kitchen with an armload of outerwear. She dresses in layers – Beth sees to that. She is smiling, a big broad smile, and her eyes aren't red.

"How was the game, Kitten?" I ask.

"Mommy didn't get to play either!" She marches to the cellar door and throws her gear to the cement floor below.

I pat her head as she passes in front of me to join Justin at the table.

"They won," Beth announces.

"Great!" I reply, but Beth frowns.

"That means they have to play again tomorrow," she explains.

It is tournament time. Single elimination. Kathleen's team had not won a game all season – we thought the torment would end quickly – but now they have won twice and are threatening to make the Final Four.

"I have a lot of housework to do. Maybe you and Justin can take her tomorrow."

"Sure," I say. Sure. A little time for Justin and me to spend together. We can talk about sports, girls. Manly things. I will ask him if he ever tasted beer. Perhaps he will confide in me that he and his friends once slipped into an R-rated movie and saw women's breasts. Or perhaps we'll stand together in silence, my eyes will drift over toward a hill of grass, and I will wish for the return of an earlier time.

November 9

"This really bites," Justin sighs.

We are standing along a red snow fence, watching the players run up and down the field. It is new – the snow fence. They have added it since the melee to keep unruly parents from swarming the field.

Kathleen is sitting on the bench, playing with her knee pads. She looks our way and smiles bravely. She is nervous; she might have to play today. The team is short three players because their fathers are still in jail and the players are off with their mothers arranging bail. It was quite a fight. It has made the city papers – everyone is talking about our suburb with a mixture of amusement and contempt. Property values have dropped, but they will recover once the fight is consigned to the footnotes of local lore.

"Don't say 'bites'" I say.

"Okay. Sucks then," Justin replies. "Frankie's gone and Howard's a jerk."

I have not met Howard. He is still just a voice. He guffaws a lot, and I imagine snots fluttering in and out of one of his nostrils. Justin is right – from what I've heard, Howard is a jerk.

"Why did we have to move here, anyway?" He does not look at me. He looks off toward the horizon, toward the city and his old friends.

I want to tell him that it was his mother's idea. I didn't want to come because I knew the suburbs. I grew up here; watched America's parents spread across the land like mold across a shower curtain, dragging children in their wake, searching not the land or the people, but the cold metal office buildings for life's meaning. Pursued the better television with better remote control; picture-in-picture so they could watch the news and the sitcoms together, and cry and laugh all at the same time.

Children don't really need all that. Stability is all they seek; and that won't be found in the suburbs.

And even the city. I watch the mindless scurry, the dangerous gambles – throngs of jaywalkers among the rush hour traffic, all hurrying to work. I wait for the walk light – I am going nowhere anyway – and wonder will I ever be part of them. This is not what I wanted. This is my father's dream. I am this because my father built me so.

I want to teach Justin not to surrender. Tell him! – an adult is just the shell of a child after all the joy has been wrung out. Rebel, Justin! But I see even now it is almost too late. Already, he would groan – "You're embarrassing me, Dad." – if I were to don Mickey Mouse ears and start to sing "M...I...C...." See you real soon, Justin. See you in the throng of jaywalkers.

I can't tell him any of this, though. I can't tell him that the suburbs were his mother's idea – and only hers; that I fought her in the quiet hours, whispering gentle protests into her ear as her head tossed upon the pillow. I'd like to tell him, but parents must stick together when confronted by their children. A united front. If Justin saw just a tiny crack, he would exploit it. Children are clever, they're smarter than us. He would find a way to widen that crack enough to squeeze through and make his escape – back to the city.

"Your mother wanted a house with a yard," I explain. She wanted more, but I can't tell Justin the rest. She wanted safe neighborhoods and schools without drugs and violence. She wanted girls who served lemonade on their front porches to gentlemen callers and boys with faces free of metal objects; a newspaper boy on a bicycle chased by his faithful springer spaniel, its pink tongue flapping from its mouth. Daffodils.

She got the daffodils.

"Who cares about a fuckin' yard," Justin shouts.

"What did you say?" I stare at him, and he stares back

"I said, 'Who cares about a fucking yard.'"

We are here to bond. We are not father and son, but pals. He has put me in an awkward position. I don't know what to do. But "fuckin'" – that's pal language, not father-son language. Perhaps we are bonding. Perhaps he is just being my pal.

Kathleen comes running toward us. She is crying. Her coach is yelling at us, waving frantically toward the field. The play has stopped, and everyone has turned to watch us. We are the half-time show.

"Daddy!" She throws her arms around my waist and squeezes me. "Don't make me play."

"Get in there, Kathleen!" I hear the coach yell. "It's your turn!" He throws his clipboard to the ground, and begins stomping toward us, his beer gut jiggling beneath his shrunken sweatshirt.

"Don't make me!" Kathleen screams.

"Of course not, Kitten." I take her hand, and we walk toward the parking lot.

The coach yells an obscenity our way, and Justin turns and gives him the finger. I laugh and slap Justin on the back. We are bonding, after all.

Fuckin' all right!

***

We enter the kitchen through the metal door. Beth is at the breakfast table with Eve. It surprises me. I have never seen Eve in our kitchen.

"Hi," I say.

"What are you doing back so soon?" Beth asks.

Neither Justin, Kathleen, nor I reply. The soccer game – it is not something we wish to talk about. Kathleen scurries to her bedroom. Justin moves toward the refrigerator, and Beth reaches out and strokes his hair. "Jussie?"

She is using his pet name again, the one she uses when she thinks he is angry at her. But he has been out with Kathleen and me; he could not be angry. She uses it other times, though. When? After she's been making love, right? But I've been out, too.

"Where's Adam?" I ask.

"Jail," Eve replies.

There is something wrong – Eve and Beth are not moving. They watch Justin as he takes a jar of peanut butter from the refrigerator shelf.

"Jail?" I say. "He was at the game yesterday?" At the fight, I want to say, but "game" seems more gentle, and I am among women.

Eve and Beth nod their heads stiffly. They are not moving like normal people. There is something wrong in the house.

"You didn't bail him out yet?" I squint at the two women, but they don't seem to notice my stare.

"I better go get him now," Eve sighs.

"Don't forget the cash," Beth says.

"The cash?" Eve replies.

"Yes. Remember. You didn't have cash for bail, so you came over to borrow some."

"Oh," Eve says. "Right! The cash." The two women giggle, and Beth leaves to get her pocketbook.

I look at Eve, but she doesn't look at me. She is still not moving. She continues watching Justin as he spreads the peanut butter across a slice of bread.

"So does Adam have his Bible with him at least?" I ask.

She looks up quickly. "His Bible? No, I don't think so. It's in the evidence locker. I believe he hit someone with it."

Beth returns and hands Eve a wad of bills. They peck each other on the cheek, and Eve exits through the front door.

"So old Adam's in jail," I laugh.

"Yes." Beth seems dazed. The excitement of the suburbs has been too much for her. "Yes, he's in jail."

"And Eve just let him sit there all night?"

"Yes," Beth replies absently. She stares off toward the front door. "Well, she can be quite a spitfire when she wants to be."

November 10

The doorbell rings. It is Adam. One eye is purple. He looks like a panda bear. The hillbilly is with him, and they're each carrying a beer.

"That's some shiner," I say.

Adam ignores my remark. He hands me a fistful of money. "Here. I don't know why Eve bothered Beth. She knows where we keep the emergency cash."

"This happens often?" I ask. "You keep bail money around?"

The hillbilly smiles while Adam continues to frown.

It is Sunday morning, but Adam is not at church. I have never been to jail. I have never been to a Baptist church, either. How long must a person be out of one before they can return to the other?

I look down at Adam's beer, and he realizes for the first time that he is drinking on a Sunday. He slides the beer behind his leg, out of view, but it is too late.

The hillbilly sees me eye the beer. "Got another cold one over at the homestead, if you want to come over."

"Sure," I say. I don't know why; it just comes out. Now I have to remember his name. Perhaps Adam will call him by it.

I look about my house – it is so quiet. Kathleen is probably crying by her window, serving tea to her sympathetic dolls. Beth is sleeping late – she slept badly, moaning, calling out, "More, more." Perhaps she was dreaming of me. But perhaps she was dreaming of a clearance sale at the local K-Mart. Justin went into the bathroom for his morning shower and never came out. He is lost somewhere in the fog.

I shut the front door quietly. "Just a quick one," I whisper to my new friends.

The hillbilly has dug a fish pond in the back yard. There are goldfish swimming around in the stagnant water. He picks up a rope and tugs it until a six pack of beer emerges dripping from the dark water. "If I keep it in the fridge, the kids drink it on me," he explains. He yanks a can out of the plastic harness and hands it to me. "It's pretty cold."

"Thanks." I want to say his name, but it still eludes me. The beer is not really cold; it's like tap water.

There is a vinyl car seat beside the pond. Adam and the hillbilly are sitting on that, but there appears to be room for three. I wonder if the seat belongs to the dismantled pickup out front under the black tarp, but then I remember that the pachysandra, the tarp, the car batteries – that was a long time ago. A different hillbilly.

This hillbilly is a bit unusual. For one, he only has three children. Boys. One even goes to college. I've never seen any of them sprawled out drunk in the front yard, either.

"So what do you do?" the hillbilly asks. "Harry? Right?"

I nod. "I work for an investment company." That is usually enough to end someone's interest in my work. "What about you?"

"I'm a biologist."

This scares Adam. He hops up from the bench and stares at the man. He thought he was a roofer or something; he thought perhaps he was one of the men that had repaired the roof on the Sunday School last summer. But he isn't a roofer; he is a man of science. An enemy of religion. Rearranging genes and cloning mice to once-and-for-all rid the world of God.

"What kind of biologist?" Adam asks cautiously.

The hillbilly is leaning back casually in the car seat. He has a coffee can balanced on his lap, and is plucking out meal worms and tossing them into the fish pond. "Wetlands biologist," he says, then laughs. "I count bugs, mostly."

He counts bugs. He doesn't play God, he just counts bugs. Adam sits back down, then chugs the rest of his beer like an old pro. "That's why they call you Nat!"

Nat – that's his name. Bill Abernathy, but his friends call him Nat.

Nat smiles at Adam. "Another beer?" he asks, but Adam shakes his head.

A car pulls into my driveway. Our three sets of eyes watch it in silence. I set my beer in the grass, a sign that I am more than casually interested in the car.

"That's my car," Adam says, squinting in confusion.

The car door swings open, and a pair of shapely legs appear. The delicate feet land gently on the dark surface of the driveway. A head emerges.

"That's my wife!" Adam shouts.

He throws his weight against the rear of the car seat, and the three of us fall backward with the seat. We are covered with meal worms, but Nat manages to save his beer. Together, the three of us peek up over the rim of the inverted car seat.

"She must be looking for me," Adam suggests.

Eve opens the car trunk, then the passenger door. She stands holding the door as though she is expecting someone. The front door to the house opens, and my wife appears. She is carrying a large suitcase and an overnight bag. Eve scurries up the front stoop and takes the smaller bag from Beth. They scan the neighborhood for signs of life, then run to the car. My wife has church clothes on. They must be going to church together – with suitcases. They stow the suitcase in the trunk, then hop in the car. The two car doors shut simultaneously. I know now – they're going to the fitness center. I'll buy Beth a gym bag for Christmas so she doesn't have to lug that heavy suitcase around. Through the rear window, I see the two women face each other. They kiss.

"Lesbians," Nat whispers.

Adam stands up. "What the hell is going on here?"

The car backs out of the driveway, hitting Nat's trash can before shifting into forward and screeching up the street. Nat doesn't seem to notice that his trash can has been injured; he picks meal worms from his shirt pocket and tosses them into the fish pond.

"What the hell is going on?" Adam yells again as he runs from the back yard toward the retreating car. He wishes he had his Bible now. There are passages in there that can stop this foolishness. There are passages there that will turn his wife to salt.

***

The phone rings and rings and rings. Being Sunday, perhaps Mrs. Finch has strolled to church. She might have tacked a modest hat to the top of her head with a huge hat pin, and pulled a pink veil across her face to subdue man's temptation. As she walks, her hand is ready to yank the hat pin from her hair at the first sign of seduction.

I am about to hang up, but then there's a timid voice at the other end of the phone. "Yes?"

"Beth's left me," I say.

"Who is this?" She is out of breath. She has run to answer the phone, feeling quite certain that it is just another telemarketer. But at her stage of life, attention from any source is craved.

"It's Harry," I explain.

There is a pause, then recognition. "Harold!" There is also confusion. "This is Sunday, isn't it?" Up to now our relationship has been strictly Monday through Friday, nine-to-five.

"I didn't know who else to call," I groan. "My wife has run off."

"Oh?"

"I'm still hoping she's just gone to the fitness center, but she took her jewelry case."

"You think it's another man?" Mrs. Finch's voice turns conspiratorial. She has not been privy to juicy gossip for decades, and she is relishing the moment. Her seventeen dollar investment is paying off in unexpected dividends.

"I think it's another woman," I reply.

There is an awkward silence. Oh dear. Wrong generation.

I hear a groan from behind me. My son is lingering in the background. He is finally dressed, but his hair is still wet. He has not been long out of the shower. He was definitely long in the shower; he has set a new standard for teenage cleanliness. He begins to bang his head against the metal fire door and shouts in cadence, "I am going to get so hassled at school."

"Harold?" Mrs. Finch calls to me. "Harold?"

Kathleen slinks into the kitchen, her eyes already beginning to water. She can feel the trauma in the air.

"Harry?"

"Yes, Mrs. Finch?"

"Perhaps it's a Thelma and Louise thing."

"You think so?"

She is trying to help, but it is no comfort; I prefer to think of Beth sleeping in a cheap motel with a Baptist housewife rather than being gunned down by a platoon of state troopers. I must still love my wife.

"Dad?" Justin looks at me with pleading eyes. "Can we just move? We can tell people you're a widower."

You're a widower – Kathleen hears that. She begins to cry. She thinks it's real. Why can't I have smart children?

Justin has resumed banging his head against the door.

"You know what you should do, Harold?" I can barely hear Mrs. Finch's distant voice above the noise of my frenzied off spring. "You should call your mother."

Beth has run off to be a lesbian – that is what I'm going to tell my mother. I am going to call up my mother and tell her that the woman that she said was a tramp, the woman that she said was not good enough for me, the bimbo who was going to break my heart – I am going to tell my mother that that woman has run off to have a lesbian affair. Justin? What part of the country did you have in mind for this grieving widower and his two children to move to?

"Thank you, Mrs. Finch," I reply. "I'll call you tomorrow and let you know how it's going."

November 13

Kathleen is playing with her Barbie dolls; Barbie and her little sister Kelly have put the Ken doll in a shoe box. He has no clothes on. He has no genitals.

Barbie is taunting Ken. "We don't want to play with you anymore."

"We don't like boys anymore," says the Kelly doll.

Ken tries to say something, but Kathleen drops the lid to the shoe box on his plastic head. She then looks quietly about the floor; it is littered with Barbie clothes. She picks up the prom dress – her latest acquisition. There will be no prom now. She picks up Ken's tuxedo and slips Barbie's little sister into it. There is a bagginess to the outfit; Kathleen pulls and tucks, she rolls up the pant legs trying to make it look right, but it isn't right – it's all wrong. She starts to cry.

I want to comfort her, to hug her and stroke her hair, and say everything will be all right, but the doorbell rings. It is Adam. He marches into my house with his two children in tow. His face is puffy and red; he has not slept for three nights – ever since our two wives disappeared together.

Adam leads me into the kitchen. He has his Bible open and is reciting a passage from Leviticus.

"And you shall not lie carnally with your neighbor's wife," he reads, lingering on the word "carnally," drawing it out and seeming to enjoy the word much too much for a Bible reading.

"I think that refers to men," I say. "Men can't lie with another's wife." I offer Adam a beer from the refrigerator, and he takes it without comment.

"Okay, okay." He scans further into the Bible. "You shall not lie with a male as with a woman."

"Men again," I say. "A man can't sleep with another man."

Adam slams his Bible shut. "What is this? Men can't do anything, but women can do whatever they want?"

"It also says you can't sow your fields with two different kinds of seed."

Adam looks at me. He doesn't see the connection.

"It sort of puts homosexuality on the same level as crop rotation," I suggest.

Adam does not blink – Bible jokes are not something he can deal with.

"Drink your beer, Adam."

"You know, this is all your fault."

Yes. Of course. I am the one who brought my wife here, to a land devoid of richness. But you too, Adam, brought your wife here, and we must share the blame.

I can guess how it all happened. They met over coffee, without a common interest; Beth from the city, and Eve from somewhere in the south – a city perhaps, but a much different city than from the north. "Which do you prefer, phonetics or whole language?" they asked each other, having nothing but children in common. They argued, then agreed, then argued some more. They decided they liked them both – language with a whole bunch of phonetics.

Perhaps Beth reached first across the Formica table to admire one of Eve's buttons. "Are they real pearls?" Her bored fingers, clumsy from months of inactivity, tugged too hard. Oops. The button popped off. So innocently. Two bored housewives comparing PTO notes over coffee, admiring buttons.

"Don't worry. They're all a bit loose," Eve replied. She tugged another button to prove she was not lying. Oops! That one also popped off, and Eve's breasts fell into view. "I don't wear a bra around the house," she giggled.

"They're lovely," Beth commented, free as women are to admire each other's bodies.

"They're real," Eve said.

"Of course they're real," Beth replied. "You're a Christian."

Beth felt the urge to show hers to Eve, to be admired in a purely aesthetic way; and not have to worry about arousing the other party and following the act through, performing a bit of acrobatics in a pool of sweat. Slowly, as if in a dream, Beth unbuttoned her blouse. "I don't think mine are as firm as yours."

"I've been going to the fitness center longer than you," Eve replied softly. They touched. "Yours are nice, though."

Their gentle fingers sent subtle shivers through each other's bodies, to regions long dormant, to areas that they never dreamed were even a part of themselves.

Through the languid daylight hours, the two women slowly undressed. Their coffee turned cold, became forgotten, as they moved without realizing it – across the kitchen floor, to the carpeting of the staircase, and into the discreteness of Eve's bedroom.

Without the noise of the city to distract her, Beth was able to examine her true thoughts as the two women sat cross-legged on the firm mattress. What was it she sought? Not the suburbs – moving here had been the wasted motions of a desperate woman, the flailing about of a drowning housewife dragging her spent body onto the illusion of a tropical island. It was the subtle intimacy of this that she had sought all these years, not the hurried thrusts of a man.

But is it truly my fault? Or Adam's? Or any man's? No, it is nature, and it is evolution that is to blame. That is how time has programmed a man to be. We must quickly plant our seed and be gone before a larger ape happens along, yanks us from our frantic embrace, and tosses us into the jungle foliage.

"What the hell is wrong with you?" Adam yells.

I awaken from my dream, and find that I am slowly massaging my nipples. "Just trying to see what they get out of it," I reply.

There is yelling in the back yard. Adam and I hurry to the kitchen window and look out: Justin and Cain are sprawled in the dirt. Justin has Cain in a headlock – he is not really hurting him, but Cain is bawling anyway. I open the back door, and Justin releases his hold.

Cain wipes the tears from his eyes with the back of his dirty hand. Justin sits staring at us, tugging at a lone dandelion in the dust – he thinks perhaps we hadn't noticed the fight.

"Aren't you gonna say something?" Adam asks.

"Boys!" I shout. "I'm trying to grow grass there."

It's not what Adam had in mind. He steps in front of me. "All right! Who started it?"

Both boys point at the other.

Justin stands up and kicks dust at Cain. "You said it's my mom's fault 'cause she's not God fearing."

Cain jumps up and kicks dust back. "You said my mom was

the one that ate pussy first."

The two boys leap at each other. A swirl of dust swallows them up.

"Boys! Boys!" Adam runs into the dust storm and emerges with his own son. He leads him swiftly past me and into the kitchen. "Sarah! We're going home."

"I'm sorry about this, Adam," I say, but he ignores me and keeps looking about the kitchen for his missing daughter.

The two girls run down from upstairs. Kathleen has on my pajama bottom, but nothing else. Sarah has on my pajama top, and nothing else.

"What have you two... Never mind." Adam grabs Sarah's hand and marches his offspring out the front door.

He does not say good-bye.

November 17

There is a postcard in the mail from Beth. She says she's sorry, but this is something she has to do. She and Eve are headed for San Francisco – not because of the liberal atmosphere there, but for the sourdough bread. Eve has heard they have wonderful sourdough bread in San Francisco, and Beth and Eve are Bohemians now. They are following their whims, and their latest whim is for sourdough bread. She thanks me for not canceling the credit card. She asks how Justin and Kathleen are doing, and wants me to tell them she still loves them. She writes, "continued on page two." There is no page two. Perhaps she forgot she was sending postcards. Perhaps she forgot she needed to address and stamp page two, also.

I pretend I know what page two says. It says she still loves me. It says she and Eve have almost gotten this strange urge out of their systems and that she'll be coming home soon, that she will toil beside me in the yard so that we can have the green lawn she's always dreamed of.

The front door flies open, and Adam storms in. Eve's been charging motel rooms on his credit card.

"They charge meals on my card," I reply.

This makes him more angry. He feels it's his wife's deliberate attempt to mock him. "See? Two women eating together, there's nothing wrong with that, but two women in a motel together..."

"I don't think she means anything by it," I say.

"Why couldn't they alternate days?" Adam asks. "Whoever pays for meals one day pays for the motel the next." He's pacing around the kitchen. He looks in the refrigerator, but there are no beers. There were two beers there last night: I'll have to talk to Justin about that when he comes down for dinner. "She's going to put all her sins on my card for the world to see. She'll charge lubricant next." Adam blushes; he thinks he might have given one of their little secrets away. "Do women use lubricant?"

I shrug my shoulders.

"What do they do, anyway?" Adam really doesn't know. He knows very little about women's bodies. He wishes there were something in the Bible – thou shalt not explore too deeply the softness of thy wife – something explicit that would let him off the hook in that department.

"They do a lot of touching," I suggest.

"Touching? Is that all?" He seems to calm down.

"Kissing, too."

"Kissing?" This is beginning to sound not all that bad to Adam. They're doing all the things he doesn't care to do. Perhaps when Eve gets back, she will have had enough of touching and kissing, and they can resume their familiar missionary position – a quick release, then he can roll off to face the opposite wall and get a good night's sleep. "Well, I don't think we should be supporting such perversion. I canceled Eve's card. You should cancel Beth's, then maybe they'll come home."

No, Adam. They won't. It's not that easy.

I point toward the refrigerator door. There is a crude map of the continental United States taped to it. It is a place mat from the town's newest restaurant, proudly displaying the abundance of sibling restaurants that have sprouted like mushrooms across the country ever since the venture capitalists infused them with cash. There are magnets – little fruits – scattered across the map.

"I'm tracking them," I say. "That banana's Connecticut. Sunday night, they ate at a seafood place there."

Adam tips his head closer to the map.

"The cherry is where they ate Monday, some home-style place in Lancaster County." As I speak, we are beginning to taste the food. It has been over a week since anyone familiar with kitchens has prepared us a meal. "Tuesday was a rib joint in North Carolina."

That one worries me. Get further north, Beth! It's not safe for two lesbians to be traveling too far south.

Wednesday they moved into Kentucky – and I felt better.

Adam studies the map. "Any pattern?"

"They're eating regional," I say.

"Any ideas where they might be headed?"

"San Francisco," I reply.

Adam runs his fingers along the magnets. He doesn't understand San Francisco – the upturn to Kentucky has his fingers headed toward Alaska.

"Beth sent me a postcard," I explain.

There is a box of cold pizza lying on the counter; leftovers from last night. It is concealing the gas range from me; my children are safer if I don't try to cook.

"You want a slice?" I ask.

Adam shakes his head. He doesn't remember all the forbidden foods; animals of the sea without scales, animals with cloven feet. Or is that uncloven feet? He is sure day old pizza is mentioned somewhere in there.

"They're asking questions at church," Adam sighs. "I tell them Eve is on vacation with Beth."

"That's sort of true," I reply.

"The women seem to know, though," he says. "Nadine Meredith said she's bringing a casserole over tonight. Macaroni and cheese."

Macaroni and cheese. That's second marriage food. It shows an ability to provide basic sustenance – nourishing, but without the frills.

"She's divorced, I take it?" I ask.

Adam nods sadly. "She has three teenagers. They eat like horses."

The front door flies open again. This time it is Cain. "Dad! Mrs. Meredith is at the house."

"Okay," Adam yells back.

"You gotta get home right away," the boy continues. "She's doing our laundry."

"Yeah, okay, Cain."

"Dad!" Cain is begging now. "She's picking through my dirty underwear."

Adam rolls his eyes. "I gotta go."

"Your boy's growing up fast," I say.

Adam does not reply as he hurries through the front door.

The house is silent for only a moment, then Justin runs down the stairs. He must have heard Cain's whining – he is carrying a basket overflowing with laundry. He's worried that Mrs. Meredith will visit here next. He's had a vision of a strange woman holding up one of his jockey shorts, examining the spot where his approaching manhood has stretched the cotton into a comfortable pouch. It has propelled him to take matters into his own hands.

***

Kathleen is smug. She's been brushing up on her Swahili. She says we're moving back to the city.

My rice is boiling over on the stove, and I curse.

Kathleen laughs and says something mysterious – kwahani oog bagonda. She says it's Swahili for "the path to home is always smooth." I think she made it up. She laughs again when I pick up the phone and press the quick-dial button. She likes it when I ruin dinner.

"There's takeout back home," she says.

"There's takeout here, too," I reply.

"Yeah. Pizza." She laughs even more as she looks at the stack of pizza boxes beside the refrigerator.

I am keeping them there until recycling day, but I don't know – are pizza boxes really recyclable? They've got food stains on them. I tried tossing them in the trash, but the garbage police dug them out and left them beside our driveway.

"Justin," Kathleen calls. "Daddy's getting pizza again."

I hear a groan from the laundry room.

"One large cheese," I say to the Italian at the other end of the phone. I don't give him my name – he knows my voice.

Justin is doing laundry again. He has mixed his colors and his whites. He comes into the kitchen with a pair of pink underpants on his head. "Dad, Dad," he shouts. "Look! I've turned gay, too."

My kids are so damn cheerful all of a sudden. Beth would still be here if we were always such a fun group.

I set the phone down, but it calls me immediately back. It's Adam.

"What'd she make tonight?" I ask.

"Baked chicken," he says.

"At least you're eating."

A moment of silence.

He's made a decision. He's not ready to trade in Eve for Mrs. Meredith. He's moving the family to San Francisco, to wait for Eve's arrival.

"There's Baptists there," he says. "They'll help us."

They're leaving first thing in the morning, before Mrs. Meredith comes over to clean the bathrooms.

"She doesn't spend the night?" I ask jokingly.

The phone goes dead.

Adam has no sense of humor about this.

November 18

The moving van is already in front of the Greenley's house when I step outside for the morning paper. There is no one at the house except for the movers – Adam slipped away before daybreak, just to be safe. Women have instincts he can't explain – he was worried Mrs. Meredith might come over just a bit early this morning.

Nat is sitting on his car seat tossing meal worms into his stagnate puddle; he wants to fatten up his fish before winter sets in. Roger is already at work, with a piece of spinach stuck between his teeth. Mrs. Finch will sleep for several more hours. That is the extent of my network of friends. Except – I also know a lesbian. She is in a car headed for San Francisco, searching for the perfect sourdough bread. She is kissing my wife's ear as my wife takes her turn at the wheel.

Justin and Kathleen leave for school together. They are pals now. They are happy. Kathleen will arrive early, but that's okay. She'll play on the swings while she waits for the school bell to ring, pumping higher and higher, hoping to catch a glimpse of the city as she soars over the tree tops. Kwahani oog bagonda.

The suburbs will not last, Justin and Kathleen feel. The suburbs are for whole families. We are falling apart – look at the kitchen if you want proof. It's just a matter of time now – I will take them home. That's what they think. But they've forgotten – Beth is coming back. Someday. We must wait for her.

***

Mrs. Finch calls with an update. She has written a missing person notice and sent it to newspapers and magazines around the country.

She sent a detailed account to *Penthouse* – she thought it was a magazine for wealthy people. They will send a rejection slip back. They will include a note saying they liked the general premise of the story, but it needed a more heterosexual theme; perhaps if the two women were with a younger man...

"Mrs. Finch," I say. "She's not really missing. It's more like she's run away."

Mrs. Finch laughs. She remembers a time when her daughter ran away, long ago. Her daughter was Kathleen's age then. She tied cornbread in a red handkerchief and stuck the handkerchief on the end of a stick. A neighbor's dog smelled the cornbread and chased her up a tree. "Did you look in your trees, Harry?"

"I only have one tree," I say. It still has one brown leaf at the top – I can see at a glance there are not two lesbians up there with it.

My boss is glaring at me. I mouth to her a "Mrs. Finch" and wink. She storms away. She knows Beth is missing, but she doesn't know the whole story. My boss sleeps with women; she'd like to sleep with men, too. She'd like to sleep with anyone she can dominate. If she knew Beth ran off for a lesbian affair, she'd see me as weak, and she'd want to sleep with me. She'd pinch my dick off and laugh.

Mrs. Finch says she has to go; she has more letters to write. She has the address for a magazine called *Hustler*.

"No, Mrs. Finch. That's not a magazine for busy people," I say. "I'd try somewhere else."

Roger is waiting at our lunch table with pamphlets. He printed up a hundred on the copy machine in the mail room. He photocopied a color photograph of Beth. Along the top says "MISSING." The setting was too dark; Beth looks like a Polynesian.

At least my friends are trying to help. Except Nat – he's tossing meal worms to his fish. But then he's a biologist – he knows which forces of nature he can battle. Winter is coming and he must fatten his fish. Beth will have to come home on her own.

December 18

The days are too quiet. Winter is settling in. Nat no longer sits on his car seat flicking meal worms through the air. Mornings there is ice on the top of his pond – the fish are on their own now.

Soccer season is over. It ended for us the day Justin gave the coach the finger. Kathleen's team went on to win the championship – they were on local cable TV – but Kathleen was not invited to the awards banquet. She didn't seem to care.

The children are being too quiet. Their earlier euphoria has died down – they see now that I am not whisking them back to the city, but they are not sure what I will do next. They are always hovering nearby, watching me, pretending to read teen magazines. Sometimes I see Justin staring out from behind one of his old *Hardy Boys Mysteries*. It is either a ruse, or he is trying to learn detective skills. Perhaps he plans to find his mother himself.

Beth has stopped using her credit card. There have been no more postcards. I worry she has been abducted by a feminist cult. Her trail went cold in Nebraska, though. It is not an area of the country that I think of when I hear of feminist cults.

Adam called once. He has a small apartment with a view of the Golden Gate Bridge. He has been watching it through a pair of opera glasses, but he has yet to spot Eve's car.

"Maybe they passed at night?" I suggest.

"No," Adam says. "Eve never liked to go too far after dark."

That's not quite true. It was Adam who wouldn't go too far after dark; that's why Eve is sharing the darkness with Beth.

The phone at work has been quiet. Mrs. Finch has not called in over a week.

It must be the quiet before the storm.

***

My boss is standing beside my desk when I arrive in the morning. I am on time, but she is smiling nonetheless. It is a wicked smile. If Adam were here, he would know just by looking at her what passages of the Bible she was lusting after. There is a fire behind her blue eyes – she has been in contact with Satan.

"Mrs. Finch died this weekend." Her grin widens. She is getting to the part she has wanted to say for years. "This is your last check. The guard will be here in one hour to escort you out. Be packed." She hands me an envelope and spins around. She is so happy, I expect her to keep spinning, just like a ballerina.

So Mrs. Finch died; that is why she's so quiet. Perhaps she ignored my advice and sent Beth's story to "Hustler" after all, and in return received a contributor's copy through the mail. It came in a plain paper wrapper, but she failed to understand the significance. Then heart failure, right there at the kitchen table as the magazine fell open to raw flesh – a man and a woman, and several small animals. Later, the coroner arrived and tried to shut her eyes, but they were bugged out beyond the reach of her eyelids.

I don't have time to tell Roger what's happened. He works in the mail room – he knows already. He's known for several days but hasn't found the courage to tell me.

The guard is polite. He is very efficient, too. The company has had many layoffs – he no longer thinks about the people he escorts out the front door. I have filled two boxes with personal items – coffee cups and family pictures, mostly. He has to search them to make sure I'm not running off with company property. He holds up a box of paper clips.

"Those are mine," I say. I bought them during one of the company's periods of austerity. The guard places them back without a word, then lifts up one of the boxes. It is not part of his job description to carry boxes, but he does it anyway as a final service to a fellow worker.

We walk quietly through the halls, each carrying a box. At the front door, the guard places his box on top of mine. I step into the daylight, then hear the door close behind me. The guard does not lock it – the whole ceremony is purely symbolic. They do not expect me to attempt a violent return. My boss – ex-boss – is staring down from an upstairs window. She is still smiling, but the smile is beginning to fade. She has lost something important to her – she is beginning to realize that now that I'm gone. I will turn the corner and disappear from her life, and she will panic. She will hunt the desks that stretch out before her and look for a new face to fill the void in her life.

There are no trains this late in the morning. I wait on the platform beside my boxes. The train station is cold and lonely – it is a metaphor for life. There is a grayness to the air that I never noticed before. Perhaps the trains have returned to burning coal.

The only other person at the station is a woman in a wheelchair holding a can full of coins – I recognize her. She has gotten a bad corner for panhandling. She wheels toward me, and I prepare to pull out my wallet. She stops in front of me and smiles, then pulls out a stick of gum. "Here, honey," she says.

No one has called me "honey" since Beth left. I fish around in my wallet for two dollars, but she waves the gesture away. She has seen this many times before – the midday departure, the small stack of boxes. Perhaps she herself was once a victim of the corporate world.

"I'm all set for today, honey," she says, and wheels back toward her spot on the platform.

She's all set for today. She has seven teeth and is stuck in a wheelchair, but she feels she's all set.

A lone train arrives. It's bell clangs like an old cow lost in the woods. There is a hiss of brakes, then the conductor leaps onto the platform. He struggles to get the woman's wheelchair over the small chasm that separates the platform from the train.

"Thanks, honey," she says to the conductor.

I'm disappointed. I thought her "honey" was a special gift to me.

It is snowing when I get back to the suburbs. The fallen snow lays undisturbed upon the pine needles as I hike through the forest. The trail to my secret forest glen is also undisturbed. Even teenagers lack the virility to stand up against the cold winter air; for now they must sneak occasional moments together in their darkened family rooms while their parents sleep unknowingly in the bedrooms above.

I brush the light snow from a rock and sit down. In the snow, I find a familiar object from my youth. It is a roach – the spent end of a joint – the remnants of an exhilarating gathering of friends. I see them passing the joint between themselves, inhaling deeply, laughing as the smoke bursts from their mouths. They cuss about their stupid parents, they talk about all the morons in their pin-striped suits, they laugh at the politicians with their false sense of importance. Someone plays Bob Dylan on a portable cassette player. *Everybody must get stoned*. I see now that they are not the unfamiliar faces of the neighborhood teens; they are my classmate's faces – my old friends – and among them is my face. Someone passes me the joint, and I laugh and wave it away. "I'm all set for today, honey."

Boy was I stoned that day.

We all were. We were stoned, we were witty, we were chummy. We had music, we had values, we had truth, we had friendship. We had popcorn – mouthfuls of it.

We had no money.

We were all set.

I look around the empty clearing and realize my boxes are not with me. I left them on the train, in an overhead bin. They will travel back and forth, city to suburb, continue my daily commute for me. Perhaps the blind lady will sit under them. Her dog will lift his nose, smell my scent, and remember me.

Back home, I gather the contents from the mailbox before heading up the snow-bleached driveway. Nat is sweeping snow from his fish pond. He spots me and waves the broom my way.

"Some guy's been hanging around looking for you," he says as I wander over and join him at the edge of the pond.

I look down and expect to see fish frozen in place, but there is only ice. "Some guy?"

"Yeah. Looked like a lawyer or something." Nat continues sweeping. He sees me eyeing him curiously. "My youngest wants to try out for hockey this year."

"Nat, your pond's only six feet across."

"Eight. Anyway, he just wants a spot to practice dropping

his gloves and swinging his fists." Nat stops sweeping; the ice is clear now. There's a rope leading into the ice. Looking closer, I can see the outline of a beer can beneath the surface. Nat follows my gaze. "Yeah, there's three of them stuck down there." He picks up the rope and gives it a futile tug. "Oh well. Now I have a reason to look forward to spring."

"I better get home," I say.

Nat nods. "Hey Harry, send your boy over. He must be Brucie's age. They can practice body checks together."

"I'll tell him," I say.

"Maybe they can try out for the team together."

"Yeah, okay." Yeah, okay, but fat chance. Justin doesn't do team sports. He won't wear a uniform. He says it's dorky. He'll wear his baseball cap backward, he'll leave his baggy pants fluttering around his butt like a wet flag, he'll follow the latest, oddest fad along with eleven million fellow teenagers; but ask him to enter a playing field with six or eight other boys, and he'll say the matching uniforms are dorky.

Justin, you've each got your own number!

Nice try, Dad.

***

Justin trots into the house and slams the door shut. He does not expect to find me at home. He is singing about sex. *Oh Baby baby baby.* Yes, soon he will be using those corny lines. His lips will stick out like Mick Jagger's, and the girl will swoon into his arms.

Justin, you're not just using me?

Baby, feel that and tell me it's not the real thing.

"Justin, that you?" I shout. He needs to know I'm home before he does something to drive me over the edge.

"Dad? What are you doing home?"

"Took a little time off."

He squints at me. "You got fired."

Kathleen enters the house on this note. She should start crying, but she doesn't. The suburbs have dulled her emotions.

"I was laid off," I explain.

"Same thing."

"No, it's not the same," I argue. It just feels the same.

The two children are quiet for a moment. They are thinking. Little wheels are spinning. I hear a ticking, but it is only the kitchen clock.

"What do we do for money?" Justin asks.

Kathleen says nothing, but a smile is creeping across her face. She is smarter than Justin – she takes the world as she sees it and projects it into the future. That's probably why she's always crying. It's surprising that she doesn't cry more. Justin is a teenager – he lives strictly in the present.

The kids have won. The suburbs were never my idea anyway.

"We'll have to sell the house," I say.

"And?" Justin still can't see past today.

"We'll go back home!" Kathleen shouts. "Maybe our old apartment is still empty."

Justin squints again, and I send him a confirming nod.

"Yes!" he shouts.

The two children run up the stairs. They are going to start packing.

"Whoa, whoa," I shout. "We won't be moving right away. There's a lot to do."

They ignore me. I hear them digging through their closets. For once, Justin is looking beyond today.

December 19

I hear Kathleen typing at her computer. I peek into her room and see her sitting at her desk, bundled up in my trench coat, the collar turned up, a brown fedora hat pulled down around her ears.

"What are you doing, Kitten?"

She is startled and spins around. "It's a secret mission," she says.

"A secret mission." I laugh.

"I'm tracking down Mommy."

"Oh." I envision she's sent an E-mail to her little gardener friend in Michigan. "Any luck?"

She rolls her mouse across the desk top and a picture of a swami appears. "Well, I've contacted this psychic in Calcutta through his web page, and he's probing the universe." She slides the mouse further, and a screen full of messages scrolls by. "I found this psychologist in Frankfurt who's done a lot of work on sudden homosexual impulses. I set up a private chat room, and he's talking to his colleagues in Montreal and Buenos Aires right now. I don't understand it much, so I'll wait until they've come up with the profile." She flicks the mouse again, and a mountain stream appears. "I've entered her as a missing person in the Wilderness Club's home site, so any hiker in North America will be looking for her..."

My mind begins to swim. The image of a quaint bouquet of Michigan snapdragons wilts.

"I've contacted my gardener's club, the pet lovers, and the after-school mystery club. I also threw in the shoppers club, but I don't think they'll help much. They never leave their houses."

"How many people are looking for Mommy?" I ask.

"I think about half a million, but once I get my web page set up, it should go higher. I'm using *sex* as a keyword."

I slowly back out of her room, a feeling of inadequacy pervading my very soul. Beside her on the desk, Kathleen's Barbie doll sits at a toy computer – pink and plastic with no internet hookup. Her red lips are grinning at me, mocking – even Barbie knows more than me.

***

A letter arrives – Beth's handwriting is on the outside. The postmark says Omaha. Inside are seven sheets of paper with careful handwriting running the length of each side. There is also a photograph of a group of five women. Eve and Beth are smiling from the right side of the group. On the left are two women in matching tee shirts. They are smiling, too. All four are sporting crewcuts – it looks good. They look younger, healthier. They look a bit like boys. Perhaps I'm turning gay, too.

In the middle of the group is a woman with long blond hair, a black eye, and a cut lip. She is smiling despite her injuries. There are dried cornstalks hovering over her in the background. The cornstalks seem to be waving. It's such a cheerful picture.

I can just make out the writing on one of the women's tee shirts – "Women's Rescue League."

I read Beth's letter, and I am strangely happy. Beth and Eve have joined the underground. They are rescuing battered women and taking them to safe havens. Beth reads them women's poetry and Eve inspires them with passages from the Bible. Eve is a bit jealous of Beth's job because Eve has found there are very few passages in the Bible that are inspirational to battered women. After Beth reads her poetry, all the women sigh. They make dreamy comments like, "Isn't that beautiful." After Eve reads, she is met with silence, or worse yet, "Well, it's getting late."

They drink wine sometimes, but then they don't comment on beauty. They say, "Men! Ha! Who needs them!"

I expect her letter to say good-bye. Fourteen pages is a lot; no one writes that much unless they have something important to say. But no, it is all chit-chat. She speaks well of Eve: she is warm, she is gentle, she has compassion. I read between the lines: Beth sees now that something is wrong. Physical and emotional attraction and sexual attraction are not the same thing. You need not sleep with all that you admire in the world. Humor, intellect: you would have to fill your bed up with an odd assortment of clowns and elderly professors to start meeting all those needs.

It's obvious: she wants me again. She doesn't say it, but it is there in what she doesn't say. Words like "passion" and "excitement" are missing from the pages. There is no heat searing my fingertips as I hold the letter. There is no jealousy in me as I read about Eve.

"From Mom?" Justin asks.

"Yeah," I say. "She's helping troubled women."

"She could of stayed home for that," he says.

I stare at Justin and smile. He has insights I never knew he had. He'll catch up to Kathleen yet. Perhaps one day he'll start crying.

"She coming back?" Justin asks.

"Not yet," I say.

Kathleen is hovering at a distance. "We're still moving back home, though?"

"Yes, Kitten."

The movers are coming tomorrow. Beth's letter has arrived just in time to throw a bit of doubt in my decision, but not early enough to change it.

I continue reading. Beth misses the children, but the value of her work compensates her somewhat for that. She seems to have forgotten that she ran away; she writes as though she is doing a job we had planned all along, like she joined the Peace Corps and we threw her a proper sending-off party.

She won't tell me where she's living; she's been sworn to secrecy. There are laws broken sometimes; there are dangerous men prowling the woods in search of the women they once owned. One slip, and freedom – or even lives – could be in danger.

They never made it to San Francisco. The importance of sourdough bread faded in the smoky haze of an Omaha coffee shop.

They sing inspirational songs sometimes. The lyrics are rather foolish and would make men laugh, but it's more the entire atmosphere rather than the loose collection of verse that creates the inspiration. They sing them around a campfire after a successful rescue while coyotes howl in the distance. Women have surpassed men for high adventure. Headlights flash from a distance mesa, and secret passwords are exchanged. A rendezvous

– and the rescued woman is handed off to another group, to be smuggled off to another part of the country.

Melancholy falls over the four women.

But tomorrow there will be another rescue. The adrenaline will pump once more.

Beth says she will write again. She sends the children her love. She would have signed off with a little heart and a "p.s. I love you," but she can't – Eve might be looking over her shoulder.

"Dad? You okay." Justin gently nudges my elbow.

I open my eyes and see I'm sniffing a corner of the letter. It is still soaked with the smell of Beth.

December 20

I watch the movers struggling to remove a large sofa through the front door. I had told them that it was originally brought in through the sliding glass doors in the rear, but they insist on removing it their way. A man in a business suit appears on the front stoop, blocking their path. He is carrying an umbrella. There is no rain in the forecast; there is no snow, either. Christmas will not be white this year.

I recall what Nat had said several weeks ago, about a lawyer man prowling about. Six months ago, a lawyer on my stoop would have been of no more concern than a milk bottle, but now... Beth is out there somewhere. She's found conviction; that sounds too much like convict. It's a strange language; conviction being a belief and guilt all at once. Perhaps that is why Kathleen prefers Swahili.

I remember convictions. It was long ago. It started with a war. They tried to beat our convictions out of us. In the end, we sold them. I am standing in the remnants of my convictions. At the time, I would have thought they'd be worth more.

It is with extreme caution that I approach the man with the umbrella.

A slight smile sends the tips of his pencil-thin mustache skyward. "Good day, sir."

He tips a black bowler hat, then tries to hand me his business card, but the sofa keeps us apart. One of the moving men pushes him aside while the other grunts, heaves his huge body against the sofa, and sets it free.

"Jolly good," the man with the umbrella says.

He holds out his business card again as he fills the void left by the escaping sofa – he is a solicitor, the card says. He pretends he's British, but I know better. He's a lawyer for god sake; the paperwork would have been easy. A simple name change, and the disguise would have been complete. But Antonio Spinozzi, that is not British.

The two burly movers haul the sofa across the dismal lawn to a waiting van. We are violating rules here, moving in December. It's a special case though; the children are returning to a school system they already know. We do not have to wait for June.

The solicitor pulls an envelope out from inside his top coat. "And you would be the elusive Mr. Lascome?"

I nod slightly. Anything you say can be used against you in a court of law. Nods can not, perhaps.

"I represent the estate of Mrs. Constance Finch. You knew her?"

"We talked on the phone," I say. "I never met her."

"Yes. Well, you must have been quite a talker. She has named you in her will." The tips of his mustache shoot skyward again. "May I come in?"

My children are huddled behind me. There is tension around them. They stand like two filaments; an arc of electricity jumps between them; they are charged and ready to go. This man can only delay their departure for home.

I stare at the envelope. It is thin, but it could easily conceal seventeen dollars. "We're in the middle of moving," I say as I step clear of the door. "You'll have to excuse the mess."

Mr. Spinozzi steps in and hands me his umbrella. "How well did you know Mrs. Finch?"

"She grew tomatoes," I say. I want to say something about the Hustler magazine the coroner may have found, explain that Mrs. Finch was not a collector of pornography, that she was merely looking for my wife. I catch myself before I do, though. It might restore Mrs. Finch's good name if the real reason behind the girlie magazines was known, but it would do nothing for my family's reputation if folks knew Mrs. Finch was scanning pictures of naked women looking for Beth.

"Tomatoes. Yes, she and her tomatoes." Mr. Spinozzi scans the empty rooms. "Is there someplace we can sit down?"

There is only one room the movers haven't touched. "The bedroom," I say.

He stares at me for a moment. Perhaps he's heard about Beth; he might be thinking it's a family affliction. "We can stand at the kitchen counter, I guess," he replies. He has abandoned his accent, worried that I've mistaken it for something less masculine than British.

The envelope he carries is stuffed with more papers than seventeen dollars warrant.

He hands me a photograph. "Your benefactress."

It is an older picture: she is standing among her tomato plants. She is smiling as she stands in the hot sun dressed in black. Her husband is recently dead. I'm not sure which she is smiling about, her vibrant tomatoes or her dead husband.

"That's her farmhouse in the background," Antonio Spinozzi

explains as he spreads his papers across the cheap Formica countertop.

I look for a seventeen dollar check from my former employer, but there are just legal documents.

"Her will is a bit complicated. For starters, you'll have to move to her farm if you want to collect anything."

"Dad!" the children shout in alarm. Mr. Spinozzi's words have just touched them; a jolt of static electricity has been released.

"No," I say, waving my arms about, pointing out the emptiness of the house to him. "We're moving to the city today." I turn to smile at my children, to reassure them. They smile back with cautious, uncertain smiles.

"You were her financial advisor, were you not, Mr. Lascome?"

I nod my head slightly.

"How much do you think she was worth?"

"She had seventeen dollars in the account I handled."

"Seventeen dollars?" Mr. Spinozzi chuckles. "Isn't that precious. No, Mr. Lascome. Mrs. Finch was a wealthy woman. Her husband was a miser and never let her spend any of their money. It was a habit she carried with her to her grave." He chuckles slightly. "A habit that has worked to your advantage, but one that I'm sure you won't adopt." He shows me a bank statement. There are numbers stretched along the bottom. "That's not her account number," he says. "That's her balance. Almost eight million dollars."

Justin whistles low.

"That's not so much," Kathleen says. "That's two hundred to the third power." She smiles impishly.

How does she know these things? Sometimes she scares me.

"Come on," she says. "Let's go home." She heaves her backpack onto her shoulder. It contains all that she needs to resume her normal life – her Barbie dolls and a Christmas list for Santa. A strange list – land for peasants, freedom for dissident writers, and something called a "Beanie Baby."

"All we get are two hundred dollars each?" Justin is not good at math. He has no innate feeling for correct answers. At school, he once had to calculate the circumference of a softball; the number of miles he came up with would have been incredible even to a space traveler, but he wrote it down on his test paper anyway. His teacher wrote "wow" beside the answer and gave Justin half credit, figuring the question must have been poorly worded.

Mr. Spinozzi waits patiently for the excitement to die down, then becomes brisk and businesslike. He places pencil marks on his list as he reads. "You have to stay on the farm for one year," he explains. "You have to make a pretense of working the farm – grow some tomatoes, some corn if you think you can keep from getting lost in it." He scans down the list, skipping the little details he will explain later; the types of tomatoes (heirlooms not hybrids), the best fields for planting. "You can not make any changes to the farm, no improvements, no hired hands." Mr. Spinozzi flips to the last page. "Finally, you must care for the cat."

"Mittens is still alive?" I ask.

"Yes, alive." Mr. Spinozzi stares briefly at me. I claim ignorance of Mrs. Finch's personal life, yet I know her cat's name; he finds something odd in that. He begins to fold up the papers. "The cat is actually the heir to the estate. You are named as her caretaker. Stay on the farm, take care of the cat, and after one year you become the heir. Come down to my office tomorrow morning at ten and we'll do the more tedious paperwork. Then I'll get you the keys and directions to the farm, and you'll be on your way."

He snatches the umbrella from my hand, and spins to leave. His accent returns – only stronger, more exuberant – as he spots the "for sale" sign on the front yard.

"Take that down," he orders. "And tell these good chaps to put the furniture back. The estate will take care of your normal expenses while you're off feeding the cat. I say, there's nothing more normal than a mortgage payment, right, right? You do have a mortgage? Of course you do. Wouldn't be the suburbs without one. Buy as much house as you can bloody well afford, not as much as you need. Ha ha. I love America." He nudges the brim of his bowler with the tip of the umbrella. "Good day, sir, children."

I watch as Mr. Spinozzi retreats toward his car. A thin smile spreads across my face.

Look Edna, we's rich! We's headin' for the boonies!

"Daddy," Kathleen whines. "You promised."

"But kids, a year isn't so bad, and then we get eight million dollars."

Kathleen shakes her head. "A year's a long time."

"Yeah, Dad," Justin agrees. "You're so old, a year doesn't mean much, but I'm only fourteen. That's like a quarter of my life."

"Four, Justin," I say. "If you were four, it would be a quarter of your life." His math is still off, but he's right about a year being a long time for a kid. I think back to when I was fourteen. One year. Three hundred and sixty-five days. That was about seven hundred and thirty untapped hard-ons.

Eight million dollars, though. That's a lot of money. I look at Justin and imagine how he will spend the year. I look at Kathleen and imagine how she will spend the year. I think of myself and imagine how I will spend the eight million dollars.

The two moving men stomp through the foyer, seeking out

remnants they may have overlooked.

"Ah, I'd like to put the furniture back for now," I call. "Can I do that?"

The two men are silent for a moment. They each hope that the other knows the answer. The smaller man finally speaks. "Most folks don't change their minds at this juncture."

"Yeah," the other man agrees. "What happen? Someone die and a better apartment coming available?"

"Something like that," I say.

"Dad," Justin implores. "You promised."

I try to ignore him. He's fourteen. He'll spend the next year lying in bed listening to bad music through tiny headphones, his pants slipped down around his thighs, his fingers discovering things about himself he never knew. He can do that anywhere.

"Yeah! You promised us, Daddy."

Kathleen – she'll spend the year sitting in a corner of the apartment building's dank basement with her friend Rahana, their Barbie dolls talking gibberish to them, the two little girls pretending it's Swahili. Dank basements are not healthy. Farms are.

There's eight million dollars out there. I can buy a red convertible and park it outside my old office building. I'll stare up at the second floor windows, then drive off when I see the cold blue eyes appear behind the glass. I can wait in my bedroom for Beth to return, my pants slipped down around my thighs; I can learn new things to show her so that maybe this time she'll stay.

I have a thought. I pick up the wall phone and punch some numbers into the hand set. I hope there is someone at the other end so this can all be settled now.

A woman picks up on the fourth ring. I look at my children and whisper, "Grandma." It is Beth's mother, not mine. My parents live in the suburbs; they've bought cemetery plots in the suburbs. Beth's parents live in the city. Beth and her mother used to shop for handbags together. Sometimes we went over there for brunch. They wish to be cremated and placed on the mantle.

"Hi, Sue," I say. After our wedding, I tried to call her "Mom," but it felt so odd, I found myself calling her nothing at all. "Sue" works much better. "You know how you've wanted the kids to visit for a while?"

I turn and look behind me. Justin and Kathleen are smiling. They're standing side-by-side, each with an arm around the other's waist. I've got such a cute family sometimes; it's always for the wrong reasons.

"How long?" I'm almost afraid to say it. "Oh, about a year." There is silence at the other end. Justin and Kathleen are standing with their fingers crossed. "It'll be shorter if the cat dies."

There is distant talking on the other end. It sounds like cartoon chipmunks. My children's smiles have stretched out into tense grins. Kathleen has crossed the fingers on both her hands. She has crossed her legs and is bouncing up and down. She looks like she needs to pee.

"Sure. I'll take them for summer vacation. Yes, I know Walter has a heart condition." Walter is my father-in-law. I never tried to call him "Dad."

There are chipmunks again.

"Justin help out at the shop a little? Sure, he'll be glad to." I see Justin's grin fade, and I shrug my shoulders. My father-in-law sells wedding gowns. Justin doesn't know it yet, but he'll enjoy being around young brides-to-be. They emanate a certain sexual awakening that will be in sympathy with what he's feeling. The young women will stand on the alteration block and send secret smiles his way as he pushes a broom around the perimeter of the shop; a pleasant shiver will shoot through his lower body. Sometimes the future bride will come with her bridesmaid or a younger sister; there will be electricity in the air then. Justin will catch a glimpse of pure white legs – legs that he knows will soon be wrapped around the ass of a naked man. He will think then that he has the coolest job in the world.

"Then it's okay? Great!" I turn to face my brood. I stretch out my arms in triumph. Ta da!

Justin is smiling broadly. *You are the coolest, Dad. The coolest!*

Kathleen uncrosses her legs. She uncrosses her fingers and claps her hands. "Kalunga cow tonga!" Then she falls silent; she is thinking, poor girl. "Daddy? Where do they make millionaires live?"

"Anywhere the millionaire wants, Kitten."

She smiles smugly. She knows once I'm a millionaire, I'll spoil her. I'll buy her anything she wants. I'll buy her the city.

December 21

A small caravan winds its way through the gray country side – a blue minivan followed by a white Cadillac. My son and daughter are in the back seat of the van; they are singing songs I have never heard before. They say I've heard them; it's just I could never understand the lyrics when the professionals sang them. Justin and Kathleen are not talented enough to garble up the lyrics. Walter is sitting beside me, while my mother-in-law is following along in the Cadillac – an arrangement that has something to do with Walter's heart condition, but I don't ask for specifics and the connection remains a bit vague in my mind.

"Countryside's not very pretty," Walter says, looking out the side window at the snowless December landscape.

"It's winter," I say. "It'll be pretty come spring."

"A lot of bugs in the spring, I'll bet." Walter hasn't smiled since we left the city line marker.

"What's our next turn?" I ask.

Walter looks at the piece of paper unfolded on his lap. "French

Fry Lane," he says.

"French Fry Lane?" The kids laugh. Then they turn serious; maybe there's a McDonalds out there somewhere.

Up ahead is a wooden sign with hand painted letters: Finch Farm Lane. This is the closest Walter has gotten with his directions. Earlier, he had us looking for Saturn; when the sign for Shelburne appeared, he yelled, "That's it! Saturn!"

"Jeez, Walter. Will you get some glasses."

"Nothing wrong with my eyesight."

He's adapted to a life of limited vision. He and Sue visit Florida each winter. He thinks all animals are border collies, but he's avoided falling into the jaws of hungry alligators by developing a renewed fear of dogs – a fear he had overcome in his childhood.

"French Fry, Finch Farm." The kids laugh again.

"Hey, don't sass your elders," Walter yells.

A few weeks with my father-in-law, and the kids may want to give up the city yet.

A big white farmhouse looms ahead on a hill. Its green shutters hang at odd angles; a brick chimney leans outward in sympathy. I pull out the photograph that Mr. Spinozzi had given me; the building is somewhat reminiscent of the house in the background of the photo. It has not been painted since the photograph was taken – late 1960's I would guess. It has become a bit obscured by the growth of shrubs; arborvitae and rhododendron reaching the rim of the rotted gutters. A layer of wet brown leaves covers the roof, making it hard to tell whether the roof is still slate. The lawn has not been mowed in years; small maples are sticking up among the brown grass. The forests are trying to reclaim what was once theirs.

There is a barn to the left side of the house, but the snows of many winters have brought the far end to its knees.

The children laugh again. This is even funnier than french fries. They start singing the theme song to "Green Acres." Even Walter joins in, though I doubt he sees clearly enough to understand the humor.

"All right, all right" I say. "You won't be laughing when I come home with a suitcase stuffed with hundred dollar bills."

There is a strange car idling in front of the barn. Mr. Spinozzi steps out at the sound of our tires crunching up the long driveway. He is holding a cat. The cat is black with white feet; it can only be Mittens.

"Mr. Spinozzi," I greet him.

"Ah, Mr. Lascome. You found it okay."

"My father-in-law kept wanting us to go to New Jersey, but we got here anyway."

Walter climbs laboriously from the van, grumbling about vehicles that are too high off the ground. "That's because there's a Shelburne in New Jersey, too," he says. "We used to take Beth there when she was a child."

"That was Ship Bottom, Walter," I remark.

Mr. Spinozzi hands me the cat. "Take good care of Mittens," he advises me. "Remember, she's the heiress, you're the caretaker."

Justin and Kathleen leave the van only long enough to join their grandmother in the Cadillac.

"You kids don't want to see your old man's new home?" I ask.

They stare out the car window with apprehension. "That's okay, Dad," Justin says.

"Afraid of ghosts?" I tease.

"Afraid we'll fall through a floor," Justin says.

Mr. Spinozzi hands me another of his business cards. I have four of them now. "Call me if you have problems. I can't really help you any – the will's quite specific – but you can still call."

Walter tries to get into the driver's side of the Cadillac, but Sue won't unlock the door. He reluctantly enters through the passenger side and slams the door shut.

I wave slowly as the white Cadillac crawls backward down the steep driveway. Mr. Spinozzi smiles awkwardly at me. "Well, good luck," he says. He puts out his hand to shake mine, but sees Mittens is sleeping in my arms. "You might actually like it here." He tips his bowler and climbs into his car.

Slowly, he backs his car around by the barn, then drives from the farm, spinning gravel out his rear tires. I watch with a sense of sadness; not that I have any feelings for Mr. Spinozzi, but seeing his bowler leave is like saying good-bye to civilization.

December 25

It seems strange spending the Holidays among the in-laws without Beth. I remember the first Christmas we spent with her family. We were not married then – we were living together. It was strange then, meeting everyone for the first time, being a sinner and all, but this is stranger yet. There is still that tension in the air; from Beth's sister Laura in particular. She eyed me that first time with a stony interest, seeing me as the despoiler of virgins, like I was Christopher Columbus planting my corrupt flag pole into the pure white sands of an untouched continent. *Hey! There were cannibals inhabiting those shores before me, baby.*

Come to think of it, Laura has always watched me with a certain cool detachment, compiling an encyclopedia of my failures I suppose. We're on the zees for sure by now.

"What's with the cat?" Laura asks harshly.

I am sitting opposite her, perched on a wooden piano stool with Mittens in my lap. "This is my eight million dollar cat." I swing gently back and forth in half circles on the stool, hoping the subtle motion will keep Mittens, my benefactress, calm. She does not like strangers. She does not like me, come to think of it, but she is partially deaf and mostly blind, and thinks my legs are an inanimate stretch of denim carpeting.

"Looks like it has mange," Laura growls.

I look down at the cat. She's right: it needs a bath, but I'm afraid it will catch pneumonia if I put it in water. I tried to brush the knots from its fur, but the damn thing yowled like I was torturing it. The will only states that I am the cat's caretaker, not its hairdresser, so I've abandoned my attempts at being a feline beautician.

The children finally arrive.

They rode up here in the white Cadillac with their grandfather. Justin went along as navigator, but the car still disappeared from Laura's rear view mirror as Laura and her mom blazed the trail in an aging gray Ford. I asked if we should send out a search party, but Sue said he'd show up. "He always does," she sighed, seeming almost sad about that. Then she went to put some things in the refrigerator. I heard her gasp as she entered the kitchen.

She's still in there rattling pots and pans about. Words like "mess" and "disgusting" filter out into the parlor.

Kathleen runs toward me with open arms. "Daddy!"

"Don't squish the cat," I reply.

Justin stands in the doorway with his hands in his pockets. "Hey, Dad." He looks around, at the bare white walls, the three chairs, the faded green sofa, and the yellow cotton drapes that make up the front parlor of the old farmhouse. "So this is your pad." The way he says it – pad – he is mocking me. Mocking my generation, anyway. Pad is no longer cool. He is not mocking the room, though. He has little interest in decor. Justin thinks underpants draped over a bare light bulb makes for a perfectly fine lampshade – until they start to smoke.

Kathleen shows absolutely no interest in the house. She kneels in front of me. "Hi, Mittens." She pets the cat vigorously. "She's kind of lumpy, Daddy."

"She's a girl then?" Laura asks.

I don't really know. I'm not aware of any cat needs that would be altered on the basis of sex, so I have never checked.

"Of course she's a girl," Kathleen says. "Can't you see by how kind and gentle she is?" She looks into the cat's eyes. "Macala too nooka."

The cat perks up her ears. Perhaps that was Swahili for "the mice are everywhere." It would be the only comment Kathleen has made about my new quarters.

Walter struggles through the door with his arms filled with brightly papered packages. Justin steps out of his way, but keeps his hands in his pockets.

"Justin. Help your grandfather," I order.

Laura pats the empty space beside her on the sofa. "Papa's fine. Sit here, Jussie." She is the last one to call him "Jussie" on a regular basis; she will never accept that Justin is no longer seven. Justin will not accept that she used to bathe him; he still blushes when they brush past each other outside a bathroom door. He wishes there was some way he could show her that he's not so little anymore.

"Sure is getting cold." Walter stomps his feet even though his boots are dry. He thinks foot stomping is the universal sign for cold toes, and not a method to clear shoes of small snow drifts. He looks into the corner of the parlor. "What's that thing?"

"That's our tree, Walter," I say.

"Where are all the branches?"

"That's how they grow in the wild," I explain.

I had found a journal in a desk, penned in Mrs. Finch's handwriting. It held a detailed account of Mr. Finch's farming efforts. For a number of years he had grown blue spruce and white pine in a part of the farm call Brookside Meadow. Every December, suburban folks journeyed out, each to cut the perfect tree and to tie it to the roof of their car. They stood like statues among the trees, staring from one frozen pine to the next, debating in their minds the relative merits of each one as gently falling snow accumulated on their shoulders like uncontrolled dandruff. They forgot the lesson of the prior year and again bought the fullest tree, then got it home and found there was no room among the thick branches to hang the ornaments.

I followed Mrs. Finch's hand drawn map to Brookside Meadow, but it was gone. The forest had reclaimed it. I found myself instead among neatly spaced rows of towering pine trees. I looked up and saw the lower branches of blue spruce and white pine. I was a leprechaun concealed in a forest of Christmas trees. I chose one of the trees at random, then sawed it down in three hours with a hack saw. It crashed through the surrounding trees and landed softly on the bare ground with hardly a sound. I cut the top off, leaned it against a boulder, and stepped back; the branches were sparse, set along the trunk at irregular intervals, a victim of the crowded conditions in which it was forced to grow. I looked up through the small hole my handiwork had left in the canopy. There were other treetops up there, ones that from my distant view looked fuller, more like how I wanted my Christmas tree to look. But there was also howling from deep within the forest, almost like wolves, but more like... Indians? I grabbed my treetop and trotted back to the farmhouse. Once safely inside, I tried to close some of the green shutters, but the hardware would no longer move.

"You know, if you put a few lights on it, it might not look so bad." Walter examines the tree closely. He rubs several pine needles between his fingers. He's been doing that – rubbing the pine needles – for as long as anyone can remember, but no one's ever asked him why he does it.

"I couldn't find any lights," I explain.

"Go out and buy some. You that hard up for cash?" Walter pulls out his wallet. "Here, here. Have a few twenties."

I wave them away. "That's not it, Walter. I'm not allowed to improve anything."

"What? Christmas lights would be improvements?"

I shrug my shoulders. There's no point in saying more. Someone's pitched a tent on the hill on the other side of Finch Farm Lane. Sometimes I see dark shapes moving on the hillside among the mountain laurel, the glint of a binocular lens giving their exact location away. They're watching this place, waiting for me to slip up so they can turn me in. I imagine the Finch Family has posted a reward for anyone with information that would disqualify me from receiving the inheritance. Funny. None of Mrs. Finch's relatives ever knew she had eight million dollars; now that they do, they can't live without it.

Kathleen has been listening intently. She spots my newspaper beside the only comfortable chair in the parlor – the chair is vacant, waiting for my mother-in-law to return from the kitchen. There are scissors lying on top of the newspaper; I've been clipping out help-wanted ads – lumberjacks are desperately needed. Kathleen slides across the bare floor, picks up the scissors, and starts cutting chains of paper dolls from the folded newspaper – Christmas elves to hang on the tree.

There's a woman's scream from the kitchen. Walter and I jump from our seats and run to investigate. Justin also tries to rise, but Laura pushes him back – this is man's work, Jussie.

Sue has dropped the tray that held the Christmas ham, but her hands still think they've got it – her two fists are held out before her gripping an invisible serving tray, shaking visibly.

"There... there... there was a face in the window," she says. "A big hairy face."

Justin has freed himself from his doting aunt. He runs to the back door and throws it open. "Big Foot!" It is a reckless teenage impulse to open the door – we do not want Big Foot in our kitchen. Walter nudges Justin aside and closes the door. He turns the dead bolt for good measure.

"Oh yeah," I say. Everyone turns and looks at me – Laura and Kathleen have joined the rest of us in the kitchen. "I forgot to tell you about him."

"You knew about him?" Walter leans over the kitchen sink. He pushes back the curtain and scans the overgrown herb garden.

"He seems harmless." I say. "He likes to watch me cook." I know the suburbs – property rights are a treasured principle. The country, though, is all new to me – hunters and snowmobilers traversing the fields of strangers, nature lovers stopping to snip cattails beside a farmer's pond. Free range chickens. Perhaps watching neighbors cook is a country tradition. Perhaps we should have invited Hairface in to join us for Christmas dinner.

"Hey, Dad. You got a gun?" Justin still thinks guns are cool. He and his buddies talk of weapons. They know how large an area a nuclear warhead can destroy. They don't imagine they'll be living anywhere near that area, so they can talk about it with a sense of awe, not horror. They have not seen a real war yet. They've seen a few little teeny-weenie feel-good wars on television, but not a real ugly long swampy black-body-bag war. They have not seen fires burning in the streets of Chicago. Justin thinks it's cool when Arnold Schwarzenegger uses a machine gun to wipe out every commie in the Southern hemisphere. If only we had had Arnold thirty years ago. Hasta la vista.

Girls are starting to look cool, too, though. There's turmoil in Justin's soul. He and his pals know that the cowboy and Indian thing is childish, but... damn, that new stealth fighter is so cool. No one's ever seen it, of course, but it's just got to be cool. *Cindy Wyman sucked my dick last night*, one of the boys will say. *No shit!* the others will shout. He'll nod his head with a new sense of confidence, and the other boys will fold up their *Soldiers of Fortune* magazines and toss them to the back of their lockers. Weapons might me cool, but these boys have got missiles of their own they'd like to launch.

"How'd you get her to do that?" Justin will ask.

"I told her I loved her." The other boy will make kissy lips, then laugh.

Justin will try to make a kissy face – metamorphosis has begun. He'll stop and look longingly toward his locker stuffed with soldier magazines. He doesn't know if he's quite ready for girls – the penis, it's such a private thing. He doesn't know if he wants a stranger hanging off the end of it.

"Dad. You got a gun?" Justin asks again as I fade in and out of consciousness.

"There's a gun over the fireplace," Kathleen says. She's smug – she knows how important weapons are to her brother, yet she spotted the rifle and he didn't.

"No bullets, though," I say.

"Oh, Harry! You live way out here, and you don't own a gun?" Sue has finished picking the ham from the floor. It was on a metal serving tray, so glass shards are not a problem. She has lived in the city for sixty-four years and has always had a gun nearby. She's never used it, but she says it's like insurance – you only need it when you don't have it. I've used my insurance plenty of times, but I've never needed a gun.

Walter keeps a gun at the bridal shop. He reads about armed robberies at other stores and almost wishes for one at his; it would break up the tedium created by a steady stream of future brides, each one demanding to be treated like the only one. He thinks robbers might be easier to deal with. Robbers do not hit bridal shops, though. They could not case the joint easily; they would not blend in with the other customers. Robbers rarely look like brides.

"You know how I feel about guns, Sue," I say. "Besides, I'm not going to shoot someone for looking at a ham."

Sue clamps her mouth shut. Talking is over; she will ignore me now for three hours – that is the usual punishment. This is a treatment normally reserved for Beth, but Beth is not here, so I am her proxy.

"I'm sorry, Sue," I say. "But guns are dangerous when you've got kids around."

The others look between my mother-in-law and me. The Christmas gathering, the family meal, the fights – tradition has begun. Laura is relieved; she is usually first.

Why aren't you married, Laura? Uncle Ed normally asks that, but he's skipping Christmas this year. I phoned him to invite him and Aunt Miriam over, but he said, "What are we, the three wise men? Have to journey out into the country and find a manger?"

"I've got a barn, Uncle Ed, not a manger," I said. "And it's fallen down."

"So that makes us want to come?"

Aunt Miriam was yelling in the background. "Tell him about my hay fever." It's winter Aunt Miriam; don't worry about your hay fever.

"We're going over to Aunt Sophie's for Christmas," Uncle Ed explained. Aunt Sophie is Ed's and Walter's sister. She and Uncle Ed haven't talked since he got her a deal on a Studebaker. Apparently, the country has brought them back together.

With much relief, I scratched Uncle Ed from the guest list.

Laura is now smiling, pleased by my failure to lure Uncle Ed and Aunt Miriam to my green pasture. *Why aren't you married, Laura?* She does not have to hear that this Christmas.

"So you couldn't surprise us with a boy friend." Laura's pleasure is short lived; Walter has taken on the role vacated by his older brother. Uncle Ed is not the problem after all; it is Laura's strange situation – not being married – that's the problem; a situation that cannot be disguised by shifting the ham dinner to the countryside. It is a stranger situation still since Laura has easy access to a wedding gown.

"Dad!" Laura storms from the kitchen. She will throw herself in the only sofa and sit sideways, staring out the parlor window, wishing for snow to blot out the world. Perhaps Hairface will come along. He'll look in at the sad spinster and think her loneliness is beauty. He will forget about ham. She will view his hairy face with a serene sense of wonder – why did her mother scream? The windowsill will hide his lower body, and she will not have to think of what manly functions flame below. She will think he is as harmless as a puppy. They will marry, in the spring, in the last standing corner of my barn. I will be the only guest – all the others will claim hay fever. We will all wear overalls. They will honeymoon in my straw.

"What's wrong with Laura?" Walter shouts.

Laura has her mother's genes. She will not talk to her father now. It is all happening too quickly – who's speaking and who's not – I won't be able to keep track. Walter wags his finger at my mother-in-law. "Sue! Go say something to that daughter of yours."

Sue places the ham beside the sink, then goes to the parlor. "Come on children," she calls. She has picked up a subtle message from her husband – Walter wishes to speak with me.

I start carving slices from the ham. Walter will behave better if I'm wielding a butcher knife.

"So, Harry," he says. He snatches a slice of meat from the plate. He knows this will be his last chance to nibble. He knows after he says what he is planning to say, he won't risk placing his fingers near my knife. "We hear odd things about Beth."

"Odd?" I say. "What do you mean?"

"Well, the children said something about Beth and a preacher's wife." He stares at me with hard black eyes. It is a look he normally reserves for brides when they try to return their wedding gowns after the service.

"Eve and Beth? No, nothing odd. They're on a crusade." I don't tell him that they've shaved their heads, or that they are sleeping together. He lives in the city, but he'll still find that odd.

"You aren't having problems... down there." He looks at my zipper. He stares for too long.

It makes me self conscious. I feel something stir. If Walter sees me stir now, he will have a new cause for concern. I have to turn away.

"Well, when I was young, I could keep my wife satisfied," Walter sneers. "She didn't have to go looking for crusades."

"What about Freddie Wright." Oops. That one slipped out.

He looks at me with disbelief. Freddie Wright is a family secret, and I am not really family. Besides, there was a war then and Sue was home alone. Freddie Wright was honoring Walter's memory, that's all. In fact, if Walter hadn't been so good at tickling Sue's secret world, Sue wouldn't have felt the need to find a new feather. And when he came back from the war, didn't Walter accept Laura like she was his own child? He never showed Beth any favoritism: if Laura was to get married, she too could have any gown in the shop. Or if she would at least get laid – so her smile wasn't always so tight.

Walter storms from the kitchen. "Don't throw Freddie Wright at my face, sonny. That was long ago."

I am alone now – except for a faint tapping at the window. Hairface is smiling in at me. His hands are empty – he is not a mad slasher. I wave him toward the back door. A tie-dye tee shirt shows around his neck where his coat of leather fringe is missing its buttons. He turns as he heads toward the door, revealing a large peace sign drawn with a felt-tipped marker on the back of his jacket. He is obviously a hallucination. Perhaps my entire life is a hallucination. It is still 1971, and I am trapped in a mushroom dream.

I turn the dead bolt and open the door slowly. He stands before me, wearing old paisley bellbottoms with an American Flag sewn on each knee.

"Peace," his timid voice says.

"Merry Christmas," I reply and hand him the ham. I shut the door softly and join the rest of the holiday revelers in the parlor. There is nothing but silence.

Kathleen is sitting beside the Christmas tree – she has a string of paper elves stretched between her hands. She starts singing *Joy To The World*, but then stops when she sees that it is not the right song for this crowd.

"Merry Christmas, Kitten," I say. Kathleen jumps up and runs into my arms. We squeeze her eleven Christmas elves to death between us, but for once Kathleen does not cry.

***

It is an angry group that storms from the dining room table when I announce that the ham has disappeared.

"A five-hour drive, and you don't even feed us," Walter shouts toward me.

"Keep it down, dear," Sue says as she helps him into his coat. "You know what the doctor says about your heart condition."

"Keep it down! We feed his damn kids all week, and he can't give us one lousy meal!"

"They're Beth's children, too," Sue whispers.

Laura is already in the car. She didn't want to come in the first place, but she hasn't had a date in forty-one years, so her social life was looking rather pitiful even by her standards.

"Daddy, I don't want to go home with Papa," Kathleen cries. "I want to live in the country with you."

I look toward Justin, searching his face for his view on this. He returns to me a blank stare. He looks about at the white room and the sparse furniture, and digs his toe into the wooden floor as the yellow drapes hang limply behind him. Sorry Kathleen, but your brother does not see this as a viable alternative.

I could split the children up, Kathleen to the country and Justin to the city; but a knock at the door disturbs my thinking before the plan is fully realized. Sue opens it, and a young girl is standing on the other side. She is blonde. She is fourteen. But she is a female fourteen – she exudes a sexuality that boys can only dream of possessing at that age. She exudes it through her thin winter jacket and the tips of her well-formed breasts. She has on tight round shorts, but does not feel the cold. Justin and I move as one toward the door. Despite our quarrel, Walter is drawn into our tight male pod. There is stirring within the three of us – three generations sharing a similar holiday experience. It is Christmas joy, no?

"Hi!" she says. "We're your neighbors, the Moon family."

I look past her to see if there are other Moons hiding in the underbrush, but she is alone. She hands out a dish. It is not a neighborhood fruitcake. It is a fresh baked pie; the sweet aroma of hot apples and cinnamon fills the room. "Daddy sends his thanks for the ham." She eyes my son and smiles innocently. "He says come visit us once you're settled in." She points toward the tent on the hillside. "We live up there."

Justin steps forward. "Hi," he says, his voice failing him like a rusty hinge.

"Hi!" she lilts. "Will you be taking my bus to school?"

Justin looks toward me for the answer, but I look away. It's time to grow up, son; time to make your own choices. City friends and soldier magazines or... hot apple pie.

"It's kind of lonely out here," she says. "I'm glad you've moved in."

Justin is afraid to say more. He doesn't trust what might fall from his gaping mouth.

I nudge him forward. "Introduce yourself," I whisper.

"Um, I'm Justin." He says it quickly before any guffaws can escape through his awkward lips.

"Hi, Justin. I'm Light."

"Light Moon?" I ask.

She smiles serenely. "Moon Light," she says, without a hint of conceit; to be so young and so beautiful; and to have a name like a soft summer night, silver against a darkened pond. Let Beth come back, and we will all fight over this girl. "I've got to go. I'll see you around, Justin?" She waves her fingers at him as she spins to leave.

She steps onto the front stoop and walks toward the driveway. I think steam should rise as her body hits the cold air.

Justin heaves his shoulder against the door, to close it quickly before we all drop dead from lack of oxygen. Three males – three generations – gasp in what air remains together. The power of our lungs nearly sucks the spindly Christmas tree from its stand. But then we exhale and relax as one, wilting against the wall; and the contents of the room settle back into their proper spots.

Walter does not wait to hear Justin's response – Is he going back to the city? Ha! Walter is no longer upset about the missing ham – he wishes he owned a delicatessen rather than a bridal shop so he could shower this sweet country flower with a steady supply of honey-glazed hams. He smiles at us as he takes his wife's hand. "You'll keep in touch?"

"Of course." I stick out my hand and Walter shakes it. "I'll call you when Beth comes home," I say.

"Thanks," Walter replies. "Justin. Be good." He winks, then opens the front door. "We'll bring your things out to you tomorrow." He scans the driveway for one last glimpse of Moon Light, but sees only Laura sitting in her gray Ford, reading a tattered road map. His gaze shifts toward the distant hillside; he hopes that perhaps Moon Light has an older brother, a blond-haired, doe-eyed hunk of young muscle that could soften even Laura's permafrost legs. But there is only mountain laurel.

Walter smiles. "When the time comes, the wedding gown's on me."

December 30

I step into the winter air with a bag of Christmas debris in either hand. Kathleen is outside by herself, playing in the snow. She has covered the front yard with little snowmen. Broken twigs lie in straight lines running from snowman to snowman.

"Very nice," I say. "What's it suppose to be?"

"I'm setting up a chat room," she says.

"With snowmen?"

Kathleen does not respond, but continues working on her newest chat buddy, imbedding a huge smile of gray pebbles across its cold white face. There is no Internet access at Finch Farm, and adding it would be an improvement – or some would say it's an improvement and some would say that it's not, but there's no point in risking a violation of the will. School will resume shortly, anyway, and Kathleen will be with real children once again.

Something cold and wet touches my nose. I look up and see dark flakes swirling across the gray sky. "It's beginning to snow," I call as I hurry off toward the distant street, dragging the remnants of Christmas morning along behind me in their green plastic bags. "Don't stay out too long."

When I return, I think Kathleen has gone in, but then through the growing fury of a winter storm, I see her sitting in the snow between to snowmen. There is a twig sticking out of each of her ears, and she is typing furiously at an old keyboard.

***

There's a knock at the front door. Moon Light and Hairface are standing on the other side.

"No trash pickup out here." Hairface's voice is unusually soft, as if muffled by the thickness of his long beard. He points toward the bags of Christmas debris I've placed by the side of the road. They are disappearing under a steady fall of snow.

Damn. Even in the country, I have run afoul of garbage bag rules. I wait patiently for Hairface to pronounce sentence, but he says nothing as he continues pointing into the falling snow like the ghost of Christmas future.

"Daddy!" Moon Light shouts. "That's not how you introduce yourself." She smiles pleasantly.

The snow is swirling about their heads and tries to fight its way into the farmhouse.

"Come in, come in." I say to my two guests.

Justin runs down the stairs, taking three at a time. He's changed quickly into gym shorts and a tight tee shirt. It is role reversal – this time Moon Light has on thick jeans and a bulky sweater under a winter jacket. "Hi, Light," he says.

"Hi, Justin," she replies. She nudges her father, and he sticks out his hand toward me.

"Hey, man. I'm Crater," he says.

"Harry Lascome," I reply as I shake his cold hand. "Is it

Moon Crater?"

"Piss poor name, ain't it?" Crater smiles shyly.

"He joined the Moon family late. All the good names were taken," Moon Light explains. "My mother was Moon Beam, and my biological father was Moon Dog – he just provided the sperm, though. I've always thought of Moon Crater as my real daddy." She wraps her arms around Crater's waste and gives him a squeeze as she smiles up at him. If she weren't so pretty, I might just puke.

Justin is blushing. The girl has mentioned sperm, and now he's feeling slightly naked in his breezy gym shorts. He's mistaken her innocence for ignorance and believed she thought all boys looked like Ken dolls underneath. But no – she knows what lies behind that lumpy facade of his.

I take the coats from our two neighbors and lead them into the parlor. "Justin, two beers. And get three cokes for you kids."

Justin smiles his thanks – I have given him the graceful exit he needs. He returns shortly with the drinks, wearing the warm jeans that were drying in the kitchen behind the oven. He has remained in the tee shirt, though – it gives him that macho touch without making him feel vulnerable.

Kathleen comes down the stairs with a strip of eight paper Christmas elves dangling from her hand. The Christmas tree is gone, but she is still making ornaments. Nobody will laugh at our Christmas tree next year, she says.

Next year, we'll have eight million dollars, Kitten. You better believe no one will laugh at our tree.

She has painted the elves with water colors and sprinkled glitter on their heads. The glitter falls off as the paint dries. There is glitter throughout the house – but we live in the country now, so I don't complain.

Moon Light wiggles her fingers at Kathleen. "Hi, Kathleen."

"Ko-omana waki." Kathleen waves back.

I let Crater take the comfortable chair, and I perch myself on the piano stool. "So," I say. "You live in a tent?"

"We had a kinda emergency," Crater replies. "Mother Oak fell on Moon Base." It is too many words for Crater; a dreamy resonance invades his voice as the oak falls on the moon.

I reek of puzzlement. It shows in the way my beer can tips in my hand; and I don't seem to notice the beer dribbling onto the floor.

"Oh Daddy!" Kathleen mops my spill up with her paper elves. "Mother Oak is the big tree that guards their home."

"Yeah, Dad. You should see it," Justin exclaims. "They got this really cool house. It's round."

"That's Moon Base?" I ask.

Justin nods. "And it has a long hall going right up the middle and two little halls going off the side, so the whole thing looks like a big peace sign."

"You want to see it, man?" Crater asks.

"It's snowing out," I say.

I have just said something really stupid; it is always snowing or raining in the country. Or the wind is blowing or the sun is beating down; but the country still rolls on. It is not like the suburbs, where the first snowflake sends crowds to the supermarket to horde a winter's supply of rice, where the buses stop running and school children huddle around the radio listening for news that their community has also been struck by this unrelenting disaster. In the country, the cows and the chickens do not seem to care that it's snowing out.

Justin throws my coat at me. "Wimp."

The others grab their coats eagerly. I am out-voted. In the country, democracy still rules. Parental dictatorship seems to have disappeared along with the oxen yoke – it has been replaced with playful insubordination. I like the way Justin said wimp, though – it is the way he would talk to his friends. There is an odd element of respect and acceptance in it.

"Bone head," I say, and I see him smile as he slips out the door to lead the way.

We walk down the driveway, the three children ahead chattering to one another as if we were on a summer outing. I pull my coat collar tight and shudder as each snowflake touches my skin. I am a wimp. Too many years of luxurious suburban living have turned me soft. Will I be man enough to grow tomatoes? Or will the first sighting of hornworms send me gagging to the bathroom?

Crater lights a cigarette. He moves closer, and a strange aroma infiltrates a dormant region of my brain. "You dig some?" he says.

I take it without thinking. It is 1971 again. But I hesitate to inhale, and it is 1997. I am stuck between eras. I am in the country, living the life of a tomato farmer, and drift toward 1971. I have a lesbian wife, and stagger confusedly toward 1997. My daughter is smarter than me – it is 1971. My son listens to a radio station where they play David Bowie and call it "oldies" – it is 1997.

Why is the snow so warm and my feet so light? I hand the joint back to Crater and exhale a cloud of sweet smoke. "Groovy." It is 1971.

Crater smiles at me. "Far out, man."

We walk along the winding trail through the mountain laurel, climbing slowly toward the tent. It is a boxy white canvas tent, like something the military might use on maneuvers for an officers' mess. Off in the distance, there is a lake.

"Walden Pond!" I shout.

Crater laughs. His laughter forces him to gag. "Piss Hole

Lake, we call it. Man, tourists flush their toilets in it all summer long." He waves in the other direction. "I'll show you Walden Pond."

The children have been talking quietly ahead. Kathleen turns and shakes a finger at me. "Daddy, drugs are bad. You're supposed to just say 'no.'"

"It's excess that's bad, Kitten," I reply. Excess of anything. Excess of food, of guilt, of romance. Excess of work, of play. Excess of speed.

Excess of money.

Is eight million dollars excess? I can't wait to find out.

Crater thinks of something funny and laughs again. He fights hard to hold on to his last toke, but the smoke pours from his mouth. "They had a parent's day at Light's school. The teacher pointed around the room, and each parent was suppose to tell the kids that they never did drugs." He stops walking. His voice grows serious. "I couldn't lie to the kids. I told them not only did I smoke pot, but I enjoyed it, too."

"Ow," I say.

"Light's teacher flipped out. No point in lying, though, man. The kids see through it."

Light turns and smiles. "My class voted him 'Daddy of the Year,' but the principal wouldn't let him come back for his prize."

"Rahana says that drugs are used to enslave her people," Kathleen says. "She says the CIA is involved."

"I don't think that's true, Kitten," I say. "The CIA usually operates outside our country. She probably meant the FBI."

We reach the tent. Inside there are two cots with more white canvas. At the back of the tent is a small wood stove, vented through a slit in the back wall. The kids bypass the tent and keep marching toward the crest of the hill, in the direction Crater indicated lay Walden Pond. Crater and I, though, we need to rest. We each stretch out on a separate cot; I stare up at the ceiling and see strange shapes come and go as the falling snow melts on the warm canvas.

"So, Crater," I ask. "What do you do out here?"

"Do? Do? Do do." Crater starts laughing. I am not as stoned as him and only manage a short chuckle.

"Yeah," I say. "Work – like, for money."

"You mean bread, man?" Crater pauses as he draws another hit off the joint. "I whittle some."

"You whittle?" I roll over on the cot and stare at him. He does not look like a whittler. Overalls are whittling garb, not tie-dye tee shirts and paisley bellbottoms. "You can support a family whittling?"

"*Support* a family? That sounds too strenuous, man." He rolls over, too, and hands me the joint. "Mother Earth provides us our needs. You just can't get caught up in all the bullshit."

"Like what?" I lie back as I exhale and watch the blue smoke coil toward the roof of the tent.

"Like what? Like satellite dishes and televisions so you can sit and watch nature shows, when nature's right outside your fuckin' door."

He, of course, can say this; but most people don't live in a tent.

"So what do you whittle?"

"Flutes mostly. Tom-toms, too. You'd be surprised how much the tourists will pay for something that's not made in Japan."

"China," I say.

"Huh?"

"We get our junk made in China now, not Japan."

"China? What ever happened to Mao Tse-tung?"

"He died, man," I say.

There is silence in the tent. History has betrayed him. Crater spins his legs to the ground and stands up. "We better find the kids."

The children are waiting for us at the crest of the hill. They are standing in the falling snow, but don't seem to notice it. In the little valley below is Moon Base, and beyond Moon Base is Walden Pond. There is a large tree lying on the roof of Moon Base. There are fields on the left stretching up from the pond to where the opposite hill crests. Most are overgrown with white birch, but a few show signs of recent cultivation. There is a long stone foundation, perhaps a hundred feet long; and at the end sits a little shed. I imagine the shed once covered the entire foundation.

"See, Dad?" Justin points down at Moon Base. "It's round. If you slice the roof off and look in, it looks just like a peace sign."

Perhaps that's what Mother Oak was trying to do, slice the roof off.

"Come on, man!" Crater waves us forward. The three kids join him and rush down the hill, but I take my time, unaccustomed to the old sensation of being stoned.

The other four are already inside when I reach the walls of Moon Base. The structure is made of heavy logs. The logs are curved to follow Moon Base's circular pattern. I rub my hands along the length of one of the logs.

Crater sticks his head out the door. "Pretty cool, huh?"

"How'd you bend them?" I ask.

"Don't know," Crater replies. "We were all tripping and it just happened, but no one could remember how we did it when we came down."

"It's big," I remark.

"Had forty Moons in orbit here at one time," Crater replies. "Just Light and me left now."

I step in through the door and look about the interior. Mother Oak has shattered the roof, showering debris throughout the complex.

I can hear Justin's voice – he and the two girls have worked their way down the hall, weaving and ducking through the tangle of branches. "Wow, look at all these posters," he is saying. "They're ancient." Perhaps he will develop an interest in archeology from this experience. "The Mamas and the Papas?" He has found the music room. "This is like a museum."

"Justin. Don't touch that," I hear Kathleen shout.

"I know how it works," Justin replies. There is the sound of a needle scratching across the black surface of a phonograph record, then more scratching as the needle is pulled back. Then finally... music.

No one's getting fat except Mama Cass.

"Good one, Jussie," Kathleen says.

Kathleen has called her brother "Jussie." That is one step short of "pimple-face."

"Kids," I yell. "Get out of there before someone gets hurt." Mother Oak isn't posing any danger, but I worry that Kathleen and Justin might start hurting each other.

I look up at the ceiling near the entrance. There are white spots where branches have been cut away. "You cleared some of it."

"I got an ax and a bow saw," Crater replies. "It's slow going."

"There's a chain saw in my barn," I say. "We could probably clear this pretty quick with that."

Justin pokes his head out of the branches. He has heard me say *we*. "All right!" he shouts.

We have only lived here two weeks, but Justin and Kathleen have already developed a strange attraction to the Moons. Perhaps they are in orbit now themselves.

"I'm not sure it works," I say. Who knows how long the chain saw has been sitting unused in the barn; I can't imagine Mrs. Finch was out cutting trees when she wasn't busy with her tomato plant.

Light follows Justin out of the branches. She is holding his hand. It is not the awkward hand-holding of a teenager's first love – the kind you see when children first start dating and they're not sure why. No, it is the natural hand-holding of a mature relationship. I worry what they might have done to achieve this. Then Kathleen comes out. She is holding Light's other hand. They are a little elephant family leaving the jungle, lumbering tail in trunk.

Outside, the snow is falling faster. The crest of the hill is obscured in white. The dark outline of mountain laurel is our best guide. Crater runs first, breaking a trail. We put the children between us for safety, and I go last to pick up any stragglers.

I hear laughter ahead as feet slip and slide on the snowy embankment. This is not a laughing matter – haven't any of them heard of the Donner Party?

The wind is howling at the top of the hill. I see from this angle that the tent is actually pitched in a little hollow, protected from the worst of the elements.

The others are in the tent, sitting on cots when I arrive. Crater is kneeling before the wood stove, striking a match.

"I'll have us warm in no time," he says. He watches as the paper flares, then turns and hands me a flask of Southern Comfort.

We are going for instant warmth now.

"Daddy can't drink that." Kathleen eyes the bottle suspiciously. "Mommy says it makes him silly."

"Mommy's not here," I say. I want to say that if Mommy really cared about me, she *would* be here, but I know better than to wade into those waters.

I take a little swig, then hold the bottle between my knees as the spicy warmth creeps from my belly to my head. Justin reaches over and takes the bottle. He holds it for a moment between his knees to see if I'll say anything. I stick out my hand, and he places it in my palm, flashing me a silly grin. He was just kidding, yes, but he was also testing limits. What was there to lose? Perhaps I wouldn't have said anything. Perhaps he could have taken just a little swig and felt the warmth, too. Ah, but see, I could have scolded him, embarrassed him in front of Light. There is a cost to all risk-taking, Justin. That is why they call it risk.

"So where'd all the others go?" I ask.

"The others?" Crater replies. "Oh, the other Moons. To orbit another system – that's what we used to say." The fire is crackling good now, and Crater sits back on his heels to avoid the heat. "Last I heard, Moon Kitten, Moon Song, and Moon Shadow were doing a gig in Vegas dressed up as nuns. They're now Sister Anne, Sister Margaret, and Sister Mary. They play maracas and guitars. Moon Beam – Light's mother – married a computer salesman and became Susan Glickman. She worked as a bank teller last I heard." Crater shakes his head as if there is something eternally sad in all that.

I look toward Light and wonder how a mother could have abandoned such a beautiful child. She is showing Kathleen how to do tricks with string and does not notice my stare.

Crater rocks back and forth on his heels as he recalls all who have deserted him. "Moon Dog and Moon Roof took off for California to start their own business – organic root beers. Seven flavors."

"I always thought root beer was its own flavor," I observe.

"Man, not in California," Crater says. "Everything is something else there."

Justin stands up and pulls the canvas flaps apart. His eyes dart around at the darkness outside. I see the snow blowing at a sharp angle; the tent feels very cozy. Crater pulls a guitar out from under his cot and begins strumming. He starts to sing. It is an old song, a song that inspired a generation to say *no* to their government, but it sounds very sad tonight.

"You're letting cold air in, son," I say.

"Sorry, Dad, but I need to..." He darts his eyes toward Light. He can't say it in front of a girl.

I understand; preserve the myth of purity between two future lovers. When I first met Beth, I found it hard to believe she did such things. She was so beautiful... so virginal. After I watched her give birth to Justin, that changed. After that, I could believe anything could fall from her body.

Crater looks up from his guitar. "It's around back, kid. Little wooden shed. Can't miss it." He plucks the flask from my hand and takes a swig, then hands it back. "A little parched from singing," he says, then resumes his song.

I expect to hear a toilet flush, but except for the wind, there is silence. The tent flaps separate and Justin steps in, blushing slightly as Light looks up from her string and smiles at him.

It is only when I lean back and close my eyes that I hear that Crater has the perfect voice for what he is singing. Of course, there is no market for such songs now – that is why he whittles – but it would be nice to preserve a few Craters. Set up a living museum, like they do with old-time blacksmiths and apothecaries; sit him in a room with Jimi Hendrix posters and incense, and let him sing to the tourists.

And it's one, two, three. What are we fighting for?

December 31

When I open my eyes again, Justin and I are wrapped up together on Crater's cot. Crater is curled up before the wood stove, his guitar case for a pillow. The other cot is empty, but two pairs of feet are on the floor, their toes wiggling as if speaking sign language to each other.

"What are you girls doing?" I ask.

"Shush," Kathleen replies softly. "You'll scare the deer."

"Here come two more," Light whispers. "The big one there, that's Lily Belly, and the little one is her fawn."

They have the canvas flap pulled up just enough so they can see out. I try to remove my arm from beneath Justin's head, wishing to join the girls on the floor, but my arm is asleep and refuses to respond to my commands – it has been in contact with Justin for too long and has adopted his ways.

Light throws a handful of seed and bread crumbs out into the snow. I can not see under the flap myself, but Kathleen's widening smile tells me that they have lured the deer closer. I have seen many deer, but I wish that I could be on the floor and see these now; it gives me a sense of hope watching animals wander freely about. I worry for them, though.

Kathleen reaches a hand out through the flap and brings back a snowball. “Brrrr,” she says. “I wish I had my mittens.”

Mittens. The word is like a bell. Like eight million little bells clanging at once. A finicky old cat, a cat worth eight million dollars, a cat worth more than most human beings – worth more than some third world countries, even – has been abandoned and neglected through the first real snow storm of the winter.

I rip my arm out from under Justin’s peaceful head.

“Emily,” he sighs and feels around for the missing appendage. “Don’t go, dear.”

I am not going to sleep with Justin again.

My boots are hiding under the cot. I yank them out by their laces, thrust my feet in, but don’t stop to tie them; then grab my coat and leap over the two girls, through the flap and into the new fallen snow. Deer scatter. There is gracefulness to their fear.

There is no longer a sign of the path. The snow sits a foot deep, but it is a light snow, and the wind has cleared it from the trees.

The road below shimmers in its unplowed state. On the far side sits the farmhouse, a wisp of blue smoke rising from its flue. From my vantage point on the hill, I can see with frightening clarity how much the chimney has tipped through the years.

I run straight toward the farmhouse, the steepness of the hill adding to my speed. One arm has found its home in my coat sleeve, but the other arm struggles to find an opening as the coat flaps along behind me. The hill drops off, and I slide on the balls of my feet until a branch reaches out and grabs me. My momentum carries me out of the coat, and I tumble through the icy snow until my legs straddle a birch tree and I stop.

Shit, that hurts.

But I am beside the road now, and the way up the hill to the farmhouse appears easier. The driveway is a vague outline and the snow is deep, but there are no trees to block my way. I rub my crotch to reassure my little friends that there will be no more birch trees. My right foot grows cold; I look down and see I have lost a boot. My fingers grow cold – I have lost a mitten. I am Charlie Brown on the pitcher's mound.

The door to the farmhouse is locked. Crater laughed when he saw me lock the door – you're in the country now, he said. My keys are not in my pocket; they are still in the tent. I never sleep with keys in my pocket, even when the sleep is unplanned.

I would wrap my hand in my coat and punch a window out, but my coat is on the opposite hillside, hanging from a tree, waving an empty arm in insolence at me.

The yellow cotton drapes in the parlor hang open. I press my face against the glass and look in. Mittens is stretched out on top of the radiator. She looks out at me; her tail twitches and she smiles. We have a Cheshire cat. There is a bowl of kibble below the radiator. I don't remember putting it there. She's spent eighteen years with a forgetful old woman; perhaps she's learned to feed herself.

I struggle back through the snow, retracing my steps, checking each hole for my missing boot. There is no feeling in my right foot; that is good from a comfort level, but it is not healthy. If it weren't for the boot and the coat, I could take the winding path back up to Moon Base Two, but instead I am forced to climb the embankment. My boot is near the birch tree – it must have ejected on impact. I do not feel my foot going in, but I look closely and see that the boot is on snugly. This time, I stop to tie it.

The slope above is too steep. I grasp saplings; they bend as I hoist myself higher. They threaten to snap and send me hurtling once again toward my favorite birch tree. But in time, I reach my coat. I have conquered Mount Everest.

Inside the tent, Justin is sitting on the cot in his underwear. He doesn't seem to care that Light is crouched beside the wood stove frying eggs. He looks at me. "Where'd you go?"

"I had to feed the cat," I say.

He leans over and picks fuzz from between his toes.

"Where's your sister?" I ask.

"Crater's showing her how to milk the cow."

"She went out there?" I think of my own journey; the tangled coat, the lost boot, the missing mitten, the tumble down the hill, the birch tree. Well, straddling a birch tree is more a boy problem, I guess.

"It's just snow, Dad."

I sit down beside Justin and take my boots off. There is laughter outside the tent. Kathleen enters carrying a wooden pail.

"Daddy!" She sets the pail down and hobbles to my side. There are three of us on the cot now; one in his underwear, one in her winter coat and snow shoes, and me. I am the normal one. Kathleen looks down at my feet. "Why are your toes blue?"

"I was feeding the cat, Kitten."

Justin is still hunched over, picking at his toes; he must have gangrene. I rub the fine hairs on his neck. "Don't you want to put clothes on, Son?"

"We're camping, Dad."

He is a different boy today. In the suburbs, he felt naked without his baseball cap. A month ago, he was worried Mrs. Meredith might launder his underpants. Yesterday, he felt vulnerable in gym shorts. Now he is sitting around a campfire in his undies, picking at his toes like a ... god, like a hillbilly.

"Crater says if it was summer, we could all go skinny dipping," Justin adds.

I must check the date on my watch. I'm not sure now how long I've been gone. Perhaps I slipped into a snowdrift and slept most of the winter away, like Rip Van Winkle. My watch is not on my wrist, though. It is sleeping with my keys.

"Daddy." Kathleen shakes my arm. "Crater showed me how to milk Moon Moo. She was upset because we were late, but she has such big brown eyes, she didn't look cross at all. She switched her tail in my face. Crater says that's how she says 'thank you.'"

"Moon Moo is a cow?" I say.

"Of course she's a cow." Kathleen giggles. Fathers are so silly. "And on the way back, I found out where all the birds go for winter." She looks at me and smiles proudly. "Right here! The whole valley is filled with birds."

Crater enters carrying a basket filled with eggs and potatoes "I got some more eggs, Light. If you and I are gonna take that tree down, we'll need a good breakfast."

Justin looks from his toes to me. "We're helping, aren't we, Dad?"

My son wants to do physical labor. MY SON WANTS TO DO PHYSICAL LABOR! Get that guitar strumming, Crater. I feel a country jig coming on. My smile is too obvious – even a teenager can read the meaning in it.

"It's not like I never helped at home," Justin says, and reverts to toe picking; his ears carefully tuned, though, for my response.

"Sure, we'll help."

I can feel Justin smile, even as he takes pains not to look toward me.

***

The chain saw is in working order. There is no gas, though, so I siphon some from the minivan. A path has formed in the snow connecting our two homes. On the other side of the road, the main path winds among the mountain laurel, but the children have been using my short cut on the downhill runs, sliding through the trees on sheets of plastic.

"You don't want to stay with us?" I ask Crater. "Lots of room in the farmhouse."

Crater looks puzzled. They would be too far from their farm animals. The tent is cozy and warm. Suburbanites can be so hard to understand. "No thanks, man. You can crash with us, though, if you want."

I have a warm farmhouse. It belongs to a cat, but she doesn't mind our being there. I work for her, actually. I work for a cat. Before that, I worked for a dog, a bitch, a mutant gene infecting man's best friend. "No. I got to get home later to feed Mittens," I say.

"Mittens is still alive?" Crater grins. "That is one cool cat. We used to get her stoned. Funny thing with cats, you can't tell the difference."

"Then you knew Mrs. Finch?" I ask.

"Sure," Crater says. "Some of us used to do work on Finch Farm back when Moon Base wasn't so prosperous."

We are working in the main hallway of Moon Base. There are tree limbs dangling around our heads. Snow melt is dripping from the branches and down my neck. Prosperity has a cold feel to it.

"Her son was the one who started Moon Valley," Crater explains. "But he's dead now." He pulls the cord on the chain saw and blue smoke fills the hallway. "I never met the dude personally." Using the end of the chain saw, he nips at branches. The branches fall and begin to cover the floor. There are grooves worn in the floor's heavy planks; many feet have traveled up and down the halls of Moon Base. Justin darts in and drags a handful of branches out toward the front door. Outside, a bonfire burns.

"Justin, if you see your sister, ask her to run over to the farm and fetch us two beers." I look at the sweat drenching the back of Justin's flannel shirt; there is soot from the bonfire streaking his face. "Tell her three beers," I say as I smile at my son.

He grins back. "Sure, Dad."

There is an impatience to the winter sun, and it sets before we are finished clearing Mother Oak away. Crater lights a hurricane lamp; there is electricity, he says, but there is too much water around to risk using it.

The children are in the music room. They have decided to take that risk and are playing old record albums. Sometimes they laugh, but other times they say, "Oh, cool." They play "Feeling Groovy" and they laugh. I laugh, too. Even Crater laughs.

Groovy. Groovy. Groovy.

The drone of the chain saw has become annoying.

"We're there," Crater says.

He sets the chain saw down and picks up the hurricane lamp. There is a room laying vacant before us. It smells of cedar, and the walls are draped with towels. Crater enters first and sets the lamp on a bench. He turns and grins at me; it is a ghoulish grin, shimmering in the odd light of the flickering hurricane lamp.

"What's this place?" I ask.

"This? Man, this is a shrine. This is like the center of the universe." He walks over to one wall and grabs a corner of a towel. "Moon Rocket's," he says. "He was one freak. Never made it home, though."

He doesn't say from where, but there is the pain of a nation in his voice, and I know from my own past from where he speaks.

"But what is it?" I say.

"It's a dressing room. And back there is a freaking steam bath!" He strikes a match and lights a fire under a rusted metal drum. "Behind that door, a hundred of our nation's finest patriots sweated out the plans for the end of the military-industrialist complex." He waves his arms in a grand arc about the room we are in. "These towels belonged to some of the greatest."

"They're all gone now, I guess?" I view the odd assortment of beach towels. They hang from the walls like the retired jerseys of famous ball players.

"Yeah. Dead. Vancouver. Wall Street."

"Seven flavors of root beer," I say.

Crater laughs. "Seven fucking flavors of California root beer." He sits down on one of the wooden benches that encircle the room. Leaning his head back against a towel in the design of an American flag, he lights a joint. "Today's work is officially over," he announces.

I can hear the flames licking at the metal drum. From the distance comes the sounds of the children playing Janice Joplin on the old record player. *Summertime, and the living is easy.* Crater hands me the joint; and I suck in the smoke, close my eyes, and feel the presence of a hundred radicals.

There is a hissing sound. Steam. Crater rises and removes his shirt. There is fog before my eyes, but it is not from the boiling drum. He wiggles from his paisley bellbottoms; he does not wear underwear. I move without thought and disrobe beside him.

Justin steps into the room. "Hey Dad!" He sees two naked men and forgets what he was about to say.

"We found a steam bath, Son," I explain. It is preemptive, to assure him that his father is not adopting his mother's liberal ways.

"A steam bath! Cool!" Justin hops around the room as he yanks his socks off; his boots must be in the music room. He wiggles out of his jeans; he does wear underwear. He grips his sweatshirt and flips it off over his head, his arms continuing downward toward the ground, removing his underwear in one fluid movement. My son is standing naked beside me – it is all so strange. We have not stood naked together since I taught him to pee into a toilet. *Just aim for the center, son, like this.* It seems so long ago. The seat was wet when he was done, but I patted his head anyway. *Good job, son.*

"Justin? You in here?" Light steps into the room with Kathleen in tow. They see three naked men.

I expect Justin to flee, to hide the horrors of his masculine body from these young girls, but he doesn't move. Crater does not move, either. My legs, though, are turning slowly, involuntarily, twisting my hips sideways to present a less threatening view to the innocence of these female eyes.

Light glances from her father to the metal drum. "Great! You got the steam bath going." She yanks off her sweatshirt and wiggles out of her jeans. She does not wear underwear.

Kathleen sits on the floor and struggles with her boots. "Daddy, can you help me?"

I hesitate. There is no graceful way to hover over her.

"Here, I'll get them." Light leans over Kathleen's shoulder. Her youthful breasts sway gently as her hands work the laces.

I look down, fearful that the image that lies before me may cause me to rear my ugly head, but all is calm. It must be this place: the towels, the memories. I am viewing beauty, nature; and for once it is not being confused with sex.

Crater opens the door that leads from the dressing room to the steam room. He and Justin step in, but I hesitate for a moment, unable to take my eyes from our lovely young neighbor.

"Dad? You coming?" Justin asks.

"Oh yeah. Sure." I tear my eyes away and turn just in time to see that Justin is watching her, too.

***

Evening, and we are once again in the tent. After dinner, Crater and I sit before the fire and share the rest of the Southern Comfort. A sweet voice begins to sing an old folk song. I turn and see Light sitting on her cot. She is topless and is brushing her long blond hair.

She smiles at me. "My mother used to sing me that song when I was little."

"It's very pretty," I say.

Kathleen is asleep behind her. Justin is sitting cross-legged on the other cot. He seems to be counting the brush strokes. He thinks he is in a luscious dream.

That night, Justin and I lie pressed together on the cot. I whisper in his ear, "Did Light brush her hair last night while I was asleep?"

"Yeah, Dad. Why?"

"Oh, no reason," I say. Only, I know now that I have not gone mad; all that I have seen today in my children makes a little more sense.

January 2

It is a magical place, Moon Base. Mother Oak is now Baby Firewood, to continue on in another life, no longer sheltering the Moons' home, but providing warmth instead. Crater says that is the religion of nature. He says when there is a full moon, we will have a proper ceremony and thank Mother Oak for her self-sacrifice.

Some of Mother Oak has been split into shingles. There is justice in that; the roof that she destroyed she will now rebuild. Justin is on the roof pounding shingles over the holes. The winter air has warmed and the sun is shining through the clearing where Mother Oak once stood. Justin has removed his shirt. The first signs of youthful hair have formed on his chest, and sweat glistens there among the twisted brown strands. He stands holding a hammer against his hip and yells down to me for more shingles. We have put him in charge of this project and he is performing admirably.

Crater is swinging an ax, building a stack of new shingles. It is something he has done for years, and he now makes it look easy. I select the best ones from the pile and carry them to an improvised lift. A rope hangs over a tree branch; I pull the rope and the shingles rise to Justin's eye level. He tosses the first few back on the ground.

"I told you, Dad. Not so thin."

The rest pass inspection, though.

Deer watch us from a distance; there has been no hunting in Moon Valley for thirty years, and their fear has been replaced by a mild distrust. The pound of a hammer, the crack of an ax – those are sounds implanted in the deer's genes, and they feel they should run – but Kathleen has scattered hay in a nearby clearing, and they feel they should eat, too.

"Daddy. See? Three of them," Kathleen whispers and points toward the deer.

"Aren't you helping Light?" I ask.

The two girls are supposed to be mopping up the floors; much of the snow melted and flooded the inside of Moon Base while we frolicked in the steam bath.

"She said to feed the animals."

"I don't think she meant the wild animals," I say.

"Moon Moo didn't want all her hay." Kathleen tips her head back and spins around in the snow. She laughs as she stretches out her arms and flaps them like wings.

"Do you want to go feed Mittens with me?" I ask.

Kathleen stops spinning. "Poor Mittens," she says with fake sorrow. "Poor poor Mittens is all alone."

"Come on, goof ball," I say and rub her shoulders.

We take the winding path through the mountain laurel. Kathleen wants to race, but I tell her I am too old for such things.

"Light says you have a young moon rising."

"She does, does she?" I don't know what it means, but it

sounds sort of groovy. Um, cool. "What else does she say?"

"She says she's a virgin. That has something to do with kissing boys, doesn't it?"

I smile down at her. She is too young for that little talk. We will wait until her mother returns. "Yes, Kitten. Something like that."

"Justin said he's a virgin, too." Kathleen skips along the snowy path. We could be talking of her favorite television program for all she knows.

"Justin said he's a virgin?" I ask.

"Yeah. But I saw him kiss Emily McBride once, so I think he was lying."

"I think if a boy admits he's a virgin, you can believe him, Kitten," I say.

"Light says she'll stay a virgin until she meets the right boy. She says he has to be a farmer, like her daddy."

"You're a fountain of information," I reply.

We reach the mailbox. There was no delivery yesterday – "neither rain nor sleet nor gloom of night" is something of an exaggeration, at least in the country. There is mail today, though. There is a letter from Beth with a Chicago postmark. She and Eve have been promoted. There is no glass ceiling in the women's movement. Chicago is much better than Nebraska, she says. There are slums and gangs; prostitutes, drugs, and homeless victims of neglect. There is a lot more to save than farmers' wives with black eyes.

I am not happy she is in Chicago, but the eastward migration is a trend I hope she continues.

Kathleen sees my face and knows who the letter is from. "Mommy's coming home?"

"Soon," I say. "She's heading back." I take Kathleen's hand, and we walk together toward the farmhouse. There is other mail;

I scan it as we walk. There's a postcard from Adam. He has moved back to the suburbs. San Francisco was strange, he says. The men whistled at him, and the root beer tasted like cherries. Mrs. Meredith was waiting for him when he returned. Her three teenagers were playing basketball in his driveway when he pulled up in his car. At her age, Mrs. Meredith knows the pickings are slim and has learned to move fast.

March 17

It has been a long winter, and my children have been yokeled, but they don't seem to care. Justin and Kathleen sing "Old MacDonald had a farm" as they stroll toward the barn. There are eight chickens roosting in the splintered rafters, and that means fresh eggs for breakfast.

Justin pauses as he exits the barn door – he looks toward the hillside and searches for Light's blond hair. He thinks he spots her, and holds the egg basket up for her to see. *I'm a farmer. See?* he's trying to say.

The eggs sizzle in a cast iron skillet. Justin and Kathleen sit at the kitchen table, each with a knife and fork in either hand.

"We'll be late for the school bus, Daddy," Kathleen complains.

"Almost done." I inhale deeply. "Ah, fresh eggs, kids."

"Dad?" Justin's voice has deepened considerably as of late, but he has found his little boy voice again, and this has me suddenly worried. "Can I get a pig?"

"Justin, what's all this interest in farming?" I smile coyly as I flip the eggs. It is not the pig, but the poke he is really interested in.

"Well, you know," he says. I know, but I'm not going to help him out. "Since we live in the country..."

"Yeah, but Justin, in nine months we'll have eight million dollars, and we'll live someplace else." I lay two eggs on a plate and slide it across the table toward Kathleen. The plate stops in front of her, but the eggs don't.

"Live where, Dad?" Justin reaches across the table and grabs his plate before I can give it a shove. Kathleen stares down at her eggs, but won't eat them. The two eggs stare back up at her from the table top – they won't eat her, either. It's a Mexican standoff.

"Live where? I don't know." I flip Kathleen's eggs back onto her plate. "Someplace else."

"The suburbs again?" Justin sighs.

"Not the suburbs." I sit down between Justin and Kathleen with my own eggs. I like mine runny, and the two children groan when I burst the yolk.

"Then the city?" Justin asks.

"God, no," I say.

Justin shakes his head. "And parents say kids are weird."

"Okay, you can have the pig," I say. "But before we move, you got to eat him."

"Eat him?" Justin looks at me. He sees I'm smiling and knows it's in jest.

"Sure," I say. "Bacon to go with our eggs."

"No, Daddy!" Kathleen squeals. "We can't eat a little piggy."

"Of course not, Kitten," I say. "But Justin, if you want a pig, you got to fix the barn up first."

"No problem!" Justin jumps to his feet and grabs his lunch

bag. "Light already said she and her dad will help us." He runs to the parlor and out the front door, grabbing his coat from a hook as he leaves. Outside he leaps about in the gray snow, sending odd hand signals to the opposite hillside. The tent is gone, though; Moon Base has been restored. There is no way the Moons can see him from their valley, but Justin is too excited to think rationally.

"Justin! Wait up!" Kathleen yells. She hangs from her coat as she struggles to remove it from its hook.

"Here." I flick the coat free for her, and off she goes.

Light's beautiful hair shows above the mountain laurel as she works her way down the hillside path. She will meet Justin and Kathleen by our mailbox. Together, the three will wait for the school bus. Justin and Light will sit together on the bus and talk about the future. Light thinks one day the valley will again be full of Moons. Hordes of new Moons will crowd the steam bath and discuss philosophy; they will smoke pot, raise chickens, and mow hay. In the winter, they will whittle flutes and sell them to the tourists.

Justin likes the idea of a new crop of Moons; he hopes that Light will choose him to be her breeding stock. He is itching to be the father of a nation.

Kathleen will sit behind Justin and Light. She will pretend to read a comic book, but she is really my spy. It's not a planned arrangement; Kathleen will tell me everything because there is no one out here for her to talk to when Light and Justin are together. I will pretend to know Swahili so she will tell me more than she should.

It is quiet with the children away at school. I read an old newspaper – it is advertising winter clothes. It is a very old paper if the sales are in step with the season. Mittens climbs onto my lap and purrs as I gently rock in Mrs. Finch's chair.

The winter air is silent. The migratory birds have gone south, while the rest are wintering in Moon Valley.

There is a knock at the front door, then the door slowly opens. A hairy face appears in the doorway.

"Hi, man. Thought you might want to whittle." Crater steps in with an armful of logs. "I got some good cedar here." He sets the wood down in the middle of the parlor. "I don't like cedar flutes myself 'cause the smell is right there in your face, but the freaking tourists love 'em."

"I don't know how to whittle," I say.

He looks at me like I just said I couldn't pee or something. "It's not something you learn, man. It's something you do, like doodling, only you use a pen knife."

"Do you drink beer when you whittle?" I ask.

"Oh yeah. You got to."

I push the cat aside and walk into the kitchen. "Do we need a pot belly stove?" I yell back toward the parlor. There's an old one sitting in a corner of the kitchen. It is disconnected and has no flue pipe, but I could set it in a corner of the parlor for atmosphere if it would help with the whittling.

"No, just the beer, man," Crater calls back.

When I return to the parlor, a cold can in each hand, there is a pile of wood chips on the parlor floor. Crater holds up a finished flute.

"That was fast," I say.

"Tourists don't care how it sounds," Crater says. "And the rougher the better." He runs his fingers up and down the length of the flute as he blows through one end. The difference in sound is more random than scalar. "I call them Indian flutes, so folks expect them to sound a bit sour." He trades me his knife for a beer. "You try."

The knife cuts too deep on me and gets stuck in the log.

"You're supposed to be whittling, man, not carving up a salami." Crater chuckles. "Just drag the blade along the surface." He slowly rolls a joint as he twists back and forth on the piano stool.

I try again, but the blade gets caught in the gouge left by my first attempt. "You do the whittling," I say as I hand the knife back. "I'll just watch."

"All right, but if you're staying in these parts, you better learn to whittle." He is caught with too many objects. He hands the joint off to me and sets the beer on the floor.

"I've got eight million dollars coming," I say. "I don't need to whittle."

"Whittling's more than money, man." He sends chips of cedar flying about his head. Despite the appearance of random flight, they are all carefully aimed and land in an arc about his feet. "Why, even Mrs. Finch whittled."

"Really?" I take a drag off the joint and hold the smoke in until my lungs rebel.

"She had a real fondness for wood," Crater says. "She and Mother Oak were like married or something."

"How do you marry a damn tree."

"It was the sixties, man. We had imagination then." He finishes the flute and hands it to me. "Here. Play, man. It's good for the soul."

I take the flute and blow, but nothing happens. "There's no hole."

Crater takes the flute back and looks into one end. "Damn Winslow didn't bore it all the way." He flicks at the end with his pen knife, cutting several inches from it, then hands it back. "Here. You get a soprano."

I play a few notes, then stop. "So how the hell did Mrs. Finch marry a tree anyway?"

"I wasn't here then, man," Crater says. "But what I heard was her son got killed in the war."

"The one who started Moon Valley?"

"Right," Crater says. "And after the funeral, she moved into the tree fort he built here as a kid."

"In Mother Oak?" I ask.

"Sure thing, dude. She stayed up there and cried. Watered Mother Oak with her tears till she was part of the tree. That's why the tree fell over after she died. Weren't no storm."

I point a finger at Crater. "You're getting spooky, smoking that stuff."

He looks in his hand and sees that it is empty. "What'd you do with the bone anyway, man?"

"The bone?"

"The joint," he answers.

Except for the flute, my hands are empty, too. I look around the rocking chair, but the joint isn't there. "I dunno."

He shrugs it off.

I look once more around the room and see that the cat is also gone. There is a tail sticking out from under the sofa, though. I look under and see Mittens there; she has dragged the joint with her and is smiling as she inhales the smoke. I reach beneath the sofa and grab the joint. Mittens swipes a paw at me, but is otherwise too stoned to move.

"Let's get out of here," I say. "This place is giving me the creeps."

"You dig ice fishing?" Crater asks.

"Sure," I say. "What's to do? You sit in a shack and drink beer."

"Come on then," he says and rises from the piano stool, giving it a little spin with his finger for good luck.

I look once more into the parlor before shutting the door. The shadow of the rocking chair is moving against the wall. I see that I am living Mrs. Finch's life for her; using her furniture, cooking in her pots, and tending to her cat. I will spend her eight million dollars, too. Perhaps her head has been frozen somewhere. Perhaps one of the odd unmentioned conditions of the will is that I must suture it onto my shoulders and allow Mrs. Finch to live again.

Outside, the driveway is still covered with snow. The minivan sits unused beside the barn. When the weather is cold, the chickens stand in the gaps between the barn boards and peek down through the windshield, dreaming of a new, cozier home.

"You don't have a car, do you, Crater?" A path has been worn between our two farms, but it is icy, and I grasp the fringes of Crater's coat for balance.

Crater wears snow shoes and does not notice the ice. "A car? No. Had a motorcycle once, but it's at the bottom of a lake."

"How'd that happen?"

"I was in the can, man, and missed the announcement about the brown acid being no good."

It is an odd explanation, but it is probably as much as he knows. I remember my own college career and the beer parties with their unfathomable finales; waking one morning to a foul odor, finding my face suffocating in the plump arms of a gigantic woman. She was naked. Worse yet, I was naked. But thank god it was her bed we were in and not mine. She snored like a mule as I searched the room for my clothing, finally finding it stuffed in the freezer of her efficiency refrigerator, hidden there so that I could not abandon her as so many others had. I looked over at her puffy pink face – I could never be her love slave. Her snoring stopped, and her eyes popped open. I ran in panic from her room, sat naked in the early dawn light in a bus shelter until the frozen crispness left my pants and I could once again dress.

I staggered back to my dorm room as ice melted against my testicles.

I have used the memory of that night on many occasions to deflate an unwanted erection.

Crater smiles at me and sings, "I don't want a pickle. Just want to ride on my motorcycle."

It is in the way he sings "pickle" that frightens me. I wonder if Mother Oak has taught him to read minds? It is just a coincidence, though, isn't it? But that is such a cop out, calling something a coincidence every time the alternative is uncomfortable.

"Well anyway, old Dylan's sitting on the bottom of a lake now," Crater says. "I guess technically speaking, I still own it."

We cross the street. It is plowed even though no one lives beyond my mailbox. Sometimes a car travels slowly up the road, moving quietly between the snow banks, disappearing into the gray underbrush; but it never returns. Only the snowplow returns; whatever is up there, the snowplow is too big for its mouth.

We reach the spot where the tent used to be. Moon Base lies a short distance away, behind the hill's crest, and beyond that – Walden Pond. There are two red dots moving upon the snowy surface of Piss Hole Lake.

"Damn snowmobilers," Crater says.

We watch as the red dots move toward the near shore. Then they disappear.

"Shit!" Crater shouts. "They broke through."

"Broke through what?" I ask.

"Through the ice." He runs downhill toward the lake. There is no path going in that direction. Crater whacks the laurel branches aside with his coat, leaving a trail of suede fringe for me to follow. "Come on, man!" he shouts over his shoulder. "They'll be dead if we don't get them out quick."

I run after him, but my eyes keep darting toward the farmhouse and the curl of blue smoke rising from the chimney, beckoning to me with its promise of warmth. "Maybe I should go call the fire department," I yell.

"'Department' around here is a loose term, man," Crater yells back. "The Dalmatian answers the phone until the nightly poker game arrives."

Crater reaches the shoreline first. The snow is slushy where the water meets the sand. The lake is spring fed, and there are areas where the ice is only safe in the coldest part of winter.

Two boys struggle along the jagged edge where the ice and water merge. One of the boys spots us and waves his arms frantically, held afloat by the soft, airy down of his red snowmobile suit. The other boy slips below the surface – perhaps the thin synthetic insulation of his suit lacks the natural buoyancy of down.

"Run, man," Crater yells to me. I have fallen well behind – my boots do not stay upon the surface of the snow like his snowshoes do. He points to a fallen tree. "Grab a side." He heaves hopelessly against the tree until I arrive and help him with the heavy trunk.

We run as though storming the castle gates, the rotten end of our battering ram wobbling before us, but holding together. Dead branches crackle and break as they scrape along the frozen surface. We are still short of the break in the ice, but Crater yells "Heave!" anyway, and we both let go, sending the projectile skidding toward the two boys.

The one boy is safely below the lake's surface, but the other is waving frantically as the tree careens toward his skull. He sees it coming and reluctantly throws himself deeper into the icy water. The tree stops. Crater and I stare apprehensively until the boy's head bobs above the surface once more.

Crater kicks off his snowshoes and steps warily toward the

tree. "Get my fishing pole." He points toward the shore, to where he had swapped the small stick for the large. I turn and run.

When I turn back, Crater is straddling the tree trunk, pulling the one boy to safety. "Fishing pole, man," Crater screams.

I pick up the pole and run across the ice toward the two figures, forgetting for the moment the weakness of the ice. Then, like an amateur acrobat, I tippy-toe the length of the fallen tree to where Crater and the boy sit. We listen to the groan of the ice and the crackling of the dead tree. "Take the boy to safety," Crater suggests, lowering his voice to a whisper as though it were avalanches, not thin ice, that threatened us.

The boy is blue. I take his trembling hands and tip-toe backward as I guide him toward solid ground. I slip from the log and think I am doomed, but the ice, despite the appearance of a long crack, holds firm. The boy remains behind on the log, staring at the blue tint of his outstretched hands, unsure whether he is supposed to follow me onto the thin ice.

I climb back onto the log. Crater has dropped his fishing line into the lake. I can feel the tree shift as he moves from place to place, yanking the pole in different directions, hoping that blind luck will snag the missing boy with the bare hook.

"Fuck," he yells. "Oh, shit. Where'd he fuckin' go?"

The pole bends. Crater stops swearing and starts gently working the reel. "Come on, kid. Hold on," he calls.

The other boy and I reach the end of the log. "Come on, kid," I call. "Run!"

The boy responds as best he can; jogging along stiffly like he's encased in a suit of armor. He keeps his blue hands stretched out before him. He's riding his mighty stead. The Blue Knight is in retreat.

"I'm gonna need help, man," Crater yells.

I halt, but the boy keeps running, not stopping after we've

reached the safety of the beach, but continuing blindly into the woods, his hands whipping away the underbrush with unseen reins.

"Come on, man," Crater yells as he pulls two red arms from the water and lays them across the tree. "This one's more dead than alive already."

I am an acrobat again. I scurry across the log with the confidence of a major circus attraction. The tree complains with a series of creaks and groans, but it is the silence of the boy to which I am responding.

Crater and I each grab an arm.

"This ain't gonna work, man," Crater says as we interfere with each other's movements. "Just hold me steady."

I grip Crater's hips while he grabs the boy by the armpits and hoists him over his back. Water dribbles from the boys mouth. "Come on. Run, man, run."

There is coughing behind me as my feet skim across the tree's fragile bark surface. My foot slides sideways as the aging bark peels away. The world spins rapidly, and I find myself sprawled across the snow and ice, afraid to move. Spider webs form beneath me where my elbows struck the ice. Crater carries the boy past me to safety. I see the boy crying as he hangs upside down from Crater's huge shoulders – he thinks a Yeti has stolen him.

"Where's the other boy?" Crater yells. He sees I am down. "Come on, man, before it gives way."

Jumping to my feet, I run toward shore. I think I hear the ice breaking up behind me, but it is only the lake itself crackling a warning to all comers – beware the ice of March.

Shards of ice do not rise up and snap at my retreating heels, like some Hollywood picture show; and it is not relief, but disappointment I feel when I turn and see that I am not safe because of any heroic feat, but because I lack the manly bulk necessary to shatter the lake's surface.

Crater is standing over the boy, gently shaking him as he examines the young face.

"You've got my boy," I say as I look into the youth's teary eyes.

"No, he's mine," Crater replies. "Yours is in the bushes."

"They all look the same when they're blue," I suggest.

"We've got to get them to the steam bath before they go into shock." Crater lifts his boy onto his shoulder again.

The boy screams lightly, his brief moment of freedom yanked to an end – once again the prisoner of the Yeti.

I retrace my boy's tracks and find him hiding in a spread of junipers. He is crying softly and shuddering loudly. I see that it is more than the soft blue color of their faces that makes the boys so similar – they are twins.

"Hop on, kid." I crouch before him. I do not have Crater's strength and will not attempt to toss him across my shoulder. "We'll get you someplace warm."

He wraps his icy fingers around my throat. I adjust them lower so I don't choke, then set off at a jog, carrying the boy piggyback up the hill. Crater has not bothered with his snow shoes – he has broken a trail for me, and the climb is easier than I expected.

"What's your name, kid?" I ask.

He does not answer right away. Perhaps his parents have told him not to talk to strangers. They have probably told him not to play on thin ice, either, but he apparently forgot that.

I am about to remind him that I just saved his life, but before I do, he says his name softly. "Rick."

"How old are you, Rick?"

"Twelve," he replies quickly. "Is Nick okay?" There is fear in his voice. I can not see him as he dangles from my neck, his icy fingers once more closing in around my throat, but I know his eyes must be squeezed shut as he tries to block out the vision of the last few minutes. I can feel his Adam's apple struggling against my collar bone – he is working hard to keep from sobbing.

Once again, I adjust his fingers. We reach the crest of the hill, and it is all downhill now. Crater has already reached his destination – he has the history of the woodsman in him and can move fast to avoid capture by Indians. He has leaned his boy against the heavy log walls of Moon Base and is opening the door.

"Nick's your brother," I say. "You're twins, right?"

The boy does not reply, but I can feel his cold chin nodding against my cheek.

"Well, twins share everything, so if you're okay, he's okay," I suggest as we enter Moon Base.

Crater has already reached the dressing room and released the steam from the heating system There is a cloud bank rolling down the hallway toward us. I charge into it, dragging Rick behind me.

His brother is leaning against a towel. It is an old towel, decorated with a dove and an olive branch. Nick is struggling against Crater's efforts to remove his wet coat – he is delirious and thinks he's being raped by the abominable snowman. There is no strength to Nick's struggle, though. He throws punches no more real than his dreams.

"Come on, Rick," I urge. "Get this wet stuff off."

He struggles, but in a helpful way, as I peel off his coat and his snow pants. Underneath, he is wearing red long johns. Good enough. I spin him around and shove him gently into the steam room.

Crater grabs Nick around the waist and lifts him off the floor.

I slide over and battle to remove the boy's snow pants.

"No, not again. Not tonight. Not again," Nick gasps weakly as the elastic waistband slips over his feet. Then he falls limp – he's a puppet, and his strings have been cut.

We carry him into the steam room and set him beside his brother. They are matching red candles. No, they are Christmas elves.

"I'll stay here, man. To make sure they don't spazz out," Crater says. "You go call for help."

Rick's eyes widen; but Nick is oblivious to us, still swatting the air, battling invisible demons.

"No," Rick shouts. "Don't call anyone."

"We gotta," Crater says. "Your brother needs help."

"They'll send us back," Rick whines.

"You were running away?" Crater asks.

Rick nods his head. "From our dad."

Crater becomes excited. It has been many years since Moon Valley has given refuge to a runaway. These two, though, are too young and will have to be returned. Crater laughs. "You were running away on snowmobiles?"

"We aren't old enough to drive a car."

Nick's eyes are still closed. He starts slapping air away from his stomach. "Please, Dad. Don't," he moans.

"I better get some help." I shut the door to the steam room and leave Crater with his new wards.

Outside, there is the sound of a helicopter out toward the lake. Dogs are barking on the ice. I crawl to the edge of the former tent site and take up a position beside the abandoned outhouse, where I peek cautiously through the mountain laurel toward Piss Hole Lake. A dozen men are scattered across the ice, each one led by an excited dog. The helicopter is hovering over the hole where the boys fell through. I watch as a man is lowered from the helicopter by a cable. His boots dip into the water, then out again. He pokes slabs of ice away with the end of a golf club and peers into the depths of the lake. The dogs are released. They run across the frozen lake surface and leap bravely into the frigid water. They're not sure what they're hunting for; they grab chunks of ice in their mouths and swim around in circles. One of the men on the ground climbs out onto the tree that Crater and I had slid across the hole; he grabs a dog by its collar and tosses it safely onto the ice. Another dog swims near, and he grabs that one, too. Soon all the dogs are out of the water. They shake silver droplets from their wet fur. I can almost hear the droplets tinkle to the ground, like a sprinkling of diamonds. Then the dogs stand obediently and wait for their owners to reclaim them.

One of the men points into the woods, toward where I am hiding. He has spotted footprints in the snow. The other men gather around the tracks; they examine them and are disappointed to find only large man-boot prints. One finds the snow shoes and holds them up. Another finds the fishing pole tangled in the branches beside the hole. They are excited; this opportunity to play detective has erased some of winter's blandness.

The helicopter lands on the ice, and disappears in a swirl of snow. A man walks out of the cloud – an apparition – and stands before the gathering of would-be rescuers. He is wearing a red snow suit and smoking a pipe. His hair is white. He has no beard, but when he lathers up to shave, he looks like Santa Claus. This man is the leader – I can tell by the way the other men stop their activities and look toward him. He sucks in as much air as his lungs will hold and slides his free hand into a pocket. He takes the pipe from his mouth and waves it toward the hill on which I am hiding. He seems to be using it to search the underbrush – it is his little periscope. He yells commands to the other men, but they are short staccato words, and by the time they reach me, I can not distinguish them from the barking of the dogs.

I crawl cautiously backward. A hand grabs my shoulder.

"Shhhh." It is Crater. He is alone – the boys are not with him. "Let's go down and introduce ourselves," he whispers. "Don't say anything to them cats about Rick and Nick, though."

I nod my head as I stand up. The men below are detectives, but we are secret agents. Our roles are more fascinating. Crater knocks the snow from my knees – a good spy should never look as though he's been spying.

We have barely proceeded down the hill when the men below spot us. All the others point like they've just sighted the Star of Bethlehem, but the man in red pops his pipe back into his mouth and stares, his hands planted on both hips.

The dogs strain on their leashes as we leave the forest and walk across the beach. They bark because they view us as strangers – I blame Crater for that.

We stop halfway between the beach and the hole.

The man in red removes the pipe from his mouth and taps the embers onto the ice. "We're looking for two boys – twins. You seen them?"

"No," Crater says. "We saw the hole and came down earlier to check it out. Thought the dudes must of drowned."

"No. The sons of Preston T. Service cannot drown," the man in red says. "You saw no footprints?"

"Um, no," Crater replies.

"Does your friend speak? Or is he some sort of Indian deaf mute?"

The other men have gathered around Preston. They grin at his cleverness. One man hands him the fishing pole. "Here, boss."

"You think there's a dead man in the water, so you stop to do a little fishing?" Preston returns the fishing pole to Crater. Another man hands Preston the pair of snow shoes. “Only you were so excited to start your fishing that you jumped out of your snow shoes back there.” Preston waves his pipe vaguely toward the beach.

“Are you a detective?” I ask.

“Ah, the deaf mute speaks.” Preston smiles at me. It is the smooth, well-practiced smile of a pickpocket. “No, I am not a detective. I am a businessman. A very successful and powerful businessman, and I have become that by always deducing what my opponents are really up to.”

“We ain’t your opponents, man,” Crater says.

“No? No, you wouldn’t think so. But you are not on my payroll, so I must place you somewhere.” Preston snaps his finger at various men. One scurries back to the helicopter. Another starts moving toward the woods, creating a crude path by shoving snow aside with his boot. “It’s cold out here. I see smoke ahead. Your *estate*?”

The other men snicker at the taunting way Preston says “estate.”

Crater nods.

“Well, let us talk where it is warm.” Preston waves an arm forward.

The dozen men and their dogs respond, lurching toward the forest and the serenity of Moon Valley. Crater’s grim smile speaks of the sadness of this moment: he has always feared that capitalism would one day encroach on his haven and create everything he has not built.

We enter the main hall of Moon Base. I can see that Mr. Preston T. Service is actually somewhat impressed by Crater’s home. It has size, and Mr. Service likes to judge first on size. Tree branches are no longer sticking through the roof – that counts for extra points.

There is complete silence within – even the hissing of the steam bath has ceased. The fluorescent lights flicker dimly after the brightness of the outdoors. Crater tries to steer Preston T. Service into the first room, but our guest insists on continuing forward. At each door, one of his men peels off and disappears into the darkened room or down the unused hallway that the doorway marks. When we reach the steam bath, only Crater, Preston, and I remain of the original horde.

"So you have your comforts out here in the wilderness," Preston remarks. He opens the door to the steam room and looks inside.

"It's not really wilderness," Crater says. "Harry here has a farm across the street."

"A farm?" Preston says. "Would that be the Ponderosa?"

"The Ponderosa was a ranch, not a farm," I reply.

Preston glares at me. "I liked you better when you didn't talk." He looks at the water dripping from the ceiling. "It's been in use recently?"

"Ah, yes," Crater says.

"But neither of you have wet hair." Preston reaches out and strokes Crater's long locks, then smiles. "Remarkable." He spins and marches out toward the front door. His men are pulled to him like a magnet as we retrace our route. "They're runaways, you know."

"Oh?" Crater says.

"Yes!" Preston replies. "Underage runaways. And they're troubled, too. Likely to tell you all sorts of wild tales." He stares intently into Crater's eyes – penetrating, trying to read into his mind. What he finds he does not understand – he did not understand it thirty years ago, he did not understand it last year when public television did a 60's retrospect, he is not going to understand it now that he is confronting the last remnants eye-to-eye.

He could read the truth in me, but he thinks Crater and I are one in the same, so he doesn't try. "Bah! There's a ten thousand dollar reward. No questions asked. You could get this place a few lava lamps with that." He storms out of Moon Base and sucks all of his men out with him.

Crater shuts the front door, then hurries to the steam bath. He yanks down a peace sign towel and reveals a wall of vertical cedar planks, similar to the rest of the room, except for a dark rectangle where the towel provided protection from light and steam. He raps on the planks – once, then twice – and a secret door swings open. Two red elves are crouched on a shelf, flashing their impish grins at us.

Crater smiles at my gawking face. "What? You think this is the first time we had to hide fugitives?"

"They're looking better," I say.

"I don't know, man. They should really see a doctor, but then their old man will drag them home."

The two boys hop out of the shelf. They tug at their clammy long johns.

Crater points down the hall. "First room on the right," he says. "You should find some threads there that fit."

The two boys scurry off, showing little sign that they had nearly drown no more than an hour ago.

"Who is this Preston T. Service, anyway?" I ask.

"Some rich cat, according to Rick," Crater says. "Builds skyscrapers somewhere. Owns his own helicopter. Likes to bugger his sons."

"He buggers his sons?" I ask.

"Yeah. After his wife disappeared, he started pawing the boys."

"My wife disappeared," I say. "But I'm sitting quiet and waiting for her to come back." I should say I paw myself sometimes, but we aren't playing true confessions here. Crater wouldn't be shocked, though, if I told him. He'd find that to be spiritual – self-discovery, independence, not relying on others for the most basic of earthly pleasures.

"That's different, man. Your wife left you. His disappeared. Poof."

Rick and Nick return. They are dressed in paisley bellbottoms and tie-dye tee shirts. They are miniature Craters. Rick grins as he flashes a peace sign.

I hear soft footsteps in the hall.

"Daddy, there are men hiding in our woods." It is Light. School has ended for the day. She sees the two boys and their paisley bellbottoms. "Oh, they're so cute. Can we keep them?"

Crater shrugs. "Guess we got to for a while, until those cats out there leave, anyway."

Justin and Kathleen enter. They checked the farmhouse after school and found no one home, so they came over here.

"Dad!" Justin shouts. "Some homo jumped out of the bushes and grabbed me. He stole my hat."

"He just wanted to see your face," I say.

Justin stares at Rick and Nick. "You and Crater been doing cloning experiments or something?"

"We went ice fishing today," I say.

"Yeah, man," Crater says. "We pulled these two from the lake."

Kathleen steps up closer to the twins. She stares at their paisley bellbottoms; at how they flare together so there is no daylight between their legs. "Are they mermaids?" She is looking for fins.

"No," I say. "They fell through the ice, and we pulled them out."

It is an embarrassing detail, and Rick blushes, but Nick has barely recovered from being blue. Blushing red will come later for him; he will be stretched out in the steam bath enjoying the solitude. Light will step casually in, unwrap her towel, and lay it carefully on the opposite bench. She will stretch her creamy white body across the towel and smile at the boy. *This is so relaxing*, she will say. *Isn't it relaxing?*

Yes, he will fib as he flips onto his stomach. It is then that his face will flush bright red, but she will think it's from the heat.

Justin darts his eyes from Light to the boys. "So why are they here?" He is fearing competition from two 12-year-olds. The rules out here are so unfamiliar – perhaps two 12-year-old twins make up one 24-year-old man. "Hey, do those guys out there have something to do with this?"

"They work for our dad," Rick says. "We ran away from home."

"You ran away?" Justin asks. "From where?"

"Connecticut," Rick says.

Connecticut, he calls it, but it sounds like the suburbs to me.

"Jeez, that's a long ways," Justin says. "I never made it further than the bus stop."

Nick has not looked up at the other children – he is drowning again. The water has left his lungs, but now he is filled with shame. His secret is safe, though; Crater and I will not say any more. There is nothing more that can be said. Crater may have lived in a world of free love, but he knows the difference between freedom and slavery. Even in the torrid heat of the sixties, a person could still say "no."

Tears fall across Nick's cheeks. He tucks his chin tighter against his chest and runs to the only safe room he knows, the room full of empty paisley bellbottoms.

"I better go with him," Rick says. "For some reason our dad only..." He pauses a second to think of the right expression for this group. He has already told Crater the truth, but Crater was easy, with his long hair and his faraway eyes – talking to Crater was like confessing to Jesus. And the boys were a bit delirious then, too, from the cold water. Perhaps Crater really was Jesus; perhaps they had died there in the lake. To hide the truth from the son of God would deny them eternal life, so confess Rick did; crying, shaking – cold, guilt, confusion. Light, Justin, and Kathleen though – they are Rick's peer group. They will understand it the least, they will turn on him the quickest, yet he will need them the most. He finds the words he is looking for. "...our dad only picked on Nick."

I wait until Rick leaves, then rouse my own brood. "Come on, kids. Mittens must be hungry."

I can see Justin is reluctant to leave Light's side – she said she will wait for a farmer, but these rich boys from Connecticut... they present an opportunity perhaps she never expected.

Light turns slowly and walks to the secret doorway. She shuts it carefully, then picks up the peace sign towel. Justin and I both watch as she turns the towel sideways so the peace sign is upright. She smiles, then hangs the towel lengthwise from its hooks. There is a patience to her movements. Justin can't see it, but I do – she will wait for her farmer. Moon Valley is a place where patience is rewarded – there is no getting ahead because no one is lined up to go anywhere. I think of that first morning in the tent, Kathleen and Light lying by the door flap waiting patiently for the deer to move into the campsite. Kathleen is young – she can learn from Light.

"Dad, Mittens can wait," Justin pleads. "Let's stay here until dark so we can sneak past the guards."

I look at Justin and wonder if he will learn patience, too. No, he will be a premature ejaculator. There is some sense to his plan, though. His purpose is not pure, but then many great ideas have been spawned by corrupt motives.

March 29

Spring is late. Crater has too many flutes and not enough firewood. I have suggested burning some of the flutes if the weather doesn't improve.

Light and Justin went out looking for fallen trees. They have come back with barely an armful of sticks.

"Someone dragged a lot of wood onto the lake and burned it," Justin says.

"Sounds like something my dad would do," Rick suggests.

He and his brother have been staying inside, out of sight. They play Chinese checkers and Monopoly. There is a feeling of harmony, of well being, when they sit cross-legged with the Chinese checkers board nestled between their paisley knees. A nervous sense of conflict invades now, though, as I watch the two boys grasping fistfuls of Monopoly money in the hallowed confines of Moon Valley.

"My dad once bought up all the toilet paper in some town, and kept buying it up until they let him have his zoning change." There is a sense of admiration in Rick's voice as he speaks of his father. He forgets his hatred; the Monopoly game has corrupted his mind, and for a moment he is proud of his father's scandalous ways. "He always said he could beat people with the little things, details they would overlook."

"Well, he might own a lot of toilet paper, but no way he can wipe out the whole forest," Crater says. He taps my shoulder. "Come on, man. I know a place they wouldn't of been."

We grab our coats and step outside. It is nearly April, yet there are four inches of new snow on the ground. Even though Walden Pond is still frozen, we hike around it – like Piss Hole Lake, there are soft spots on the icy surface. There is one small area that never freezes and is crowded with ducks even in February. Light collects stale bread from the school cafeteria and feeds it to the birds throughout the winter – she tells the cafeteria workers it is for a school project. Perhaps it is – Light doesn't seem the type to lie.

Beyond the pond, we climb the slopes where cultivated fields once flourished. They have sat idle for years and have now begun reverting to forest. We crest the hill and begin heading down through a more mature stand of white birch.

"I don't normally bring anyone out here," Crater says. "It's my secret garden." There is a thick spruce grove; the trees nearly grown together like a hedge. Crater leads me through a break in the trees – he sees footprints in the snow and swears softly. He puts a finger to his lips. "Shhh."

I follow him quietly, placing my feet in the footprints he leaves in the snow as if that will somehow soften the sound. There is a clearing ahead. We enter it and a broad smile crosses Crater's face.

"Far out." He points toward the tree tops. There are four men dangling upside-down from ropes. It is an odd sight – I look about for the shadow of a giant spider. "Didn't know if my booby traps would work with all the snow," Crater whispers.

The men spin slowly from their tethers. One man flaps his arms as if he has given up on a normal rescue and believes learning to fly will be his only means of escape.

Another man's face spins into view; there is a pipe dangling from his angry lips. His white hair has not lost its shape, even after hanging upside-down. "Ah, gentlemen," he says loudly. "As you can see, I have yet to find my sons. Perhaps you will cut us down."

"Hang loose, man," Crater says. "We'll cut you down once we've restocked our firewood." There is a pile of logs, stacked when the clearing was first made, no doubt. Crater picks up one end of the top log and signals for me to grab the far end.

"I suppose it wouldn't help if I offered you the service of my three men here in exchange for cutting us down now?"

"Never needed three men before, man," Crater says.

Preston Service smiles. He tries to fill his pipe, but he finds his world is flipped around, and he can't function under such unusual rules. Tobacco sprinkles from the treetops and accents the snow-covered ground like pepper. "Of course you knew, Mr. Crater, that I was seeking some sort of advantage in my offer. Men like me are always seeking an advantage over our opponents."

"I'm no one's opponent, man," Crater says.

"The boys are okay, though?"

Crater does not reply.

Yes, the boys are okay, Preston Service surmises. He continues spinning slowly on the end of his rope. I can no longer see his face, but he continues talking. "Despite what they've told you, I do love them. I love everything that's mine."

"You can't own children, though," Crater says.

"I think that's what they were trying to tell me by running

away," Preston replies. He lets the pipe fall from his hand. "You know, my men could easily storm your palace."

"Or you could knock on the door," Crater says, "and I'd let you in."

"That wouldn't be my style," Preston T. Service replies.

"Your style won't find the boys." Crater salutes Preston. "Come on, Harry." He heaves the log higher, and together we march it back to Moon Base.

The sun is going down when we return for the last log. Preston and two of his men are still spinning from their ropes, but the fourth man is lying on the ground.

"He thought he was James Bond," Preston explains. "He burned through his rope and landed on his head. I didn't hire these men for their brains."

I run to the man's side and squeeze his wrist, searching for a pulse. I have no idea what to do if he has no pulse, but checking for one is an urge I have learned from the movies – murder mysteries in particular.

"He alive?" Crater asks. There is concern in his voice. I worry for Crater – if the man is dead, Crater will blame himself for not cutting them down earlier.

The man moans as I squeeze his wrist tighter.

"These Russians have thick skulls." Preston laughs – it is a nervous laugh, but there is relief also. He doesn't need a death, either – that would bring police. He needs to find his sons without attracting the cops, to return them swiftly to his exclusive estate where the authorities would not dare intrude.

There is a large burlap bag lying in the snow. Crater kneels beside it and stabs it with his pocket knife. Sand pours from the hole. It is some type of counterweight. "Be cool and you'll land a little gentler than Boris there," Crater calls, "once enough sand's leaked out." He lifts the last log onto his shoulder. "Come on, Harry. We got our firewood. Let's go crank up the steam bath."

April 1

The children are playing Monopoly. There is a large pile of play money in front of Light. Nick has just landed on Boardwalk and fallen backward, mocking heart failure after seeing the price he must pay for a hotel room.

"You don't have to pay me anything." Light smiles and instead hands Nick a small bundle of yellow bills.

"You can't do that!" Rick shouts. "You got to bankrupt him."

"That's your father speaking," Light says cheerfully.

I look at Justin. There is something odd about him. Then I see it – he is wearing paisley bellbottoms. "Justin, where's your jeans?"

He ignores me for a moment – he has a renewed interest in counting his money. There are seven dollar bills fanned out before him, and his last piece of property – a railroad – is mortgaged.

"Justin. Your jeans. Where are they?"

"They were a little wet, so I borrowed these."

He was never a good liar; the tips of his ears always turn bright red when he is being untruthful. They flicker now like two candles; they take on a pointy shape. Justin is now the third paisley-panted elf, wedged between the original twins.

Ah, the twins. That is why Justin has exchanged pants. He is not sure what will work with Light, so he will copy the twins, imitate their every move, play them to a draw. Then come spring, he will get a pig, become a farmer – play his trump card – and score.

"Justin." I shake my head but I say no more. Justin does not remember three years ago when he was the twins' age. They are at that awkward stage. Forces are telling them they should be interested in girls – external forces, like television and near-sighted aunts; and internal forces – they are finding strange hairs, and sometimes at night they have to bend over to pee. But all-in-all they view Light's beauty with less interest than they would a new video game.

There is a knock at the front door. The twins scurry into the closet – it does not seem like a good hiding place, but when I open the closet door to cover them with a blanket, they are gone. They are little magical elves.

Crater opens the front door. A middle-aged woman is standing there.

"I'm Rick's and Nick's new tutor," she says. She sticks out her long fingers, and Crater shakes her hand meekly. "May I come in? Mr. Service is afraid the boys are falling behind on their school work."

"I'm sorry, Miss. The boys aren't here." Crater stares at the woman with more interest than her plain features warrant. He frowns slightly as though he should know her but can't recall why.

"Yes, I know. But I'm suppose to do their lessons anyway."

She slides a box full of books into the hallway, then carries in a suitcase. She looks from the dim hall to the front room where the Monopoly game was being played. "I'll do it in there." She takes the top book from the box, strolls into the room, and begins reading. She looks down at the two empty spots at the Monopoly board and flashes a slight smile.

"Come on, man. Let's finish our game." Crater sits where Nick had been. I slide from the easy chair to the floor and pick up Rick's small wad of play money – neither twin exhibited their father's flare for business.

Light rolls the dice – she passes GO but does not collect two hundred. "I'll leave some for those who need it," she explains.

The tutor holds a grammar text in front of her face and begins reading. She calls out that – wherever they are – she hopes the twins will join her in diagramming a few sentence structures.

"Miss, what is your name, anyway?" Crater asks.

"Myra," the woman replies. "Miss Myra Bloomberg." She closes the book and paces about the room. "There aren't any windows?"

"No," Crater says. He shakes his head as he tries to match her name to the memory of a face.

"Is there a reason for that?" she asks.

"I imagine there was," Crater replies. "But the next day, no one remembered what that was either."

She eyes him curiously. She is unfamiliar with men in general. She became a school teacher in the hopes of avoiding men, and was even a bit concerned with this assignment when she learned that her pupils would be 12-year-old boys. Crater, though, does not remind her of men; he reminds her of a mellow summer afternoon, sitting in a field of buttercups with her skirt spread out around her, of schoolmates playing jump rope in the nearby shade. He reminds her of the past. He reminds her of friendships and dreams; of camaraderie, honesty, and sharing. Her nipples struggle within her tight bra; she thinks for a moment of surrendering her virginity, of yielding to him because he is not a man, but an abandoned god who will coat her with golden honey, and not befoul her with man's greedy slime. She shakes these thoughts from her head. "But Mr. Crater, children need sunshine."

"They go outside for that," Crater replies.

"Even the boys?"

Crater smiles. "Miss, the boys aren't here."

"Well, as you wish." Myra picks up a different book and thumbs to the center pages. "Boys!" she yells, her bold red lips trumpeting toward the ceiling. "We're going to do fractions now."

There is a low groan from the closet. I pretend I don't hear it, but the others look quickly toward the door.

Myra grins. "Mr. Service said the boys were not particularly fond of math."

April 5

Winter has finally surrendered. Justin and I hike through the spring mud toward Moon Valley to show off Justin's new pig – a present for his fifteenth birthday. The pig was part of a trade the minivan for a pickup truck. Pig icing on the pig cake.

Kathleen has stayed home to spoon warm milk to Mittens – the cat seems ill.

There are no guards loitering in the woods. They have been gone for several days. Preston T. Service is satisfied with his choice of Myra Bloomberg as an inside agent. She can keep tabs on the boys for him, and let him know when it is best to strike. He picked her carefully, choosing her for her homely, spinster ways; doubly secure in the belief that she could not be seduced because she would not let it happen, and also, neither Crater nor I would try.

The door to Moon Base is wide open. There is no sign of anyone at the Monopoly board. Down the hall, a woman's voice is shouting, "Oh papa! Oh papa!" Justin and I follow the sound to the steam room.

Crater is lying on the floor, blood oozing from his back. Long fingers dig in at his shoulder blades as steam swirls around his head.

"Oh papa!"

The pig squeals under my son's arm, and Crater's ass ceases jiggling.

"Oh my!" Myra shouts as her head tips back, and she sees the two of us standing there, hovering over her and Crater.

I grab the peace sign towel from the wall and drape it across Justin's eyes.

"Jeez, Dad! You think I never saw two people fuck before?"

I am alarmed for a moment, wondering who he might have seen and when. But no, it was not me and Beth. What we did never had the physical passion of fucking. We screwed; like the timid twisting of a bolt into a wing nut.

It is a crass word – fuck – but it is exactly what is going on here. Crater, alone in this forgotten valley for all these years; he is tired of playing wooden flutes, and now with his own truly fine instrument is hitting chords that he thought he could no longer play. Myra, alone all her life; she has forgotten about gods for now – she is sucking the juices from Crater like a spider in the hopes of revitalizing her sagging soul. It is a mutually satisfying fuck, and it makes me horny thinking of the last time Beth and I... screwed.

Crater looks up at us. "Been a long time, man," he grins.

"Sorry. The front door was open," I say. I grab Justin's hand and lead him blindly away. We will go play Monopoly until these two are finished. They say money and sex are one and the same, anyway – but ours is play money and Crater's is real sex.

A jealous feeling creeps into me as Justin and I face each other on the floor and roll dice. I look at Justin and try to recall the moment he was conceived, to use that memory as a reminder that I, too, once enjoyed the pleasures in which Crater is now indulging. I can't recall it though. I find it hard to even think of Justin – this large man-child – as once having been little more than the end play of an erotic moment, a bit of vomit spewing from a body part that has fallen victim to acute motion sickness.

There is a picture album open on the floor. Beside it lay a pair of women's panties and Crater's jeans. I crawl over and look at the pictures. They are group photos taken beneath Mother Oak at a time before Moon Base was built. White tents are pitched among the clearing. Walden Pond sits glimmering in the background and corn grows high on the hills beyond. With their long hair, it is hard to tell the boys from the girls. Some have beards – they would be the boys. But the others – I am guessing from their respective heights that the shorter ones are the girls and not merely clean-shaven boys.

In one photo there is a boy in the middle. I recognize the beard and the eyes. It is a young Crater. Beside him is a homely woman. She looks almost middle-aged. It is Myra. She has never grown older – she is some dark spirit from the past coming to reclaim Crater's soul.

"Drug overdose," Crater says. He and Myra have entered quietly on bare feet. Crater knows without looking which photograph I am examining.

Myra is wrapped in two towels and blushes when I look up, but Crater is standing naked in the middle of the room using his lone towel to rub his beard dry. His penis is no longer the bold instigator of Myra's unabashed screams, but is a shriveled pink reminder of his celibate past.

"Her name was Moon Dance, but her parents buried her as Abby something. Never would let me know where they put her."

"Moon Dance," Myra says. "I like that."

"Do you?" Crater wraps his towel about her waist and draws her closer. "Then I dub thee Moon Dance Too."

I can't judge whether it's Justin or his pig who is squirming more. There is too much sex in the air for someone of Justin's age. "Um, is Light around?" he asks.

"She took the twins down to the pond to fish."

The words are barely out of Crater's mouth before Justin is dashing for the door. Every moment she is alone with them, there is the risk they will say something farmboyish and the pig will be a wasted effort.

He is met at the door by the twins. Behind them is Light. Justin looks at their clothing and frowns. They are no longer dressed in paisley bellbottoms, but are wearing green overalls, flannel shirts, and straw hats. They are crafty little shits, stealing his trump card on him. Justin realizes how ridiculous he looks – a junior hippie with a pig under his arm – and stomps past the three returning fishermen.

"Hey, Justin," Rick says cheerfully.

"Hey, yourself," Justin replies.

"What's with him?" Rick asks as Nick holds up a string of fish.

"He brought his pig, but you beat him to it," I say.

"We don't got a pig," Rick says.

"*Have* a pig," Myra corrects the boy, then blushes as she realizes she is no longer dressed the part of the schoolmarm. "Get in, boys, before you're spotted." She waves the twins and Light through the door, then wanders over to her clothes. They are carefully draped across a chair – except for her panties, which were the last thing she abandoned, her crotch so hot for a man's touch by then that she tossed them away as recklessly as she did her virginity. She pulls a cell phone from the pocket of her slacks. "Here, Crater."

He looks at it, unaware of what it might be, but accepts it as a gift. "Thanks." He might think it's some form of vibrator. He'll try rubbing it between Myra's thighs some night and give an operator somewhere in Tuscaloosa something to call home about.

"It's a phone, Crater," she explains. "I was supposed to call Preston Service on it if the boys left the house. Two of his men are staying in town ready to grab them."

"You're a spy?" Crater thinks back to an old adage – never trust anyone over thirty – but he had felt sure that no longer applied. Now he is thinking the old ways were truth – and truth never changes.

"Well, that was before..." Myra blushes again. "... before I *knew* you." She takes her clothes from the chair and walks into the hallway, then turns, throwing Crater a seductive smile. Crater follows her out.

There is a hiss of steam.

The door to the steam room slams shut, leaving me to sit with the three children and stare at the Monopoly board, cringing each time adult laughter peels through the timbers. I think of Beth and wonder what she might be doing. Perhaps she is laughing in a steam bath with Eve.

The front door flies open and Justin marches in. He is wearing blue overalls and a flannel shirt. He does not have a straw hat – that is too Huck Finn, something fine for 12-year-olds, but not appropriate for a teenager bursting toward manhood. He has his pig, though. He tethers it to a floor lamp with a length of frayed cord.

There is not much room on the floor between Light and Rick, but Justin squats down and nudges Rick aside with his shoulder.

"Hey, man," Rick says.

"Hey, yourself," Justin replies. He slips in beside Light and places his arm cautiously across her shoulder. There is an awkwardness to his movement that is due more to my parental presence than to any lack of confidence on his part.

A woman's sharp orgasmic scream rolls from the direction of the steam room. Fear floods Justin's eyes – he did not realize that as a man, he would wield such power at the tip of his body. He yearns to be a boy again – slides his arm from Light's shoulder and claims the toy race car as his Monopoly game piece.

"We aren't playing Monopoly," Light says. She and the twins are sitting around the game board out of habit, like Kathleen and Justin did with television in the suburbs. There I'd find them staring glassy-eyed at the TV set, their mouths hanging open – not because of the vegetarian cooking show playing before them, but because their minds had gone to sleep and they were slowly loosing muscle control.

No game? Justin looks suspiciously from Rick to Nick, wondering if there is some foul plot afoot to exclude him from the group. There is no money in front of either twin – that could mean they are indeed playing the game. But Light has no money, either, and Justin relaxes.

It is Kathleen's turn to burst through the door of Moon Base. She is crying even though she hasn't been near the suburbs.

"What's wrong, Kitten?" I ask.

"I think I killed Mittens," she howls.

"No!" I shudder. It is a strange shudder, like I've been zapped with a ray gun and an alien being has fled my body. I want to say Mittens is okay, she is just sleeping, but Kathleen is old enough to know when she's holding a dead cat on her lap. She is telling me the truth – Mittens is dead. I am surprised by how little emotion that concept evokes. The eight million is gone. But so is Beth, and it is Beth that I miss, not the abstractness of eight million dollars. I once thought such a lurid amount would coax her back, but I'm not so sure now. It would not lure Crater from his sacred valley.

There is another joyous scream from the steam room.

Eight million would not drag Myra from Crater's passionate embrace.

The twins would not go home for eight million. There are piles upon piles of millions back at their father's estate – the compost pile itself is probably made up of worn out dollar bills – but here they sit, playing or not playing Monopoly. And their father, buried up to his armpits by his vast wealth, still feels compelled to rifle through his sons' undies for loose change.

Justin doesn't want eight million, either. He wants a pig. No, Justin wants Light, and pigs are her currency.

Kathleen walks over to me and leans apprehensively against my shoulder. Tears stain her cheeks.

I grab her and hoist her onto my lap. "Mittens was old and sick. It's not your fault."

"But it is. She was cold, so I put an electric blanket over her." Kathleen tries to control her sobs, but the memory is too horrible. "Smoke came out of her when I plugged it in."

Okay, so Kathleen did execute my eight million dollar cat.

The door to the steam bath slams opens, and the two lovers enter the room fully dressed – it surprises me how quickly Myra has gained influence over Crater.

I have seen it with others. I have imagined how it works – the first time they lie naked together, the man smiles slyly as he feels the progress of his efforts. *I'm in*, he thinks. The woman smiles slyly, too, as she feels the movement within her and thinks, *I'm in*. But how can that be? Because it is sex and it is physical, but it is not physics. They are both *in*, each in the way they desire most.

Crater pulls out a joint and lights it. Myra sniffs the sweet air, stares at Crater, and pinches her legs tighter together. "Not in front of the children, dear," she says quietly.

It is not a command he has heard before, not here anyway. He remembers the early days – there were many children then. They swam naked in Walden Pond, and it was viewed as wholesome. Parents made love under the evening stars, and that was beautiful. Babies were born, their anxious siblings awaiting their arrival beside their laboring mothers. And then there was Moon Dog and Moon Roof, and all the other Moon men passing a joint along the length of a fallen log as they debated whether the tents should be replaced with a more permanent structure. Moon Dog thought since the animals had a barn, the people also deserved something sounder. But Moon Rider did not agree – the animals were kept in a strong barn since they weren't civilized enough to stay in tents on their own.

Crater squints as he tries to remember when that all became dirty, wrong. *Not in front of the children* – what does that mean? Crater shrugs and turns to face the wall. He inhales deeply and thinks – something is already wrong – then exhales, sending a thick cloud against the rough timbers.

"Oh, Crater." Myra storms out. Her footsteps echo down the darkened hallway.

Crater turns back to face us. He smiles sheepishly. "I guess I'm out of practice with this domestic stuff, huh?"

"Practice doesn't make perfect when it comes to women," I say. I think of Beth and how much I practiced with her, only to find out years later that I wasn't wearing the right uniform and was entering the game through the wrong locker room.

"What should I do now, man?" Crater asks.

I walk to the front door and beckon Crater over. We step outside into the spring air. There are three fishing poles leaning against the dark brown exterior of Crater's fortress. I grab one and hand another to him. There are two straw hats lying on the ground beside the door. We are not twelve – we do not need them.

"Tell her you're sorry, and you'll never smoke again," I say.

Crater holds up the smoldering joint. He watches the smoke rise, beckoning to him. "But that would be a lie. I'll probably smoke before dinner."

"It's not a lie. It's a weakness – you tried to stop but you couldn't. Women like weakness." I lay my arm across Crater's broad shoulders and steer him toward Walden Pond.

"So she'll like me if I lie?"

"No, she'll fucking hate you if you lie. She'll love you if you're weak."

"So, like, there's no unconditional love anymore?"

There is a spot beside the pond, the earth worn smooth and shiny – in the shape of Crater's ass – a spot at which he's sat for many years and caught fish without fail. The fish have never learned that the hairy beast that lurks upon the shoreline is a danger to them. They gather along the edge, stare up at him from the shallow water, and blow bubbles.

Crater sits down in his spot without thinking and tosses his line into the clear waters. "The fish won't bite this time of day," he says.

"That's okay," I reply. "We're not really here to fish."

Crater hands the joint toward me, but I wave it away.

"Not here to smoke, either?" Crater says.

No. Not here to fish or smoke. So why am I here? To get eight million, I thought. But that's gone now, and I'm still here. I set the fishing pole down and pick up a flat rock. I throw it and watch as it skips across the pond's surface. "One, two, three." I count each skip out loud. I could do ten when I was Justin's age. 15-year-olds don't skip stones anymore, though. They might if they thought no one was watching.

It only gets worse as you get older – you don't climb trees or draw with crayons. You don't read comic books, collect bugs, eat peanut butter, run through sprinklers, or chase down the street after ice cream trucks. You get sex and booze in exchange for all that you give up. You need the booze after you've given so much up. You really need the booze after you get the sex.

"So, Harry. What do you think of Myra?" Crater has stopped fishing. He is blowing smoke rings and comparing them to the rings my stone has left rippling across the pond.

"She's smart," I say.

"Smart's okay, I guess," Crater sighs.

A twig snaps behind us. We both turn to look. It is Justin – he has the third fishing pole. He has decided he should not be sitting with Rick and Nick – they are mere boys. He should be down at the pond with the men.

"So, Dad." He is pensive. "Where do we go now?"

"Go?" I say.

"Yeah. The cat's dead. Don't we have to leave?"

"I don't know." A feeling of panic shoots through my body. The eight million is gone, of course. But did the will state we had to leave if the cat died, or could we stay the full year whether Mittens lived or not? I can't call Mr. Spinozzi to ask. That will tip him off that something is wrong. Silence, and he will stay away until September, when he will come to see the tomatoes. He might ask about the cat then, but I'll stall, saying Mittens is off chasing mice. He will definitely want to examine the cat before he hands over the eight million, though.

"Hey!" Crater says. "I could stuff her. Set her in a pose like she's sleeping."

"Myra?" I ask.

"No, man. Mittens."

"You already stuffed Myra enough," Justin says.

Crater and I look up at him. He wants to laugh, but instead an uneasy cloud fills Justin's face. He should not have said that – that was pal talk, not dad talk. Crater and I burst out laughing, and Crater reaches up and pulls Justin down beside him.

"I sure did, didn't I," Crater says. "Did you hear her shriek?"

Justin nods his head, "Sure did." He tosses his fishing line into the clear water. "I thought girls were supposed to like it?"

"They do, man. It's just sometimes you get a virgin, and they sound a little tortured." Crater looks at Justin's worried face. "Not guys, man. They whack off so much, they're not really virgins their first time."

Justin blushes.

"See the color," Crater says, pointing to Justin's face. "Guilt."

I nod. "He's a seasoned pro."

"Cut it out, Dad."

"I remember my first time," Crater says. "I was like eleven, and we were at school playing tag on the jungle gym. I shimmied up a pole, and all of a sudden, whoa man! I hung there for a moment thinking I had peed my pants. But peeing never felt like that!" He laughs. "The other kids yelled, 'Come on, get down,' so I slid down and shimmied back up, and slid down and shimmied back up. Did that the whole recess. Took me like a year to figure out I didn't need an entire jungle gym to do it." Crater feeds his fishing line out and waits, expects one of us to continue the conversation, but there is an embarrassing silence. "What about you, man? Don't you remember?"

"It's not like a first kiss or something," I say.

"It's exactly like a first kiss," Crater argues.

"I don't know. I think my best friend showed me how."

"Come on, man. You can't 'think' about something like that."

"Okay, okay. His older brother showed him. We were ten or eleven. Twelve, maybe. And he came running over to my house all excited and said come out to the woods, he had something to show me. I thought he had a frog or something."

Crater and Justin burst out laughing. If they weren't so healthy, snots would have exploded from their noses. The laughter dies down, and Crater and I stare at Justin.

"Well," I say, overwhelmed by a voyeuristic eagerness to peek into my son's private life.

"Ah, come on, Dad."

"Well, you want to hang out with the men, you got to contribute to the conversation."

"I thought we'd talk about sports or something," Justin says. He reels in his fishing line and casts the lure toward a patch of weeds. The silence annoys him. He looks up and sees Crater and I still eyeing him. "All right." His face is not that of the animated story teller, but that of the reluctant confessor. "Christine McCarthy."

"Christine? That's a girl," Crater says. "A girl taught you how to whack off?"

"Christine McCarthy, the baby-sitter?" I say.

"Yeah. You and Mom went to Nantucket for the weekend and she sat for us."

"Christine McCarthy, the nice Catholic girl?" I say.

"Yes, Dad. Christine McCarthy."

"Jeez, and I didn't even pay her the usual rate." I stare at my fingers and absorb this new information. Our little exposé is no longer fun. Boys being boys was what we were discussing, not boys being molested. "Did you two...?"

"Fuck? No, Dad. I was only eleven." He closes his eyes to hide the tears.

I wrap both my arms around Justin's shoulders and pull him against my chest. It is odd, but I have never felt closer to my son than at this moment. "It's okay," I whisper. "You didn't do anything wrong."

Justin sobs softly. The dampness of his tears soaks through my shirt and nourishes my heart. "I was so scared, but then it felt so good."

"Damn," Crater says. "People doing stuff like that can mess up a kid's whole view on sex."

"Jeez. Christine McCarthy. Who would of thought," I sigh. "She was so ugly, I never thought of her and sex in the same sentence. I think that's why Beth hired her, so she wouldn't have to worry about me and the baby-sitter."

Justin chuckles softly against my chest. "And she smelled bad, too."

"Yeah," I say. "Your mom used to leave deodorant out when she was coming over, hoping she'd get the hint."

Justin laughs again. He looks up and wipes the tears from his eyes. "Sorry, Dad."

"God, Justin. I'd cry too if Christine McCarthy wiggled my weenie."

Crater chuckles. "I remember the ugliest woman I been with."

I think of Myra, but that is not who he is thinking of.

"She was a sociology professor. Everyone said she was a lesbian." He looks quickly at me, concerned that I may take offense since my wife is one, but he sees me smiling contentedly as I stroke Justin's hair. "She was doing research and gave me ten bucks to be one of her subjects. Then she pulled out a measuring tape and said she needed to measure my dick. I needed the ten bucks, so I said okay. I figured having a lesbian poking around down there wasn't much different than a doctor. She says 'Hum, five inches. Now I got to measure you erect,' and dropped down on her knees. She was no lesbian."

"You should always ask about a job before you accept it," I say.

Crater laughs. "Yeah, that was some job. You wonder how someone that ugly learns so much about pleasing men."

"Necessity," I suggest.

A woman's voice calls from behind us. "So there you men are." It is Myra. She has been lured to us by talk of ugly women.

Justin grins proudly – a woman has called him a man. The signs of tears are but a faint memory across his smooth cheek. "So how about those Red Sox," he says.

"Carl Yastremski still playing?" Crater asks.

Justin and I look at one another and burst out laughing. Something pulls Justin's red and white bobber below the surface of Walden Pond. He has caught his first fish.

"I think I should take my phone back," Myra says. "I've been remiss in my duties, and should really call Mr. Service and let him know the boys are here."

Crater looks at me. Be weak, I want to say. He seems to hear me.

Crater drops his fishing pole as he stands up and faces Myra. "Oh, baby. Let's try again." He reaches out to her. His bobber sinks, and the pole slithers off into the pond before Justin or I can grab it. "I want to be good," Crater says, "but I just know I can't do it without you."

It is what she wants to hear. She is amazed at her powers – why had she waited so long to adopt one of these poor creatures? All these years. She could have felt the rhythm of many men, molded them to a pleasing shape, kept them sometimes between her legs and stowed them other times under her thumb. "Well, I don't know." She smiles as she watches the fishing pole swim around the pond. Oh, he is so hopeless, she must forgive him. "Okay, but you'll listen to me next time. Right, Mr. Smarty Pants?"

Crater nods. He takes her hand and walks her toward Moon

Base. She thinks his pants are smart – he will let her experience their brilliance once more.

"Want to go back, son?"

"What? And listen to those two again?"

"You're right, son. That's something two old bachelors don't need to hear."

Justin casts his line across the bow of the runaway fishing pole, snaring his lure in the other pole's reel. Slowly he reels the line in. When the pole nears the shore, I reach over and grab it. We are a team.

June 6

The parlor at Finch Farm is scented with the mystical aroma of imported pipe tobacco. Justin, Kathleen, and I have been making what repairs we can to the barn. Crater is coming later to help with the heavy work. He says there is a trick to raising heavy timbers and if he is stoned enough, he might remember what it is. He knew better than to say that in front of Myra.

I wipe the sweat from my forehead and look around the silent parlor. A white-haired gentleman is facing the fireplace mantle, examining a family photograph.

"Ah, Mr. Lascome." Preston T. Service turns to greet me. "The door was unlocked, and the sun is quite hot for June. I hope you don't mind – I let myself in."

I nod silently.

"Your cat doesn't seem to mind strangers." Preston points with the end of his pipe toward Mittens – stretched out in one corner in the most comfortable pose Crater could affect.

"She sleeps a lot, Mr. Service," I say. "She's not well."

"Call me Preston. My friends do."

"You must not hear it often, then," I say as I walk toward the kitchen for drinks – my original mission.

Mr. Service laughs as he follows me. "I have heard that the quickest wit is found in the most rustic minds. I believe it's true."

"I've only recently become a farmer." I offer Mr. Service a beer, but he declines. I take out two, one for me and one for Justin. It is a special moment whenever I hand Justin a beer – I am showing him that I respect his maturity; and he flashes me a grin that says he admires my wisdom. I would do it over and over, just to experience that special exchange between father and son, but of course then Justin would be drunk; so it is a rare treat when he does not get a cola like his sister. "You seem to have recovered from your adventures in the woods."

"Yes, yes. Very nicely. And my man, the one who fell on his head, is much easier to control since that little incident." Preston points his pipe at me. "Locating you has been made more difficult, though. I won't go up into those woods anymore, so I've had to wait for you to come down." He holds out the family photograph he has been examining. "We are very much alike, actually."

"We're very different, really," I say.

"You have a wife who has left you," he says. "So have I."

"My wife writes to me," I say. "Can yours?"

"You are hinting at ugly rumors," Preston says as he sets the photograph on the kitchen table. "I didn't kill her, I assure you. I wouldn't hurt an ant. Of course, an ant has no assets, so what would be the point?"

The front door slams shut, and Justin appears in the kitchen doorway. He is dressed in cutoffs and sneakers, but nothing more. Although it is early June, his chest is already tanned a deep brown. His maturing biceps are moist with sweat. "Dad, where's the drinks?" He stops when he sees my unexpected visitor.

"Son, this is Mr. Service."

"Rick and Nick's father?" Justin asks.

"So you are acquainted with the twins?" Preston smiles. "I knew they didn't drown."

Justin blushes angrily. It is an anger directed at himself; he, Kathleen, and Light have been so careful not to mention the twins at school. Here, though, in the safety of his own home, he has let his guard down, and the truth has slipped out. "I met them when they were out snowmobiling. Before the accident," he says quickly. He looks at me for reassurance – don't worry, son, sometimes it's okay to tell a fib.

"You should have been in school that day. Tut tut tut." Preston pats his breast pocket, looking for his lighter. He realizes he has left it on the mantle where the photograph had been. He strolls from the kitchen, brushing lightly against Justin's chest as he squeezes through the doorway, eyeing my son's youthful body with one slow, lecherous sweep of his eyes. "Such a bad boy, playing hooky." He reaches out and pinches Justin's cheek.

I wave Justin toward the refrigerator, hand him two colas, and usher him out the back door. The beer would be wasted now – I will hold off on that and give him one later, when Preston is gone and the air is not so uncomfortable.

"So. My boys are a little bit younger than you..." Preston enters the kitchen, puffing at his pipe as the lighter flares. He looks about, and sees that he and I are once again alone.

"He had to go back to work," I say.

"Too bad," Preston says. "I had so much to ask him." Preston sits down at the kitchen table. "What I really came for is to buy your farm. I will give you a good price, but of course I expect something in return."

"I don't own this farm," I say.

"No?" Preston puffs his pipe with confidence. "But I understand you will soon."

"No," I say. "We will have to leave soon, in fact."

He looks at me with narrow, hard eyes. "Don't make this difficult." He stands up and paces from the table to the stove and back. "I am losing patience. First you take my boys, now you've taken my tutor. There is something wicked about that place, that Moon something."

"Miss Bloomberg still works for you," I say. "We haven't taken her anywhere." I resist telling him how many times Crater has taken Miss Bloomberg.

"Yes, but she calls to report to me, and ends up giggling like a drunk, like someone's... touching her. Such an ugly woman, too, it's all quite perverted."

"And touching your sons isn't," I say.

"Is that it?" Smoke pours from Preston's pipe as he fuels the burning tobacco with his hot breath. "They told you I touch them? That's their mother's doing. She has poisoned them against me."

There is sincerity in his voice. I wonder if what he is saying is true. But then I recall the way he looked at Justin, how he stared at the sturdy calves, slid his eyes up along the muscular thighs; how Preston's lip quivered ever so slightly as he scanned Justin's hidden crotch, his exposed navel, and his tanned chest; how his eyes closed slightly as he pinched Justin's cheek, as though with eyes closed he could dream it was something else he pinched. He is a dangerous man. There must be a way to get him out of Moon Valley without giving him the boys.

"I am not selling you the farm," I say. "It belongs to the cat."

"The cat! Ha! Don't defy me for too long," Preston T. Service yells as he marches toward the parlor. "You and that Crater character will lose everything if you do." He reaches the parlor and crosses to where the cat lies, then swings his foot angrily, sending Mittens sailing silently along the wall to the next corner. "That cat should see a vet," he says as he marches to the front door and flings it open. "Good day!"

June 7

From the peak of the barn, I look out over a vast wilderness empire. A steeple rises to the west. There is no longer a church beneath it, but a grange hall. The farms are dying – soon it will no longer be a grange hall. Perhaps it will become a church again. It is like a thermometer sticking up through the trees, catching the winds of time, measuring the social climate. From stern Protestants to socializing proletariats. What would be next? Perhaps a law office – folks have not been suing one another enough out here in the country. They have been under-utilizing the complex legal system set up just for their benefit.

To the east there is nothing but woods. I feel safe looking so far and seeing no smoke rising, hearing no clatter-clank of automobiles. It will be generations before vacation condos burst through the wall of trees and invade the serenity of Moon Valley.

To the south there is Crater. He has grabbed our mail and is walking slowly up the driveway. He is smoking a joint.

Justin joins me on the roof and scowls as he looks southward, seeing that Crater is alone. That means that Light has chosen to stay with the twins. Too bad, son, but now you'll get your work done at least.

As he draws closer, I see that Crater's beard has been trimmed and his hair cut short. Justin points at him and starts to laugh.

"Yeah, yeah." Crater climbs the wooden ladder as I slide to the eaves to meet him. He hands me the mail and sits on the edge of the barn's failing roof. "Wait, boy. Someday you'll be pussy whipped, too."

Justin smiles at that notion. He does not really care to be entirely whipped, but he would like a girl to stir him up a bit.

Crater sighs deeply as he adjusts his hat against the sun. "Jeez, Harry, I don't know about Myra. I'm sort of used to my own ways." Crater struggles with the joint – it has gotten too small to smoke, but he has hidden his roach clips from Myra and now he can't find them himself. "It's like she reads my mind, though. I'm about to tell her it's over, but before I can, she rips my pants off and balls the hell out of me."

"She does torture you," I say. I scan the mail and see there is another letter from Beth. There is a return address this time – Buffalo, New York. We are in the same state. Too bad it isn't a small one, like Rhode Island.

Crater scans the far end of the roof. Justin and I have removed most of the slate tiles from that half, and Kathleen has separated them in two piles below – broken and unbroken. "Damage doesn't look too bad," Crater comments.

"I thought maybe we'd just cut the barn shorter," I say. "Save the good half."

Crater looks at Justin. "What you got? Just the one pig?"

Justin nods. "Alfred."

"You named him?" Crater laughs. "Gonna make it tough, man,

taking him to market."

"Maybe I won't take him to market," Justin says.

"You got to," Crater explains. "What do you think you raise pigs for? Didn't you ever read Charlotte's Web?"

"Maybe he's a pet," Justin says.

"Daddy, are we done working?" Kathleen stands looking up from the bottom of the ladder, her dirty arm draped across her forehead to shield her eyes from the sun.

"Yes, Kitten." I turn to the others. "Break time," I announce.

"Light's making us a picnic lunch," Crater says. "She should be here soon."

Justin scurries eagerly down the ladder. "I'll go help her."

"Help her what?" I say.

"Um. Carry the picnic basket." He runs off down the driveway, tossing in funny little skips and head flips like a colt let loose in the pasture after a long night in the barn.

Ah, young love.

They will meet on the pathway and kiss among the mountain laurel. He will think they are discrete, but she may as well be wearing bright red lipstick, for the kisses will leave marks upon his mood that will show clearly to us all.

Kathleen climbs halfway up the ladder, and eyes the envelope in my hand. "Is that from Mommy?"

I nod as I tear it open and pull out the letter.

"What does she say?"

"Oh, same old stuff." I quickly scan the letter. "That she misses us and hopes to see us soon."

I tuck the letter back in the envelope: I will read it later in bed. I will show the letter to my penis. It will slowly raise its sad little eye, and together we will remember Beth and dream of what sex was once like. I might try to recreate it with creams and hand motions, but it will not be the same.

"Does she know where we live?" Kathleen asks.

I look at the front of the envelope. There is no official post office forwarding label on it this time – she has sent it to us directly. "Yes, Kitten. She must have found out we moved."

Justin comes running from the woods. He is screaming and waving a picnic basket over his head. "Dad! Dad!" He gets closer and tears begin to fall across his cheek. "Daddy," he screams. "They've taken her."

Crater and I fight one another to get down the ladder first. Neither of us is getting down it at all. Justin stops below the ladder and aims the top of the picnic basket toward us. His tears have betrayed his deception – some of his tan is really dirt. On the top of the picnic basket, someone has sprayed "trade ya" with fluorescent orange spray paint.

***

"What do we do, man?" Crater paces across the floor of the parlor. "What do we do?"

Kathleen is sitting quietly in a corner petting Mittens. She talks to the cat. That's sick, I say, talking to a stuffed cat, but she says it's no different than talking to a doll.

"So what do we do?" Crater asks for the third time.

"Sit down, Crater," I say. "You're making me nervous."

"Sit down, sit down. That's all you say, man."

"They wrote "trade ya." That implies some sort of action on their part," I say. "They'll call or something to set up a trade."

Justin bursts through the front door. His face is covered in sweat, his arms and bare chest are streaked red with scratches. "No sign of her." He throws himself wearily on the faded green sofa.

Justin wanted to organize a posse. He was hoping Light would leave a trail that we could follow – torn bits of pink silk; or crumbs from a loaf of stale bread, like Hanzel and Gretel. But other than the picnic basket, he has found no sign of her. The picnic basket is a pretty good clue to what has happened, though.

There is a timid knock at the door. Myra is there with her cellular phone. "Mr. Service wants to speak to you." She holds the phone toward Crater.

He listens grimly, saying "yeah, man" on occasion, then gives the phone back to Myra. "He wants to trade Light for the two boys."

"Light's okay?" I ask.

"Yeah," Crater says. "She spoke briefly. Said she was fine."

We are silent for a moment. There is a sickness to Preston T. Service that is hard to understand. He is willing to trade an attractive young lady for two scrawny boys.

Kathleen is too young to know the full nature of the danger the twins face, but she is the first to speak. "We can't do it, Daddy. Rick and Nick trusted us."

Staring grimly at his lap, Justin sighs. He is beginning to see that what we men carry there is not always an advantage; it can also be a curse.

"We don't have a lot of time, man." Crater takes Myra's hand and leads her out the door. "If we don't have the twins down at the mailbox in fifteen minutes, Preston said he'll ship Light off to an Asian whorehouse."

"Wait up!" I race after Crater and Myra as they hurry down the driveway, but Justin and Kathleen stay behind. They say they can't be involved in such treachery, even to save Light.

"Maybe we can overpower them when they arrive?" I suggest.

"He said only Myra was to be at the mailbox with the boys," Crater replies. "He wants you and me to take the canoe into

Walden Pond, toss the oars away, and sit there until it's over."

We hike silently through the mountain laurel. Images from past movies flash through my mind, but none hold out the promise of a successful rescue: a distracting puff of smoke, a well-aimed lasso flung from a galloping stead, a he-man swinging by on a jungle vine snatching the children to safety. But these are just scenes from well-rehearsed movies, played out by choreographed stunt men.

"We'll notify Children Services after this is over with," Myra says, knowing that our silence is more than silence. It is brooding – disappointment that we have failed the twins.

I don't really believe that Children Services can be victorious over Preston T. Service.

"We should of thrown their hats in the lake," Crater says. "Then maybe Preston would of believed they drowned."

"Naw," I say. "With the ice gone and still no bodies, he would of figured it out."

"Do we tell them?" Myra asks.

"The boys?" Crater says. "I guess we got to."

The twins are already packed when we get to Moon Base. They've tied their red snowsuits into neat bundles and have each taken an extra pair of paisley bellbottoms for souvenirs.

No one asks them how they knew what was happening. I assume that their father's command over them is stronger than we ever imagined.

I stand behind him as Crater hugs the boys. He hugs them hard – one in each arm – and tears pour from the twins' eyes like he's squeezing out two sponges. He releases them and spins around before they can see his face – he's crying, too. "Come on, man. Let's get to the boat."

***

We sit quietly in the canoe, fishing poles lying idle across our laps. Our paddles float along the shoreline, not far from where we tossed them, drifting only slightly in the still air. Crater and I stare up the slope toward the hill that separates us from the farmhouse. We will not know that it's over until we see Light running toward the shoreline to kiss her father and cry on his shoulder. She will say he did the right thing, but he will always think otherwise.

I try not to imagine what kind of greeting Preston is planning for his sons. It will probably start as a spanking, a bit of parental discipline; but once their pants are down, it will turn ugly.

It is more than a father can stand. "Come on, Crater." I pull off my sneakers and jump into the water.

"I'm with you, man." Crater removes his sandals and jumps in beside me.

The June water is cold, but it invigorates me. Crater is the better swimmer and is climbing out among the twisted roots of an old willow tree while I'm still splashing about in the shallows.

A shot rings out.

"What the fuck," Crater shouts. He scampers up the muddy embankment on all fours, then runs toward the farm, two wet trails marking his path as water pours from his soaked pants.

My feet sink into the cool sand as I reach the shoreline. "Wait up, Crater," I yell as I scurry up the embankment and chase after him toward the tent site.

He stops to catch his breath beside the old outhouse. The tent is gone, but the wood stove sits there still, like a statue in a Japanese garden. "Down there," he points, panting.

I can barely see the road through the late spring foliage. There is a long black limousine parked beside the mailbox. There are men's voices but there is no one in sight.

"Come on, man." Crater avoids the winding trail and crashes through the underbrush, taking the direct route down the steep slope – the route I first explored this past winter. I follow, sliding and tumbling past my lost mitten lying forlornly in the leaves. I reach out but can't grab it as I skid past.

I somersault the last few feet, bursting through the undergrowth and rolling into the back of the limousine. Standing up, shaking my head, I find myself hallucinating from the impact – halfway up the driveway, Moon Moo the cow and Alfred the pig are charging angrily toward Preston's three Russians. Eight chickens follow, squawking and flapping, feathers flying; and behind them are Justin and Kathleen. Kathleen is waving a hat, and Justin is waving the rifle that hung over the fireplace – they have created a small stampede.

Preston stands with his legs spread beside the limousine. His grip on Light's arm tightens – she winces in pain – while he laughs at the odd spectacle of the pathetic stampede. The twins are already in the limo's back seat. They are not laughing.

Crater looks around. There is a mailbox, but not much else. He grabs the mailbox with his big hands, squats and grips the mailbox post between his powerful legs, then heaves it from the ground. The Russians have moved up the driveway, crouching as though they each hope to grab themselves a chicken. Preston does not pay well – perhaps free chickens are one of the little perks that keep them on his payroll.

A flash of sunlight blinds me as the mailbox swings through the air, catching Preston on the side of his head. He says nothing as he crumples to the ground, releasing his hold on Light.

"Come on, boys," I yell as I stick my head into the back of the limo. Seeing my face, they smile and scamper out.

They see their father lying in the pale dust and pause, confused by conflicting feelings of love and hatred.

Justin and Kathleen are yelling "yahoo" as they charge among the panicked animals. The Russians ignore the children as they scoot past and go after free chickens instead.

"Come on." I tug the boys' hands.

Preston groans, a puff of dust rising beside his mouth from his painful gasps. He is more frightful alive than dead; and the boys turn and run toward the safety of the mountain laurel.

We send the five children up the path first. Myra and Crater follow, and I take the rear, eager to get in some licks of my own – if the Russians should follow. There is a confusion of voices below. Preston's voice is roaring among the wild cacophony of Russian profanities.

The children are leaning against Moon Base's darkened outside walls, resting, when I arrive. Myra nudges them toward the open door. "Come on, children."

Crater and I enter last and shut the door. The entrance to Moon Base has no lock and opens outward. "We can't hold them off here," Crater says. "Everyone to the steam room."

The door there opens inward. We pile benches against it. Crater tries to put the twins in the hiding place behind the peace sign towel, but they are tired of running from their father. They have seen him sprawled in the dust. They have heard him groan in pain. He is mortal after all, and they are ready to stand up and fight.

We wait. There is no sound but the slow hiss of the steam bath. The fire is not burning now, but it was earlier; and there is still pressure within the system leaking from one of the many holes in the aging pipes.

Crater presses his ear against the door. Perhaps they have given up and gone back to Connecticut. The prolonged silence gives us reason to hope.

"Even if they've gone, they'll be back," Rick whispers. "Our old man never gives up." Nick nods in agreement.

There is a loud crash, and Crater pulls his head back as though stunned. The twins have jumped into each other's arms. There is another loud crash, and caulking falls out from between the door's slats.

"Come on, man." Crater leans harder against the door. "Need a little help here."

Justin and I jump in beside him. There is another crash; wood splinters and the end of a log slides through the broken door. The twins stand beside us in frozen terror. I peek out through the hole and see the log sliding toward my face. I pull back and the log slides past my nose.

"What's that, man?" Crater says.

There is a loud buzzing sound coming from the roof. A hornets' nest has been disturbed. I look up and see the end of a chain saw slice through the newly placed shingles.

Myra screams as bits of shingle shower about her. She grabs the twins' hands and pulls them against a wall, hovers over them to protect them as though hungry chicken hawks are circling above her baby chicks. The battering ram strikes again, and the door's center board falls away. I can see Preston standing on the other side, puffing on his pipe as the three Russians run at the door a fifth time, a large log hoisted between them. It is one of the logs we took the day Preston was hung upside-down in the forest – he has selected it as a special form of revenge.

A large chunk of shingles crashes to the floor. I look up and see that there is a good size hole in the ceiling. I am expecting more Russians to pour in, but instead there is a woman – her face painted green, and twigs in her hair. She drops into the room.

Rick stares at the strange sight. "Mom?"

Nick runs to the woman warrior and squeezes her waist.

"Mom!"

Another woman drops through the hole. She is in army fatigues. Her face is painted green, also. She takes the stance of a kung foo fighter.

A third woman drops in beside the second. Justin stares at her. "Mom?"

We are raining mommies.

Light looks expectantly up at the hole. Perhaps there's one up there for her, too.

Eve falls in beside Beth. A rope ladder drops in through the hole. Three more women climb down. I see a broad smile spread across Crater's face – Moon Valley is a fighting force once again. There will be new folk songs to write after today.

"Start moving them out," Eve yells.

The twins' mother leads Rick and Nick to the rope ladder and urges them upward, into the throng of green hands wiggling anxiously above.

The door crashes open, but the Russians hesitate to enter the steam bath. The whites of their eyes expand as they stare at the group of women that block their path. They know of no explanation for this strange manifestation – sorcery perhaps. All these women – crouched with their palms extended knifelike without fear, hissing like snakes – they are as inexplicable as the valley itself. The women move toward the Russians with slow, exaggerated steps, twisting their bodies this way and that, yelling "hi yah" each time they slice the air with their able hands.

The children have all climbed to safety. Myra and Crater are also safely up the ladder. Eve grabs my shoulder – it is time I go – but I can't pull my eyes from the spectacle before me. I watch Beth as she moves with aggressive assuredness, and I get hard. I have never seen her possessed of such dominance, and it flames the fires of my desire.

With a forceful hand, Eve turns me toward the ladder. I climb two steps, then stop. I do not want my massive erection to climb past her eyes. "Come on," she whispers. "Before we lose the element of surprise." She pushes my leg, her palm so close to my crotch she almost touches it – but she does not seem to notice what has taken shape there.

I am disappointed. I thought with my shorts still wet from the pond, I would appear bigger, more impressive. Perhaps Eve is used to more; perhaps Adam is a big, big man – one of those horse dicks that used to strut into the shower room in high school. Oh my god – the rest of us boys would spin, humiliated, to face the yellow tile walls, squirt a bit of liquid soap into our palms, dab it here and there among our pubies, discretely puffing ourselves up a bit before turning once again to face the crowd. I try to remember the night of the Andersen's party, when Adam pissed on the Simpson's rock garden. Was the sound I heard that of pee falling from up high, like from a cherub fountain; or like it was being released from a garden hose close to the ground? I don't remember now.

Eve shoves me again. "Come on. Hurry."

Green faces and dried twigs greet me as I am pulled through the hole in the roof. There is a little army of women handing children down off the roof to others below. There is a ladder, too. It is my ladder, from the barn. It instills me with pride seeing that I have contributed to such a well-orchestrated operation.

The hissing of snakes dies down as the women rescuers are pulled from the steam room by their comrades. Beth comes up last. She does not climb the ladder, but stands on the bottom rung lashing out at advancing Russians with her well-trained feet while the women above hoist the ladder up through the hole.

I take one last look below. Two Russians are leaping about,

trying to grab pieces of broken ceiling. The third I hear banging on the front door – the women have sealed that off with the outhouse. Preston T. Service stands smoking his pipe, staring up through the hole that defeated him. He smiles at me, but says nothing.

"Get the boys to the boats," Eve orders.

There are twelve women in all. Eleven jog off, the twins safely tucked between them, toward an armada of canoes beached on the shore of Piss Hole Lake. The twelfth woman sits silently on a log. The twigs have fallen from her short cropped hair. I walk over and sit down beside her.

"You're not going with them?" I ask.

"No. I've done my part for now," Beth says. She turns her head and smiles.

"You're coming home then?"

"You want me to?" She looks toward the lake and sees the canoes have rounded a bend and are out of sight.

Justin and Kathleen burst into the clearing. They have come from the shoreline where they searched the green faces of the women warriors as they hunted for their mother. Failing to find her, Kathleen burst into tears, thinking her mother had been nothing more than a dream. Eve then stood up in the lead canoe and pointed toward the path that led back to Moon Valley. "Children, up there."

Justin and Kathleen race to Beth's side, drape their arms around her and kiss her cheeks, smearing their own faces with the green warrior paint.

Beth laughs as she pushes them back. "Come on, let me see you." Kathleen has not changed much in the six months Beth has been gone. Justin, though, has transformed. Beth whistles. "Jussie. You've become a man."

He blushes. "Oh, Mom."

Light steps up, takes Justin's hand, and pats it. Beth stares at the beautiful girl and smiles. "In more ways than I thought. A girlfriend, Justin?"

There is thunder at the entrance to Moon Base. Preston's men are running the battering ram against the front door.

"Come on, man," Crater calls. "Let's get them out before there's more damage."

We do not move quick enough, though. The door shudders angrily and breaks free of its hinges, falling in slow motion and crushing the outhouse with its heavy dark timbers. The three Russians spill through the doorway and into the confusion of broken lumber.

"Yes. Well." Preston removes his pipe from his mouth as he steps casually onto the flattened door and into the sunshine. He looks about at the emptiness of the clearing and listens briefly to the whistling of birds, then he looks toward me. "The women have gone?"

I nod my head.

"And the twins are gone with them?"

"Yes," I say.

"Hmm." He slaps his pockets, looking for his lighter, but he has lost that, too. "And you have no idea where they took them?"

"No," Beth says.

"Well, then I have no more business here." Preston steps off the door and into the pine needles, walking past his disheveled Russians as though they never existed.

***

We are a family again.

Beth follows the children and me down the winding path to the farmhouse. She frowns as she enters the parlor and looks about at the stark contents – the green sofa, the yellow drapes. "There obviously isn't a woman living here."

"Sounds like you flunked out of feminist school," I say. "Is that why you're back?" I take her hand and kiss it, in case she has lost her sense of humor. It smells of sweat and dirt – manly odors.

"I'm back because you need me," she says. "Look at you."

I look at the children. Their hair is a bit unkempt, but we've just climbed through a roof to escape a band of thugs – only in Hollywood would their hair still be in place. Other than the hair, though, they look pretty good – Kathleen is smiling and Justin has some brawn and a bit of chest hair.

The children look at me and shrug. I look fine to them.

Beth stares closer at me. "Harry, are those muscles?" She moves closer and rubs my shoulders.

"Would Eve approve?" I ask.

"Eve?" She lets out a little laugh that barely hides contempt. "The only thing harder than living with a man is living with a woman." She smiles sadly. "I was wrong to leave you like that. Can you ever forgive me?"

"After the entrance you made? Of course."

"Damn it, Harry. Don't be so noble. Yell or something." Beth throws herself into the rocking chair and pets the dead cat that is resting beside it.

Justin takes his sister's hand and leads her into the kitchen. They will let us talk in private.

"I'm not being noble," I say. "I understand what you did. Sort of."

"Sort of?"

"Well, remember a few years ago, we went to a neighborhood pool party, and that Ricky someone strutted out in his Speedo."

"Ricky Marshall," Beth says. "He was so good looking."

"And his Speedo. Remember his Speedo bathing suit?"

"He had tight buns," Beth says dreamily.

"Not his buns. His prick," I say.

"Women don't notice that," she says."

"How could you not notice? It was wrapped up in there like an elephant's trunk."

"I was looking at his ass."

"Never mind," I say.

"No. Tell me. Ricky Marshall had a big prick."

"And for a moment, I wondered what it would be like to sleep with him." I say it quickly, hoping that it will sound less important that way.

Beth just laughs. "Everybody wanted to sleep with Ricky Marshall. A lot of them did, from what I heard. Men and women."

"Did you?"

She looks at me in astonishment. "Of course not. I never cheated on you."

"What about Eve?"

"Eve? That wasn't sex. That was intimacy." She stops petting the cat and rises from the rocker. "Come on," she says, smiling. "I'll show you the difference."

June 8

The morning light streaks through the parlor windows as Beth and I stagger down the stairs. Justin and Kathleen are sitting on the green sofa in their pajamas. The pajamas are for Beth's benefit – most mornings there is no more than one set of underwear between them.

I am revived, and Beth is a woman again. More importantly, we are once again married. Justin smiles when he sees my flushed face and my silly grin – Mom will stay.

"You don't have to go now, Mommy?" Kathleen asks.

"No, Kitten. I just came."

Beth is too sleepy to see the pun, or perhaps she chooses to ignore it; but Justin and I smile at one another – we can barely suppress juvenile laughter. It is odd how much Justin has changed in just a few months – not too long ago, the thought of his parents having sex would have grossed him out. Now he can laugh with me about it.

Beth sits in the rocking chair and strokes the cat. She stops rocking and stares more intently at Mittens. "There's something wrong with this cat," she says.

"She's dead," I say.

"She's dead?" Beth pulls her hand away is if the cat's fine black fur were the needles of a porcupine.

"It's a long story," I say.

"There doesn't seem to be a TV," Beth observes, mistaking Mrs. Finch's small television set for a microwave oven. "Amuse me."

"It's really not that long a story," Justin says. "Dad lost his job, so we were moving to the city, but Mrs. Finch died and left her farm to Mittens."

"Yeah," Kathleen says. "And I killed Mittens with an electric blanket." She starts moving her hands about like a puppet show. "And Crater stuffed her so Mr. Spinozzi would think she was still alive." Kathleen is better than television.

Beth is confused. "So this farm belongs to the cat, and you're the cat's guests?"

"Sort of. I think it all started when I paid the cat's vet bill last year," I say. "Mrs. Finch made me the cat's guardian."

"So why did you stuff the cat?" Beth asks.

"Because we only get to keep the farm if the cat lives a year," I say.

"Dad! Dad! Tell her about the eight million," Justin says.

"Oh yeah. And we also get eight million dollars."

Beth pauses. The eight million has thrown her. I'm glad – that means she didn't know about the eight million. It means she came back for me. "You don't think they'll notice the cat is dead?"

I look at the children for answers, but they remain quiet. They only wanted to help me with the part of the story I already knew. Kathleen has eased herself onto the floor, and Justin now slides down to join her. The sofa, like the pajamas, was only for Beth's benefit. They normally sit on the hard floor with their legs crossed; something Crater has taught them; something called the locust position – I think because it makes them look like bugs.

Beth laughs. "Oh, Harry. Why don't you just find another black cat?"

"I don't know," I say. "The eight million seems sort of superfluous now."

"Superfluous. Mmmm." Beth slowly rocks. She reaches down and strokes the cat again. "I don't remember why I even left you now."

"I don't think you left us," I say. "It was a place you left."

"Oh god, the place. Yes!" Beth shouts. "Do we have to go back there? I'm sure I'll run away again, if we do."

"Well, I didn't sell the house," I say. "The cat agreed to pay the mortgage while we were taking care of her."

"The damn cat again," Beth replies. "We'll be a scandal if we return."

"We'll be scarred for live, Dad," Justin says. "The kids will tease us. They don't like homos in the suburbs." He looks over at Beth and tries to smile. "Sorry, Mom."

She nods back.

"Well, we can probably stay here until the year is up," I say. "Mr. Spinozzi won't bother coming out here until then."

There is a knock at the door. Justin unravels his legs and stands up. He leans over the sofa and parts the yellow curtains. "Uh oh," he says as he looks out onto the front stoop.

"Who is it?" I ask.

"Mr. Spinozzi," Justin whispers.

"Shit," I say. "Well, better let him in."

The door creaks open. We wait tensely to see if our fears are real, that the dreaded Mr. Spinozzi truly stands on the other side, or Justin is suffering teenage delusions.

"Top of the morning to you, young man. Is your father at home." It is Mr. Spinozzi's voice – he is English today. The door creaks open further, and then it is his face. He does not wait for an answer, but slides past Justin and into the parlor. "Ah, to be sure, I see your charming wife has returned."

Beth is sitting in the rocking chair with Mittens on her lap. She strokes the cat peacefully. She casts a smile at Mr. Spinozzi but does not reply.

I stand up from the piano stool and extend my hand. "What brings you here, Mr. Spinozzi."

He leans his umbrella against the wall and unravels a square of paper. "I received a strange call from a Preston T. Service. Something about the cat being dead." He glances over at Mittens, then stares at me. "Do you know this Preston T. Service?"

"He's a local kidnapper," I explain.

"Hm." Mr. Spinozzi walks toward the rocking chair. "The cat seems... quiet."

"She doesn't give us any trouble at all," Beth says.

"Yes." Mr. Spinozzi strokes the cat gently. He slides his hands under the cat's belly and begins to lift it. The cat does not flop about like a regular cat, but stays rigid as it rises into the air, like a young maiden in a hypnotist's act. "Very odd." Mr. Spinozzi moves the cat out over the wooden floor. He releases it, and it lands with a dull thud. "A stuffed cat, Mr. Lascome? Eight million dollars is involved here. You didn't think I'd examine the cat when that amount of money is at stake?"

"It wasn't for the eight million," I explain. "We were hoping to stay on the farm a little longer."

"I just got a pig," Justin says.

Mr. Spinozzi stares at my son with a wry smile – Justin's adult muscles bulge from the short sleeves of his "Cat In The Hat" pajamas, his wrists squeezed pink by the tight elastic arm bands. And he has a pig. It seems a bit off – perhaps we have become the Adam's Family, and any visitor is in danger if he tarries too long.

"A pig. How nice." The lawyer sighs and sets his briefcase on the green sofa. "I was actually hoping that you would succeed, Mr. Lascome, because now things get a bit complicated, and that makes my job more difficult." He pulls the will from the briefcase and leafs through the bulk of the pages. "Let's see. If you take care of the cat for one year, then you inherit the entire estate. If you do not, then Mrs. Finch's daughter is the heir. But she does not receive any of the estate until her worthless husband is gone." He stares at me hard. "You see? If you had just taken care of Midget."

"Mittens!" Kathleen shouts.

"Yes, well. Mittens." Mr. Spinozzi slams his briefcase shut. "If you had just taken care of the damn cat, my part in this affair would have ended come December. Now, who knows? I'm stuck with this case until some worthless husband kicks off. I just hope she poisons him or something so I can spend more of my time on class action suits." He yanks the briefcase from the sofa and storms toward the door. "I'll give you until Saturday to be gone. Good day."

June 14

Justin is silent as he helps load our things into the back of the pickup. Most of our stuff never left the suburbs; what we have now is mainly clothes and cereal, stuffed randomly into cardboard boxes. Mittens has her own box.

In the shade of a swamp maple, Kathleen and Light talk quietly. There are tears in Kathleen's eyes, but they do not trickle across her cheek.

"I can take Alfred, though?" Justin asks me.

"I said yes," I remind him.

He is leaving the farm with his pig and his virginity. The pig will not help him on the latter account in the suburbs. It will probably hurt, actually.

"What about the pots and pans," Beth calls from behind the farmhouse.

"Those stay," I say. "Ours are back at the house in the garage." In boxes marked "kitchen." There is also a cheese grater in there somewhere.

Gravel crunches under Beth's feet as she carries a shoe box

to the truck. "Oven mitts and scouring powder," she says as she hands the box off to Justin.

Chickens peek cautiously from their perches in the barn. One presses in too close against another, oppressive and hot like the summer heat; they squawk and peck. Feathers fly. They are easily irritated – first I traded away the minivan, then I failed to repair the barn, now I am leaving with the pickup. They must learn not to depend on humans for suitable shelter.

I look toward the hillside and scan among the mountain laurel. Crater and Myra are late. They are probably in the steam bath. They invited Beth and me for one last steam, but Beth said "no." We are returning to the suburbs, and suburbanites do not sit around naked with their friends. They cheat on their friends and steal spouses from each other, but they do not sit around naked together. Naked is sex in the suburbs.

Naked is just naked in Moon Valley.

"You've got the utilities turned back on?" Beth asks.

"I called," I reply. "I hope so."

"Cable TV?" she asks.

The word is strange, and I have to think for a moment. "Television? No, I forgot."

Justin sets another box solemnly on the tailgate. Even the mentioning of television fails to animate him. He glances over at the swamp maple and the two girls whispering in the shade. He will return to the suburbs with one of the girls, but it is not the one he wants.

There is a loud backfire. Birds flee as black smoke rises from the forest that lines the road from town. Justin, Beth, and I stop what we are doing and look toward the mailbox. An olive green pickup truck swings up our driveway. The fenders are rusted. On the driver's door is painted "Ralph's Auto Salvage" in crude hand lettering. Through the cracks of the windshield, though,

Ralph does not look out – I see Crater and Myra bouncing up and down on the front seat as the truck maneuvers up the driveway with its tortured undercarriage.

The truck stops with the crunch of old brakes and the smell of burning asbestos. The two doors swing open – one hangs lower than the other on its bent hinge – and Crater and Myra hop out, all smiles.

"Borrowed this from Ralph over at the salvage yard," Crater says. "Thought we'd drive out with you, help carry some stuff. Chance to see these suburbs all the cats dig so much now days."

Myra smiles. "I told him there's nothing to see, but he insisted."

"I think one truck is big enough," I reply.

"But what about the kids?" Crater says.

I look at my pickup. I forgot to leave a place in the back for two children and a pig. I could strap a rocking chair to the roof, I suppose, and bring them home that way. American culture rolled all into one – Green Acres, Adam's Family, and the Beverly Hillbillies.

The dark mood on Justin's face fades some. "Can Light come with us?"

"Sure thing, man," Crater says. "She's never been further than the high school."

"I'll tell her." Justin tries to walk casually, but there is a quickness to his steps that betrays his eagerness. There is a slight swishing sound as he moves through the deep grass. Light hears it; or feels it, perhaps. She looks up and smiles. Justin puts out both hands. She places hers in his, and rises from the grass.

"You know, man. You can live with us," Crater says. "Plenty of space at Moon Base."

Beth shakes her head slightly. She knows the suburbs aren't quite right, but a log fort in an abandoned farm community doesn't sound right, either.

"I don't whittle," I say.

"Oh man, there's lots more than whittling you can do. Ralph pays two dollars a piece for hubcaps."

"You want me to steal hubcaps?" I say.

"Not steal them, man. Find them, along the road. Specially in spring with all the frost heaves."

Beth shakes her head again.

"Thanks," I say. "But I've got a lead on a job with a mutual fund company."

"Oh man, why you want to go shut yourself up in some office building when you could be outside whittling, or cutting firewood, or milking cows? Or you could hike along roads and find all sorts of valuable stuff; hubcaps, beer cans."

I reach my arm out and pat Crater's shoulder. "Sounds tempting." I smile at him. He sees it is a sad smile that says good-bye. "Come on, kids," I yell. "Time to move it out."

Beth and I climb into our pickup truck. Crater and Myra climb into the cab of the flagship vehicle of Ralph's Auto Salvage Emporium, while the three children and the pig climb into the back.

I start the engine, then sit back and unfold a road map. It has been a long time since we arrived, and I need to recheck the route home. What was it we came up? French Fry Lane? I stare at the map, and I can imagine our little caravan winding along the clearly delineated highways; driving slowly so Crater can keep up, looking in the rearview mirror and keeping tabs on him by watching for the clouds of black smoke blasted into the air by the constant backfires. Fossil fuel farts.

We will arrive in our neighborhood at midday. All of our neighbors will be lining the street – they will cast no shadows – anticipating our return. They have heard the rumors; not of the farm – they know that is all silliness. They have heard of my new job; they have heard that I have an office with a clear view of the parking lot. Property values will continue to rise if my kind keep moving in.

They will hear the unfamiliar sound of an out-of-tune 1954 Ford pickup truck. They will see the dark smoke rise among the well-trimmed junipers and will wonder if they have read their watches correctly. Yes, it is noon. The Lascomes should be coming. But what is this trash rolling down between the two rows of designer mailboxes? Where are the Saabs and the Jaguars? It's not fair – some yokels are spoiling the Lascomes' triumphant return.

Their puzzled looks will turn to horror when they realize who is sitting in the front seat of the lead pickup truck. The neighborhood children will think they have slipped into the Twilight Zone when they spot Justin in the bed of the second pickup, with a pig in his lap. Justin will hold up Alfred's front paw and wave it at the crowd. Bernie Ickman will wave cautiously back; his sister will be standing pregnant beside him. She will have the taste of many boys on her lips, but she will not know she is pregnant; she will think the oddness within her has something to do with food. One morning a foot will appear between her legs. She will count her own two before realizing what is happening.

Adam will be standing out front with the former Mrs. Meredith. Her teenagers will not interrupt their basketball game to greet us. They have not stopped playing since the spring air warmed enough to give the ball the proper bounce. Several neighbors have started a petition; they want to limit the number of times a basketball can hit the pavement in one day.

Sarah will be standing alone beside a shrub, picking buds and peeling them apart. She misses her mother, Eve. Her father does not like talking to her; she might ask him things, girl things.

Adam does not know about that; he reads the Bible and sees words like "unclean." The former Mrs. Meredith tries to be a mother to her, but she finds her long running addiction to Valium interferes with her effectiveness.

We will not see Cain outside – he has discovered masturbation, and will use the solitude within the house to search his palm for hairs under Mrs. Meredith's magnifying glass.

There will be a neighborhood barbecue at the Andersen's. Troy and Donna will be watching for us from the deck of their new above-ground swimming pool. It cost twelve grand, but what the hey. They will have a secret supply of Amway products stashed under the redwood deck, and will wait for the right moment to drag them out. Their plan will be to send the orphans over to fetch us once we have arrived. No, not the orphans; they're gone.

But wait. Troy hears the rattle pop boom of the Ford pickup truck.

Donna leans against the redwood railing, and cranes her neck for a better view. This cannot be – those people, the Lascomes, look at them. To think we've had them in our house. We've shown them our Levelors and our collection of bisque statuettes.

"Should have known what sort he was when he guzzled all those beers," Troy will say as he tosses the last of his third martini into his boyish mouth.

The crowd will thin in our wake. Not so much from the dark asphyxiating cloud Crater lays out behind him – these people commute the highways every day and sit among a wild assortment of ill-timed and untuned vehicles. They have seen the orange band of pollution in the horizon and thought no more of it than they would of a golden sunset. They run because of their desire to escape that uncomfortable feeling that there are people out there that do not embrace their way of life.

The news will travel faster than our trucks. The crowd will thin out ahead of us, too. By the time we reach our mailbox, the Greenleys will be returning to their house. Adam will find Cain in his bedroom with the magnifying glass.

Cain will quickly explain – splinters.

"Let me see, son." Adam will grab the magnifying glass.

Cain will close his eyes nervously and wait for his father to discover the evidence of his sins.

Only Nat will not abandon us. He will be sitting on his vinyl car seat, tossing meal worms into his fish pond. He will hear the pickup trucks and smile. Finally! Someone's changed for the better!

I will pull up the driveway, but Crater will cut across my lawn and drive into the azalea bushes before bringing his vehicle to a screeching stop. We will all hop out at once.

The street will seem empty of neighbors, but curtains will be fluttering in the dead calm of summer. The neighborhood fruitcake will remain on the top shelf of the latest recipient's walk-in closet.

Light Moon will stand among the brown grass and stretch. It has been a long ride. Every inch of her long legs will show beneath the frays of her denim cutoffs. Her nipples will press against her tight fitting tie-dye tee shirt. Her hair will be tied behind her ears by an Indian-style headband. My lawn has never looked so good.

Wives throughout the neighborhood will use both hands now; they will pinch the curtains closed with their lefts, while they pinch their husbands' nuts with their rights to deflate any unwelcome hard-ons.

Nat will stroll over with a six-pack of beer. He will say "hi" to me and hand me a beer, then move quickly to Crater. He knows this man – not the individual, but the man in general.

"Hey," he'll say.

"Hi, man," Crater will reply.

"Want to come see my fish pond?"

"Cool."

The two will sit laughing on the vinyl car seat. A cloud of blue smoke will engulf their heads. I will see Crater with his hands out, squeezing imaginary handlebars – he is telling the story about "Dylan the motorcycle" and the lake.

Inside, the house will be set up just the way we left it. Beth and I will walk slowly through the house. She will look at the phone and see that the number has not been changed – it will seem like we never left. We will peek into our bedroom and see the naked mattress. Beth will remove her blouse and I will unzip my pants. The wall mirror will be leaning against the bureau at an odd angle; I will watch a familiar ass bounce up and down, rhythmic, like the bouncing ball on a sing-along cartoon. There will be no sweat on my chest. Beth will exhale with each thrust, but the only real sound will be that of the children chasing the pig around the front yard.

"Well," Beth will sigh when I've finished.

"I love you," I'll say.

"I love you, too." Beth will wander naked to the bedroom window. She will look out toward the Greenley's house. A sadness will cloud her eyes when she remembers that Eve is gone. The former Mrs. Meredith will walk out into the backyard to hang an endless row of boy's underwear on a clothes line. She will look up and smile at Beth's breasts as she hangs Sarah's training bra between the last of the boy's jockey shorts.

***

A horn honks, and I look up from the map. The country is

still before me.

"Ready, man?" Crater's head is hanging out the side window of the old pickup truck.

"Yeah, I guess." I shift into drive. The gears complain and slip back into neutral.

"You have to shift this thing?" Beth asks.

"Yeah," I say.

"Just great."

I rattle the stick and the truck moves slowly forward.

"Do you know where we're going?" Beth asks.

"I think so." We are going to the suburbs. It is still morning there. Breakfast. Our neighbors are poking forks under their waffles, searching for hidden cholesterol.

Beth smiles at me. It is a pensive smile. "You were great last night."

"Last night?" I ask.

"The last six nights," she says.

Six nights. It is true. We made love for six nights in a row. While the children slept above, we sat naked on the parlor floor. I rubbed my moist fingers across her straining nipples, and their color changed. I ran my wet lips gently across them, and they changed color again.

She rubbed her fingers lightly among the hairs of my chest, working ever so slowly toward my groin. Sensation awoke. Like an ocean wave, the feeling swelled as the light touch of her fingers urged my thoughts southward. I swam with a feeling of seasickness, yet it was pleasant, like the rumored pleasantness of drowning – only, I was drowning in a harmless pool of emotion.

I yielded to the pressure of her fingers, and fell back upon the cool wooden floor, with Mittens for my pillow. Beth's tongue slid across my navel and entered the tangled forest between my legs.

"Did you miss me?" she asked. Her eyes stared at me across the wild landscape of my naked body. A barren land of rolling hills and scrub brush; but there beside her cheek stood a monument; erected not for her to worship, but for her to play upon.

"Come here." I placed a hand against her chin and led her lips to mine. We kissed.

She sat upon my lap and rocked slowly. It was all very slow and patient – it was done with a woman's patience. Timeless. And afterward, I couldn't tell you whether it was ten minutes or ten hours that had passed. Perhaps it was a lifetime.

"Wipe that stupid grin off your face and drive," Beth laughs.

I have stopped beside the mailbox. I put the truck in park and open the door.

"Where you going, Honey?" Beth asks.

Crater has stopped behind us. Justin is standing up in the bed of the truck, looking out over the cab. "Dad?"

I stop at the mailbox and pull the little door open.

"Mailman comes later, man," Crater calls.

No. I am stalling. It is not the mail that interests me. I spot the entrance to the path, the twisted route through the mountain laurel that the children and I have spent the last six, seven months trampling into a well-defined trail. I cross the road and stand between the first two mountain laurels.

"Honey, what are you doing?" Beth shouts.

I turn and look at the two old trucks. Justin is standing with his arm wrapped across Light's shoulder, looking out across the rusted roof of the borrowed truck. Kathleen stands beside them holding Alfred.

Myra and Crater get out and walk to the lead truck, while Beth climbs down to join them in the morning sunshine. The sunlight plays through the trees and dances across their faces.

Even Myra looks pretty in the morning light.

"What's wrong, man?" Crater calls.

"Nothing," I shout back. "Nothing at all." I point up the slope toward where the tent once stood. "Stone!" I shout.

"Stone?" Beth says. "What are you talking about?"

"Dad?" the children say.

"Call me Moon Stone! That's my new name." I wave my arm, calling the others to join me. "Come on kids, Beth. Out of the truck. We's stayin' in the boonies!"

David Tillman lives in Massachusetts with his daughter, Kayly. His first book, "In The Failing Light", chronicles his wife's seven-year battle with breast cancer. He has written five novels since then, once again exploring the humorous side of life.